ACCLAIM FOR COLLEEN COBLE

"Colleen Coble's latest has it all: characters to root for, a sinister villain, and a story that just won't stop."

—Siri Mitchell, author of *State of Lies*, on *Two Reasons to Run*

"Colleen Coble's super power is transporting her readers into beautiful settings in vivid detail. *Two Reasons to Run* is no exception. Add to that the suspense that keeps you wanting to know more and characters that pull at your heart. These are the ingredients of a fun read!"

—Terri Blackstock, bestselling author of *If I Run, If I'm Found*, and *If I Live*

"This is a romantic suspense novel that will be a surprise when the last page reveals all of the secrets."

—*The Parkersburg News and Sentinel* on *One Little Lie*

"There are just enough threads left dangling at the end of this well-crafted romantic suspense to leave fans hungrily awaiting the next installment."

—*Publishers Weekly* on *One Little Lie*

"Colleen Coble once again proves she is at the pinnacle of Christian romantic suspense. Filled with characters you'll come to love, faith lost and found, and scenes that will have you holding your breath, Jane Hardy's story deftly follows the complex and tangled web that can be woven by one little lie."

—Lisa Wingate, #1 *New York Times* bestselling author of *Before We Were Yours*, on *One Little Lie*

"Colleen Coble always raises the notch on romantic suspense, and *One Little Lie* is my favorite yet! The story took me on a wild and wonderful ride."

—DiAnn Mills, bestselling author

"Coble's latest, *One Little Lie*, is a powerful read . . . one of her absolute best. I stayed up way too late finishing this book because I literally couldn't go to sleep without knowing what happened. This is a must read! Highly recommend!"

—Robin Caroll, bestselling author of the Darkwater Inn saga

"I always look forward to Colleen Coble's new releases. *One Little Lie* is One Phenomenal Read. I don't know how she does it, but she just keeps getting better. Be sure to have plenty of time to flip the pages in this one because you won't want to put it down. I devoured it! Thank you, Colleen, for more hours of edge-of-the-seat entertainment. I'm already looking forward to the next one!"

—Lynette Eason, award-winning and bestselling
author of the Blue Justice series

"Ever since Colleen Coble talked about the premise of *One Little Lie*, I was dying to read it. She's an amazing author and is at the top of her game with this page-turning suspense story. I think it's her best yet—and that's saying A LOT!"

—Carrie Stuart Parks, author of *Fragments of Fear*

"In *One Little Lie* the repercussions of one lie skid through the town of Pelican Harbor creating ripples of chaos and suspense. Who will survive the questions? *One Little Lie* is the latest page-turner from Colleen Coble. Set on the Gulf coast of Alabama, Jane Hardy is the new police chief who is fighting to clear her father. Reid Dixon has secrets of his own as he follows Jane around town for a documentary. Together they must face their secrets and decide when a secret becomes a lie. And when does it become too much to forgive?"

—Cara Putman, bestselling and award-winning author

"As always, Colleen Coble never disappoints. *Strands of Truth* is no exception. I was hooked from the first page. Trying to read this story slowly is impossible. Don't be surprised when you find yourself flipping the pages in a hurry to find out what happens next! This one is for your keeper shelf."

—Lynette Eason, bestselling and award-winning author of the Blue Justice series

"Coble wows with this suspense-filled inspirational . . . With startling twists and endearing characters, Coble's engrossing story explores the tragedy, betrayal, and redemption of faithful people all searching to reclaim their sense of identity."

—*Publishers Weekly* on *Strands of Truth*

"Just when I think Colleen Coble's stories can't get any better, she proves me wrong. In *Strands of Truth*, I couldn't turn the pages fast enough. The characterization of Ridge and Harper and their relationship pulled me immediately into the story. Fast paced, with so many unexpected twists and turns, I read this book in one sitting. Coble has pushed the bar higher than I'd imagined. This book is one not to be missed. Highly recommend!"

—Robin Caroll, bestselling author of the Darkwater Inn series

"Free-dive into a romantic suspense that will leave you breathless and craving for more."

—DiAnn Mills, bestselling author, on *Strands of Truth*

"Colleen Coble's latest book, *Strands of Truth*, grips you on page one with a heart-pounding opening and doesn't let go until the last satisfying word. I love her skill in pulling the reader in with believable, likable characters, interesting locations, and a mystery just waiting to be untangled. Highly recommended."

—Carrie Stuart Parks, author of *Fragments of Fear*

"It's in her blood! Colleen Coble once again shows her suspense prowess with a thriller as intricate and beautiful as a strand of DNA. *Strands of Truth* dives into an unusual profession involving mollusks and shell beds that weaves a unique, silky thread throughout the story. So fascinating I couldn't stop reading!"

—Ronie Kendig, bestselling author of the Tox Files series

"Once again, Colleen Coble delivers an intriguing, suspenseful tale in *Strands of Truth*. The mystery and tension mount toward an explosive and satisfying finish. Well done."

—Creston Mapes, bestselling author

"*Secrets at Cedar Cabin* is filled with twists and turns that will keep readers turning the pages as they plunge into the horrific world of sex trafficking where they come face-to-face with evil. Colleen Coble delivers a fast-paced story with a strong, lovable ensemble cast and a sweet, heaping helping of romance."

—Kelly Irvin, author of *Tell Her No Lies*

"Once again Colleen Coble has delivered a page-turning, can't-put-down suspense thriller with *Secrets at Cedar Cabin*! I vowed I'd read it slowly over several nights before going to bed. The story wouldn't wait—I HAD to finish it!"

—Carrie Stuart Parks, author of *Fragments of Fear*

"This is an engrossing historical story with plenty of romance and danger for readers to get hooked by."

—*The Parkersburg News and Sentinel* on *Freedom's Light*

"Coble . . . weaves a suspense-filled romance set during the Revolutionary War. Coble's fine historical novel introduces a strong heroine—both in faith and character—that will appeal deeply to readers."

—*Publishers Weekly* on *Freedom's Light*

"This follow-up to *The View from Rainshadow Bay* features delightful characters and an evocative, atmospheric setting. Ideal for fans of romantic suspense and authors Dani Pettrey, Dee Henderson, and Brandilyn Collins."

—*Library Journal* on *The House at Saltwater Point*

"*The View from Rainshadow Bay* opens with a heart-pounding, run-for-your-life chase. This book will stay with you for a long time, long after you flip to the last page."

—RT Book Reviews, 4 stars

"Set on Washington State's Olympic Peninsula, this first volume of Coble's new suspense series is a tensely plotted and harrowing tale of murder, corporate greed, and family secrets. Devotees of Dani Pettrey, Brenda Novak, and Allison Brennan will find a new favorite here."

—Library Journal on The View from Rainshadow Bay

"Coble (*Twilight at Blueberry Barrens*) keeps the tension tight and the action moving in this gripping tale, the first in her Lavender Tides series set in the Pacific Northwest."

—Publishers Weekly on The View from Rainshadow Bay

"Filled with the suspense for which Coble is known, the novel is rich in detail with a healthy dose of romance, allowing readers to bask in the beauty of Washington State's lavender fields, lush forests, and jagged coastline."

—BookPage on The View from Rainshadow Bay

"Prepare to stay up all night with Colleen Coble. Coble's beautiful, emotional prose coupled with her keen sense of pacing, escalating danger, and very real characters place her firmly at the top of the suspense genre. I could not put this book down."

—Allison Brennan, New York Times bestselling author
of Shattered, on The View from Rainshadow Bay

"I loved returning to Rock Harbor and you will too. *Beneath Copper Falls* is Colleen at her best!"

—Dani Pettrey, bestselling author of the Alaskan
Courage and Chesapeake Valor series

"Return to Rock Harbor for Colleen Coble's best story to date. *Beneath Copper Falls* is a twisting, turning thrill ride from page one that drops you headfirst into danger that will leave you breathless, sleep deprived, and eager for more! I couldn't turn the pages fast enough!"

—Lynette Eason, bestselling and award-winning
author of the Blue Justice series

"The tension, both suspenseful and romantic, is gripping, reflecting Coble's prowess with the genre."

—*Publishers Weekly*, starred review for *Twilight at Blueberry Barrens*

"Incredible storytelling and intricately drawn characters. You won't want to miss *Twilight at Blueberry Barrens*!"

—Brenda Novak, *New York Times* and *USA TODAY* bestselling author

"Coble has a gift for making a setting come to life. After reading *Twilight at Blueberry Barrens*, I feel like I've lived in Maine all my life. This plot kept me guessing until the end, and her characters seem like my friends. I don't want to let them go!"

—Terri Blackstock, bestselling author of *If I Run*, *If I'm Found*, and *If I Live*

"I'm a longtime fan of Colleen Coble, and *Twilight at Blueberry Barrens* is the perfect example of why. Coble delivers riveting suspense, delicious romance, and carefully crafted characters, all with the deft hand of a veteran writer. If you love romantic suspense, pick this one up. You won't be disappointed!"

—Denise Hunter, author of *The Goodbye Bride*

"Colleen Coble, the queen of Christian romantic mysteries, is back with her best book yet. Filled with familiar characters, plot twists, and a confusion of antagonists, I couldn't keep the pages of this novel set in Maine turning fast enough. I reconnected with characters I love while taking a journey filled with murder, suspense, and the prospect of love. This truly is her best book to date, and perfect for readers who adore a page-turner laced with romance."

—Cara Putman, bestselling and award-winning
author, on *Twilight at Blueberry Barrens*

"Gripping! Colleen Coble has again written a page-turning romantic suspense with *Twilight at Blueberry Barrens*! Not only did she keep me up nights racing through the pages to see what would happen next, I genuinely cared for her characters. Colleen sets the bar high for romantic suspense!"

—Carrie Stuart Parks, author of *Fragments of Fear*

"Colleen Coble thrills readers again with her newest novel, an addictive suspense trenched in family, betrayal, and . . . murder."

—DiAnn Mills, bestselling author,
on *Twilight at Blueberry Barrens*

"Coble's latest, *Twilight at Blueberry Barrens*, is one of her best yet! With characters you want to know in person, a perfect setting, and a plot that had me holding my breath, laughing, and crying, this story will stay with the reader long after the book is closed. My highest recommendation."

—Robin Caroll, bestselling author of the Darkwater Inn series

"Colleen's *Twilight at Blueberry Barrens* is filled with a bevy of twists and surprises, a wonderful romance, and the warmth of family love. I couldn't have asked for more. This author has always been a five-star novelist, but I think it's time to up the ante with this book. It's on my keeping shelf!"

—Hannah Alexander, author of the Hallowed Halls series

"Second chances, old flames, and startling new revelations combine to form a story filled with faith, trial, forgiveness, and redemption. Crack the cover and step in, but beware—*Mermaid Moon* is harboring secrets that will keep you guessing."

—Lisa Wingate, #1 *New York Times* bestselling
author of *Before We Were Yours*

"I burned through *The Inn at Ocean's Edge* in one sitting. An intricate plot by a master storyteller. Colleen Coble has done it again with this gripping opening to a new series. I can't wait to spend more time at Sunset Cove."

—Heather Burch, bestselling author of *One Lavender Ribbon*

"Coble doesn't disappoint with her custom blend of suspense and romance."

—*Publishers Weekly* on *The Inn at Ocean's Edge*

"Veteran author Coble has penned another winner. Filled with mystery and romance that are unpredictable until the last page, this novel will grip readers long past when they should put their books down. Recommended to readers of contemporary mysteries."

—*CBA Retailers + Resources* on *The Inn at Ocean's Edge*

"Coble truly shines when she's penning a mystery, and this tale will really keep the reader guessing . . . Mystery lovers will definitely want to put this book on their purchase list."

—*RT Book Reviews* on *The Inn at Ocean's Edge*

"Master storyteller Colleen Coble has done it again. *The Inn at Ocean's Edge* is an intricately woven, well-crafted story of romance, suspense, family secrets, and a decades-old mystery. Needless to say, it had me hooked from page one. I simply couldn't stop turning the pages. This one's going on my keeper shelf."

—Lynette Eason, bestselling and award-winning
author of the Blue Justice series

"Evocative and gripping, *The Inn at Ocean's Edge* will keep you flipping pages long into the night."

—Dani Pettrey, bestselling author of the Alaskan
Courage and Chesapeake Valor series

"Coble's atmospheric and suspenseful series launch should appeal to fans of Tracie Peterson and other authors of Christian romantic suspense."

—*Library Journal* on *Tidewater Inn*

"Romantically tense, but with just the right touch of danger, this cowboy love story is surprisingly clever—and pleasingly sweet."

—USAToday.com on *Blue Moon Promise*

"[An] outstanding, completely engaging tale that will have you on the edge of your seat . . . A must-have for all fans of romantic suspense!"

—TheRomanceReadersConnection.com review of *Anathema*

"Colleen Coble lays an intricate trail in *Without a Trace* and draws the reader on like a hound with a scent."

—*Romantic Times*, 4¹/2 stars

"Coble's historical series just keeps getting better with each entry."

—*Library Journal*, starred review, on *The Lightkeeper's Ball*

"Colleen is a master storyteller."

—Karen Kingsbury, bestselling author

TWO
REASONS
TO RUN

ALSO BY COLLEEN COBLE

PELICAN HARBOR NOVELS
One Little Lie
Two Reasons to Run
Three Missing Days
(available April 2021)

LAVENDER TIDES NOVELS
The View from Rainshadow Bay
Leaving Lavender Tides Novella
The House at Saltwater Point
Secrets at Cedar Cabin

ROCK HARBOR NOVELS
Without a Trace
Beyond a Doubt
Into the Deep
Cry in the Night
Haven of Swans (formerly
titled *Abomination*)
*Silent Night: A Rock Harbor
Christmas Novella* (e-book only)
Beneath Copper Falls

YA/MIDDLE GRADE ROCK HARBOR BOOKS
Rock Harbor Search and Rescue
Rock Harbor Lost and Found

CHILDREN'S ROCK HARBOR BOOK
The Blessings Jar

SUNSET COVE NOVELS
The Inn at Ocean's Edge
Mermaid Moon
Twilight at Blueberry Barrens

HOPE BEACH NOVELS
Tidewater Inn
Rosemary Cottage
Seagrass Pier
*All Is Bright: A Hope Beach
Christmas Novella* (e-book only)

UNDER TEXAS STARS NOVELS
Blue Moon Promise
Safe in His Arms
Bluebonnet Bride Novella
(e-book only)

THE ALOHA REEF NOVELS
Distant Echoes
Black Sands
Dangerous Depths
Midnight Sea
*Holy Night: An Aloha Reef
Christmas Novella* (e-book only)

THE MERCY FALLS SERIES
The Lightkeeper's Daughter
The Lightkeeper's Bride
The Lightkeeper's Ball

JOURNEY OF THE HEART SERIES
A Heart's Disguise
A Heart's Obsession
A Heart's Danger
A Heart's Betrayal
A Heart's Promise
A Heart's Home

LONESTAR NOVELS
Lonestar Sanctuary
Lonestar Secrets
Lonestar Homecoming
Lonestar Angel
*All Is Calm: A Lonestar Christmas
Novella* (e-book only)

STAND-ALONE NOVELS
Strands of Truth
Freedom's Light
Alaska Twilight
Fire Dancer
Where Shadows Meet (formerly
titled *Anathema*)
Butterfly Palace
Because You're Mine

TWO REASONS TO RUN

THE PELICAN HARBOR SERIES

COLLEEN COBLE

THOMAS NELSON

Since 1798

Two Reasons to Run

© 2020 Colleen Coble

Published in Nashville, Tennessee, by Thomas Nelson. Thomas Nelson is a registered trademark of HarperCollins Christian Publishing, Inc.

Thomas Nelson titles may be purchased in bulk for educational, business, fund-raising, or sales promotional use. For information, please e-mail SpecialMarkets@ThomasNelson.com.

Scripture quotations taken from The Holy Bible, New International Version®, NIV®. Copyright © 1973, 1978, 1984, 2011 by Biblica, Inc.® Used by permission of Zondervan. All rights reserved worldwide. www.Zondervan.com. The "NIV" and "New International Version" are trademarks registered in the United States Patent and Trademark Office by Biblica, Inc.®

Quotes in chapters 7 and 15 are from *The Screwtape Letters* by C. S. Lewis. First published in 1942.

ISBN 978-0-7852-2850-9 (library edition)

Library of Congress Cataloging-in-Publication Data

Names: Coble, Colleen, author.
Title: Two reasons to run / Colleen Coble.
Description: Nashville, Tennessee : Thomas Nelson, [2020] | Series: Pelican Harbor series ; 2 | Summary: "The second book in a gripping new series from USA TODAY bestselling romantic suspense author Colleen Coble"-- Provided by publisher.
Identifiers: LCCN 2020014467 (print) | LCCN 2020014468 (ebook) | ISBN 9780785228486 (paperback) | ISBN 9780785228509 (hardcover) | ISBN 9780785228493 (epub) | ISBN 9780785228516 (audio download)
Subjects: GSAFD: Romantic suspense fiction. | Christian fiction.
Classification: LCC PS3553.O2285 T96 2020 (print) | LCC PS3553.O2285 (ebook) | DDC 813/.54--dc23
LC record available at https://lccn.loc.gov/2020014467
LC ebook record available at https://lccn.loc.gov/2020014468

Printed in the United States of America

20 21 22 23 24   LSC   10 9 8 7 6 5 4 3 2 1

For the love of my life and my constant supporter, Dave Coble.

ONE

Was anyone watching?

Keith McDonald sat at the computer and glanced around the oil platform's rec room, but the dozen or so workers were engrossed in watching the final game of a Ping-Pong match. He hesitated, then hovered his cursor over the Send button. Clenching his teeth, he sent the emails. Maybe it was nothing, but if anyone could decipher the recording, it was Reid Dixon.

The back of his neck prickled, and Keith looked around again. The room felt stifling even with the AC cooling it from the May heat. He jumped up and headed for the door. He exited and darted into the shadows as two men strolled past. One was his suspect.

Keith stood on a grating suspended three thousand feet over the water and strained to hear past the noise of machinery. The scent of the sea enveloped him, and the stars glimmered on the water surrounding the oil platform that had been his home for two years now.

"Scheduled for late May—" A clanging bell drowned out the rest of the man's words.

"Devastation—"

The other fragment of conversation pumped up Keith's heart rate. Were they talking about the sabotage he feared, or was he reading more into the words than were there? He couldn't believe someone could be callous enough to sabotage the oil platform and destroy the coast on purpose. He'd seen firsthand the devastating effects from the Deepwater Horizon catastrophe. And what about the people living on the platform? Deepwater Horizon had killed eleven people and injured another seventeen.

He had to sound a warning and stop this, but he had no real evidence. If Reid Dixon blew him off, who would even listen? Maybe Homeland Security would pay attention, but who did he even call there? He could tell them about the pictures threatening Bonnie, but what did that prove? They might just say she had a stalker and he was chasing shadows.

He couldn't say they were wrong.

He sidled along the railing, and the breeze lifted his hair. A boat bobbed in the waves far below, and in the moonlight, he spotted a diver aboard. Must be night diving the artificial reef created by the concrete supports below the platform. He'd done a bit of it himself over the years.

For an instant he wished he were gliding carefree through the waves without this crushing weight of conscience on his shoulders. When he was sixteen, life was so simple. School, girls, football, and good times. He'd gone to work at the platform when he was nineteen, after he'd decided college wasn't for him.

It had been a safe place, a good place to work with fun companions and interesting work.

Until a few weeks ago when everything turned sinister and strange. He'd wanted to uncover more before he reported it, but every second he delayed could mean a stronger chance of an attack.

If an attack was coming. He still wasn't sure, and he wanted a name or to identify the organization behind the threat. If there was a threat. Waffling back and forth had held him in place. Was this real, or was he reading something dangerous into something innocent?

Though he didn't think he was overreacting.

He turned to head to his quarters. A bulky figure rushed him from the shadows and plowed into his chest, driving him back against the railing. The man grabbed Keith's legs and tried to tip him over the edge.

Keith kicked out with his right foot and drove the figure back into the wall opposite the catwalk. He searched for a weapon as the metal walkway clanged and the guy regained his feet. Nothing.

"Help!" Though he shouted, he feared the noise of the machinery drowned out the sound of his cry.

The guy was big and strong. Keith didn't stand a chance of beating him in a show of strength or agility. He rushed for the end of the catwalk, but the guy reached him first and spun him around to press him against the railing again. He tried to kick his way out again, but the guy was ready for him this time and caught him by the ankle, then used his leg to tip him up and over.

Keith saw the stars as he fell toward the dark water, then his head was under the water. The fall hadn't killed him, but he felt woozy and a bit out of it. He struck out for the surface, though it seemed impossible to reach. As he kicked out, something grabbed him by the ankle, and he flung out his arms, connecting with a diver's metal tank.

The diver held him fast and took him down into the depths.

The air-conditioning in Police Chief Jane Hardy's office whined like an unhappy dog, and she wiped a bead of perspiration from her brow. The company she'd called to work on the AC was nearly two hours late, and the Alabama Gulf Coast humidity had overpowered the ancient unit by eleven o'clock this morning. Her silky red golden retriever, Parker, lay sleeping with his head on his paws near the vent as if he wanted to get as much of the cool air as he could.

She checked her watch. Two o'clock. Will would be out of school soon, and she'd have to pick him up and take him to his father's after baseball practice. Her gut tightened at the thought of talking to Reid. She still couldn't get past his lies, even though a friendly relationship with him would make getting to know her son so much easier.

Her search on the computer ended with a ding, and she reached for her mouse to take a look. Every Monday she ran through the same search, and every week it came up empty. She glanced at the results and sighed. Still no sign of Liberty's Children and her mother. While the smart and wise thing would be to give up the search, she couldn't do it. Especially not since she'd found Will. Realizing her son was alive made her compulsion to find her mother even stronger.

Rachel Hutchins, a temp manning the front desk, stuck her curly red head into Jane's open doorway. She was about Jane's age of thirty. "Chief, there's a woman out here who says her son is missing. You want to take it?"

"Is Detective Richards or Officer Brown back yet?"

"No. Richards called in, and she's tied up with a boat that's been graffitied. I haven't heard from Brown." Rachel tipped her head to one side. "I can't get over how much you resemble Reese Witherspoon."

Jane had heard the inane comment before and didn't bother to answer. Her two new hires to replace her lost officers had just

4

started. It would take a while to get them up to speed, but she hadn't had time off in weeks, and her fatigue was starting to show.

She reached for her yellow legal pad and pen. "Show her in."

A few moments later, Rachel ushered in a fiftysomething woman Jane recognized as Ruby McDonald, the high school principal. Red eyes and a trembling mouth replaced Ruby's usual smile and happy manner. She looked like she'd come straight from campus in her demure brown skirt and tan blouse. Her brown curls were frizzy from the humidity hovering at 90 percent.

Jane rose and went around her desk to take her hand. "Ruby, what's happened?"

Though she didn't know the older woman well, they'd had several conversations at the high school about Will, who had transferred in during the final two months of the school year.

Ruby blotted her brown eyes with a waterlogged paper hankie. "It's my son, Keith. He's missing."

Jane squeezed Ruby's hand and led her to the chair by the desk. "Have a seat while I take notes."

She vaguely remembered meeting Keith in the coffee shop. If she remembered correctly, he worked on one of the oil platforms in the Gulf, a dangerous job. She guessed him to be early twenties.

She settled behind her desk and reached for her pen. "When did you see him last?"

"Three weeks ago. He was supposed to come home for some R & R yesterday, but he never showed up. I've called his phone countless times. I tried calling his best friend on the rig, and Mike said he didn't show up to take the chopper off the platform. He hasn't seen him since after breakfast on Saturday."

Two days ago. "Did Mike report Keith missing to security or anyone?"

"He says he did, but I haven't spoken to the rig manager myself. Mike talked to him and said that a search of the platform failed to find him."

"They probably called the Coast Guard to help search." She didn't want to mention that a man lost at sea would be difficult to spot from the air or from a boat. Accidents on oil platforms happened all too frequently.

Ruby gave a jerky nod. "They've been searching the sea." She wadded her hankie in a tight fist. "I know you're wondering why I'm here."

Jane wanted to show compassion, so she'd kept the question inside. "Well, finding a missing platform worker isn't in my jurisdiction."

Ruby's eyes filled with tears again. "I think he might have been murdered."

Jane stilled. "Why do you say that?"

"He sent me an email. I got it two days ago." Ruby reached into her purse and pulled out a folded paper. "I printed it out. He said if anything happened to him that it wasn't an accident." She slid the paper across the desk to Jane.

Jane unfolded it and the words tumbled into her head.

Dear Mom,

I know this email is probably going to scare you, but I have to tell you something just in case. I stumbled across some information, and I'm not sure what to do about it. If something happens to me—if I come up missing or you're told I died in an accident—go see Chief Hardy. I believe I'm in danger. I'll try to get home and talk to her in person, but I'm not sure if I'll make it or not.

I think an attack on the oil rig is being planned. Terrorists maybe, but I'm not sure who is behind the plot. I was in a storage room, and the door was open just a crack. I heard two guys talking about turning off security to let in a hacker. They said something about each of them coming away with a hundred thousand dollars. I didn't recognize their voices, but it sounded like the real deal.

Since I'm a resident of Pelican Harbor, I thought Chief Hardy would be the one to talk to first. She can call in Homeland Security or whoever would be in charge of this kind of thing.

I hope I'm not putting you in danger by telling you all this. Be careful and stay safe. Love you!

Keith

Frowning, Jane put down the printout. "Has anyone else seen this?"

Ruby shook her head. "As soon as I talked to Mike, I came straight here. I didn't mention the email to Mike. I don't know who to trust."

Jane didn't, either, but she would have to figure it out. "I'll need Mike's full name and anyone else you know there I can contact."

An oil spill would decimate the area. Lost wildlife, destroyed wetlands, lost jobs. She had to help.

TWO

Zeus. Even the name of the oil platform looming about a mile from shore inspired awe as it rose from the pristine blue waters of the Gulf.

The crane on Zeus lowered a metal cage to the boat where Reid Dixon and his videographer, Elliot Hastings, waited. The boat captain steadied the cage as Reid stepped in and moved out of the way to let Elliot crowd in behind him with the gear. With the clang of the door closing, there was no backing out now, and the cage began to rise over the pelicans riding the whitecaps below.

Wind buffeted the cage, and Reid grabbed the bars with both hands as his stomach did a slow roll. It was like a roller coaster without the safety precautions, and he hated amusement parks.

Elliot's blue eyes laughed at him. "Scared, boss?"

Twenty-five and single, Elliot never met a stranger. His blond curly hair touched his collar, and the youthful style made grandmotherly types nearly coo at him. Reid liked his can-do approach to anything he'd asked of him in the past three weeks since he'd been hired.

Reid forced an answering grin. "It's like a zip line, right?"

Elliot squinted in the bright sunshine and pointed. "Dolphins.

Wish we had time to swim with them." He pulled his camera to his face and snapped off several shots. "Good backdrop for the article."

This trip was going to be an hour-long documentary for Discovery Channel and had been instigated several weeks ago when he'd had a disturbing email from Keith McDonald, a crew member. The invitation to board the oil platform to investigate hadn't been easy to obtain, but here he was soaring over the Gulf to the noisy, clanging platform above.

A burly guy with massive, tattoo-covered biceps snagged the metal cage. His grin revealed a gold tooth. "Got you, guv'nor." His accent was all cockney without a hint of a Southern drawl.

Reid stumbled out of the cage and onto the more solid footing of the platform. He looked around as Elliot joined him. The platform vibrated under his new size-twelve steel-toed work boots, and the noise of the drills and other machinery, though muffled, was plenty loud. He'd done his homework before coming out here and knew Zeus weighed over a hundred million tons. It was forty stories high, and thick pipes tethered it to the seabed under the billowing waves. It was structured to withstand even the power of a hurricane like Katrina.

He peered through the metal grate to the water far below and felt a little dizzy.

The big guy stuck out a beefy hand. "Name's Dex. I'm one of the deck pushers, and I drew the bloomin' short straw to show you around."

The deck pusher would know all the rig's policies and safety procedures, and he would coordinate all the work done on deck including the crane operation.

Reid shook Dex's hand. "Reid Dixon."

"I've watched a few o' your documentaries and like 'ow you cover both sides o' things. What brings you to our platform?"

"Most people have never been aboard one of these monsters, and they hold a little bit of mystique. I thought viewers would like a peek inside such a difficult and dangerous job."

"You sure you ain't 'ere to see if we're another Deepwater Horizon?" Though Dex's tone remained friendly, his blue eyes narrowed.

Reid kept his smile in place. "Are you?"

"I'll let you take a gander at all the safety measures we 'ave in place. You'll be gobsmacked at all we've done 'ere."

Elliot rubbed sanitizer on his hands, then began to shoot video. Reid looked around the deck. The Gulf couldn't stand another hit like the last one.

Elliot signaled to him, and Reid started his dialogue for the documentary. "Located near here off the coast of Louisiana, Deepwater Horizon was the single greatest marine disaster in history. A year after it had sunk the deepest ever oil well, the rig exploded. The tragedy killed eleven crew members and ignited a firestorm that could be seen forty miles away. Still spewing oil, it sank two days later and continued to pump crude into the ocean. Nearly five million barrels fouled the Gulf by the time it was capped nearly three months later. The oil spoiled eleven hundred miles of beach in Louisiana, Alabama, Mississippi, and Florida. It was a catastrophe anyone alive here at the time would never forget. We're here today to make sure this rig is safe."

Reid paused and swept his hand out over the blue waters. "God has cleaned up what man couldn't, and the beaches are white again. Wildlife came back, and for the uninformed, it appears as if it had never happened. But I've looked closer and I've seen things you might not notice—things like reduced populations of larger marine animals such as whales, dolphins, and turtles, as well as lingering oil in the sediment. Some of the wetlands will take decades to recover."

He signaled Elliot to stop recording so they could proceed deeper into the rig.

Every time he stared out over the water, he saw oil platforms and wondered when the next catastrophe would occur. He hoped it was never, but his contact on this rig had hinted that something "big" was going to happen out here. While Reid wasn't sure if he believed it yet, he was disturbed enough to check it out.

He trailed after Dex through the various parts of the offshore rig. Steel girders soared overhead on every deck, and the constant hum and clang of machinery wore on his nerves. He got a peek at workers' quarters, exercise rooms, movie stations, internet cafés, and what felt like a million stairs.

There'd been no sign of Keith, though. Reid had hoped the man would approach him, but three hours later Reid still hadn't met him.

He would have to ask.

Dex gestured to a door. "Let's get a cuppa and nosh up in the cafeteria."

Reid accepted a cup of coffee in the galley and inhaled the aromas of Mexican food from the huge spread along the buffet. The workers eyed him with curiosity before he turned back to Dex. "I wanted to speak with Keith McDonald. Is he around?"

Dex's brows winged up. "Is he the bloke who wrangled you an invitation?"

"No, I did that all by myself, but I was hoping to see Keith. He's from Pelican Harbor too."

"He's missin', guv'nor. Coast Guard is searchin' for 'im now, but odds are poor they'll find 'im. Once a man goes overboard in these seas, 'is chances 'ave gone pear shaped. The whole rig is gutted about it. He was a good bloke."

"Overboard? Are you sure?"

Dex shrugged his large shoulders. "He's nowhere aboard, and he never showed for 'is flight off the rig. It happens. A guy gets cheesed off about somethin' and acts daft. Or he messes around thinkin' he's immune to fallin' off until he smacks into the waves. I'm sorry to say I think Keith is fish food by now."

Reid eyed him after his almost gleeful tone. Could Keith have been murdered? If so, it might mean his alarm was credible.

Jane eyed the oil platform rising in the blue sky. If Keith had fallen from that height, it wasn't good. The vibration from the sound of machinery shuddered through her bones, and she hailed the Coast Guard response boat on her boat's starboard side with a shout and a wave.

The Coast Guard boat throttled back as one of the four sailors gave a wave in her direction.

Her fifteen-year-old son, Will, cut the engine. "They've seen us."

She squinted in the brilliant May sunshine and squeezed around Parker to get as close to the railing as she could. "Chief Jane Hardy from Pelican Harbor," she called. "You're looking for a man overboard?" She counted three men and one woman aboard the other boat.

The twentysomething blonde woman in uniform exited the cabin and went to the bow to grab hold of the railing of Jane's boat.

"What's your business here, ma'am?" Her eyes were gray and just as steely in expression.

"I've had a report of a missing person. Are you searching for Keith McDonald?"

The woman's quick blink answered before she spoke. "We are. What do you know about this?"

A familiar set of shoulders on the oil platform distracted Jane, and she bit back a gasp. Parker whined and nudged her hand. "It's okay, boy."

"There's Dad," Will said.

What was Reid doing up there? She dragged her attention from his precarious position on a steel beam and glanced back at the Coastie. "His mother came to see me." She launched into Ruby's concerns, and worry crouched between the other woman's eyes.

"Have you reported this to Homeland Security?"

"Not yet. I wanted to verify the report first."

"Do you have a copy of the email?"

"Back at the office."

"Please contact Homeland Security with this concern. We're part of the search-and-rescue operation, and it's outside our mission for today."

"Any sign of Keith?"

The woman shook her head. "Not yet. He's been missing for forty-eight hours now, so it's more likely to be a recovery than a rescue. If we even find his body. We've got a couple of choppers in the air and several cutters out looking."

"No divers?"

"A diver isn't typically part of an operation like this."

"Did anyone see him go overboard?"

"No." The woman released her grip on Jane's boat. "We need to get back to work. Make sure you place that call."

Jane pushed away from the Coast Guard boat. "I'll do it immediately."

Will shifted in his seat. "I know Keith, Mom. He shoots hoops with us when he's ashore. He's a good pitcher, and he's helped me a lot. He worked with us on our swings too. I sure hope they find him."

"Me too, honey."

Her attention went back to the big platform blocking out the sun, and she had her hand half raised to wave at Reid before she caught herself and lowered it back to her side. The wind blew her hair into her eyes, and she couldn't tell if he'd seen her furtive movement.

She turned her boat around and headed back up Mobile Bay.

Will waved. "Hey, Dad! He saw us, Mom. Turn around."

Her fingers tightened on the wheel, but what could she say? She and Will were just getting to know each other, and the last thing she wanted was to appear bitter and mean. "I doubt he can hear us."

She spun the wheel, and the boat swept in a large circle back toward the oil platform. With the sun in her eyes, she could only see Reid's outline. He was at the platform's railing, waving. He shouted something, but the wind snatched his words away.

Waves lapped at the platform's massive under girders, and she slowed the boat so the motion didn't carry her against the steel. Closer to the beast, the sound grew more deafening.

"We can't talk to him here."

Will replied, but she couldn't make out what he'd said. It was a good excuse to accelerate away from the massive structure and pull away from Reid's gaze. As her boat left the vicinity, she heard Will shouting at his father and Reid's faint answer, but the wind snatched more than a syllable or two.

Will joined her at the helm. "How about we get pizza for dinner? We can invite Dad."

She swallowed and searched for the right words. It was the first time Will had flat out asked for the three of them to be together. For the past four weeks, he'd respected her aversion to being around his father, but she'd seen the longing in his eyes before he climbed out of her SUV to go inside the house with his dad. She'd known this day was coming, and she should have had an answer prepared.

"I-I don't think so, Will. Your dad may be on the oil platform awhile."

"I got a text from him. He's coming back to Pelican Harbor at six."

She shot a sidelong glance at him. "Did he put you up to this?"

Wind whipped his shaggy black hair around his earnest face. "We don't talk about you, Mom."

She frowned. Wasn't Reid interested in what she did with their son? When she was with Will, she'd managed to frame several unobtrusive questions and discovered they'd gone for beignets every Saturday morning and that after church on Sunday they'd gone to Jesse's Restaurant in Magnolia Springs. They both had shrimp and grits followed by Dutch apple pie cheesecake. It shamed her that she'd eagerly mined for every tidbit she could find out but discovered nothing other than a man who dearly loved his son.

Just like she did.

But he'd kept Will from her all these years, and she found it hard to forgive something like that. Maybe she never would.

THREE

Overboard. The warning might have been real.

Reid's ears still rang from the deafening noise. He parked on Oyster Bay Road in front of Pelican Pizza and flipped down the visor mirror to stare at his reflection. A five o'clock shadow smudged his jaw, and his tanned face was somber under his clean-shaven head. He seemed as scared as he felt. Would Jane even speak to him? What had possessed Will to ask them to share a pizza for dinner?

He'd nearly texted back a *no* when he got Will's message. Jane was liable to think he was behind this idea and was pushing to get past her defenses. He wanted to give her time to get over what he'd done, and she might not appreciate being crowded. But when push came to shove, he couldn't resist the idea of sitting across the table from her and searching her hazel eyes for some sign of forgiveness.

He flipped the visor back up so he didn't see the ridiculous hope in his eyes. Even allowing a glimmer of optimism would set him up for a crash of disappointment.

He exited into the aroma of garlic and cheese wafting from the building and turned toward the entrance. He caught a glimpse of Jane's face as she stared intently at Will, who was talking with both his hands and his mouth. They sat beside each other at a window booth. Reid's heart warmed when Will slipped his arm around his

16

mother and gave her a quick hug at something she said. Whatever happened from here, at least he'd made sure Will knew his mom loved him. That would go a long way with his boy.

He opened the glass door into Pelican's, and the yeasty scent of homemade pizza dough drifted his way. He hesitated, squaring his shoulders and turning toward Jane and Will. His stride ate up the distance along the wide plank floors from the door to the booth by the window.

Will caught sight of him first, and his gaze raked over Reid's face. "You got sunburned."

"Windburned." Reid stooped and rubbed Parker's ears. "You guys order already?" He hadn't dared look at Jane's face, not after he saw her shoulders stiffen from the back. This had been a monumental mistake.

Will took a sip of his soda. "Yeah, one with lots of pineapple just for you." His grin told Reid he was kidding.

Jane shuddered. "Pineapple belongs on ice cream, not pizza."

Reid slid into the booth across from Jane and Will. "My sentiments exactly. Will's French teacher liked pineapple on pizza, and I promised Will I'd never make him eat it again after that one time."

Jane's tentative smile vanished. "Your old girlfriend."

Will shifted and glanced from his mother to Reid. "Well, not really a girlfriend."

Reid sent his son a thankful smile.

Troy Boulter, the owner of the pizza place, came their way with the food. "Here you go, Jane." His brown eyes were warm with affection.

"Have you been to see your brother?"

Brian Boulter was up on murder charges after a plot to frame and take down her father. He'd harbored a grudge after Charles had arrested his dad years ago.

"I'm glad you asked. His rage has only gotten worse. He seems to be trying to figure out how to punish your dad from jail. I warned Charles already—did he tell you?"

"No, he didn't. Thanks for telling me."

Troy patted her on the shoulder and left them alone.

"What were you two doing out by the oil platform today?"

Jane's lips flattened, and she swiped her foggy glass. "Police business."

Reid studied her closed expression. "So it had nothing to do with a missing man?"

Her gaze locked with his for the first time. "You know about the missing guy?"

"If it's Keith McDonald, the answer is yes." Should he tell her about the emails from Keith? With the guy's disappearance, what he'd said took on ominous tones. "I was supposed to meet up with him so he could tell me about his suspicion that something 'big' was about to happen to the oil platform. Though he didn't say, I assumed he meant sabotage."

"He told you that too?"

"Who else did he tell?"

"His mother. He said if he came up missing, she should come see me. So she did. Do you have his emails?"

"Yeah." He pulled out his phone and forwarded the emails to her. "They should be in your in-box."

"You think the threat is credible? I called Homeland Security as soon as I got back to the dock. They promised to investigate, but I'm not sure they believed it was serious. All I have is a vague email to his mother. Why did Keith contact you?"

"He'd seen some of my documentaries but wasn't sure it was a credible threat because he had no proof. He wanted to talk to someone who could blow the story wide open and maybe prevent another Deepwater Horizon. I got the first email a couple of weeks ago and arranged to do a documentary to check it out."

She winced at the mention of the disaster from 2010 and picked up her iced tea. "Did anyone else on the platform mention a terrorist plot?"

"I didn't want to tip my hand so I didn't ask. I wanted to talk to his bunkmate and friends, but I couldn't find out who they were without showing undue interest. You think you could get that information from his mother?"

She surveyed him over the rim of her glass. "This isn't your investigation, Reid."

"No, but I can get into places and ask questions you can't. People will be more apt to talk to me than to the law or Homeland Security. You know it's true, Jane. Let me help."

She set her drink back on the table. "I don't want you asking questions on your own. It might be dangerous."

He eyed her. Did she really care if he got hurt or even killed? With him out of the way, she'd have Will all to herself. It was an unworthy thought. Though he believed he knew her better than she realized, he wasn't sure how the events of the past few weeks had changed her.

He desperately wanted to reach across the table and take her hand, but it wasn't the right time. Maybe it never would be. He might have burned his bridges for all time.

———

Well, that went better than she'd anticipated.

Jane brushed her lips across her son's cheek, then waved goodbye as Reid accelerated away from the curb. It was still light out at seven thirty, and she didn't want to go home and obsess over the day. She tugged Parker's lead, and they walked along Magnolia Street with its French Quarter brick buildings and black iron railings, then turned down the alley toward Olivia's house on Dauphin Street.

The crape myrtle tree in her front yard was about to bloom beside the oyster-shell driveway, and Olivia must have replenished the pine mulch recently because the crisp aroma of it lingered in the air.

Two figures sat on Olivia's tiny porch in a swing. Olivia Davis waved as Jane and Parker neared. Olivia had taken Jane under her wing as soon as Jane started working at the police station. Olivia had sat at the dispatcher desk for over twenty-five years—ever since her police officer husband had been killed in the line of duty—and her dark-blue eyes missed nothing. The shapely legs under her white shorts seemed thinner, and she was pale.

Megan, her fourteen-year-old daughter, was a carbon copy of her mother, though her curly brown hair was longer and often in a ponytail.

Megan patted her knee to call Parker to her. "Mom just said she was hoping you might stop by tonight."

Jane dropped onto an antique metal chair beside the swing. "I wanted to see what the doctor had to say today. Did you ask him to run the Lyme tests?"

"I asked, but I didn't get very far," Olivia said. "He seemed offended that I even considered he might have made a wrong diagnosis. I actually walked out. I kind of burned my bridges today, I think."

Jane winced. "Good grief, Olivia, I didn't want you to put all your eggs in the Lyme basket. What will you do?"

This felt like her fault. Olivia had recently been diagnosed with ALS, but Jane had urged her to get a second opinion and to check for

we're still going out. He calls a

think he gets it, he forgets and

starting to give me the creeps."

"Poor kid. Have you tried

Tyler Price's mother had d

every time Jane saw him now

high up with the oil company

hadn't remembered it until Ty

be a good resource to talk to a

Megan stared down at he

trouble. He's been through so

"Want me to have a talk w

Megan shook her head. "I

just forgets."

Jane made a note to talk

maybe Tyler would come up,

wasn't in any danger.

Lyme disease as well. Jane believed in taking charge of everything, including health, and never settling for the easy answer.

"I still have that Lyme-literate doctor's name you gave me. I left a message for her asking for an appointment." Olivia studied Jane's face. "Rough day? What's going on?"

"Do I look that haggard?" Jane managed a chuckle and tucked a strand of hair behind her ear.

"Stressed might be a better word, but it comes with the territory."

"You know Ruby McDonald, don't you?"

"Sure." Olivia nodded.

Megan looked up at the mention of the school principal's name. "She wasn't in most of the day."

Her mother lifted a brow. "And how do you know that, young lady? Did you get in trouble today?"

"Sheesh, Mom, no. I'm on the student council, and our after-school meeting was canceled." Parker nudged Megan's hand, and she went back to petting him. "I heard her son is missing."

Jane shook her head. "Small-town life. It's harder to keep a secret here than to fight off a gator."

"He works on the oil platform," Olivia said. "Was he the one the Coast Guard was searching for today?"

"He was." Jane told them about the terrorist threat and what Reid had learned as well.

A smile brightened Olivia's wan face, framed by her curly brown hair in its familiar bob. "You had dinner with Reid? That's the real reason for the shadow in your eyes, isn't it? How'd that go?"

"I don't think my nonexistent love life is more important than a missing man!"

"Oh, lighten up, Jane. You need to forgive the guy and see what the future holds."

Megan's smile was wide. "

Had Jane ever been that

cautious with her heart to be a

She lifted a brow in Mega

out with him?"

"I wish. I've seen him arou

"We're friends on Snapchat, bu

in real life."

Jane was still trying to na

erhood and wasn't sure how n

private life, but she couldn't ho

in someone else?"

"Baseball practice is his

obsessed with breaking the

pitching speed. I know all abo

Jane knew that much. W

and he practiced pitching eve

you know that?"

"He always posts his time

looked at her phone and her f

dered and put it down.

Her mother reached ove

again?" She frowned. "You ne

"I was afraid it would m

dissing him."

Jane furrowed her brow. '

you guys broke up two mont

Megan's hand stilled on

up with me, but he got hit in t

weeks ago. It affected his sho

FOUR

That bull alligator sounded too close for comfort.

Behind the house Reid sat on the pier that stretched like a finger into the Bon Secour River. Will, his legs dangling over the side, sat beside him in the cacophony of frogs trying to outdo one another. Sunset gilded the tops of the pecan trees and shimmered on the surface of the river.

Will tossed a rock into the sluggish river. "Mom seemed okay with you at dinner."

Reid snorted. "Don't tell me you didn't notice she didn't so much as lean back against the seat. She was wound up as tightly as your arm before a pitch. She couldn't wait to gulp down her food and get out of there."

"The two of you were discussing a case like old times."

The hope in his son's voice hurt. Reid held no illusions of ever seeing forgiveness in Jane's eyes. He didn't deserve it either. And it was a real shame, because that kiss they'd shared still kept him awake at night, and he'd give anything for another taste of her lips.

Reid held his son's gaze. "You haven't heard anything from Lauren, have you?"

Will straightened. "You heard from her?"

"No, just making sure she hasn't been bothering you."

"I haven't seen her since that day on the street."

"Me neither."

Four weeks with no contact from Lauren, his presumed-dead-but-resurrected ex. Her demand for money to go away again had come as a shock, but at least Will knew the truth now. Reid had begun to let himself hope she'd given up and moved on, that she was far away with no more thought about him and Will. But something in his gut told him he hadn't seen the last of her.

"Grandpa offered to take me deep sea fishing this weekend. I told him I'd have to check, but it's okay, isn't it?"

Reid gave a jerky nod. "Sure. He probably knows all the best spots."

Jane's dad had wasted no time in trying to buddy up to Will. Reid wasn't sure how he felt about that yet. If there was one place to put the majority of the blame in this situation, it was squarely on the shoulders of Charles Hardy. He'd uttered the lie that set everything in motion. Though Reid's own hands weren't clean, Charles hadn't made any attempt to find the grandson he knew was alive even though he'd told Jane the baby died. He had to have known Will was out there somewhere, but he'd waited until Reid had brought him to Pelican Harbor and revealed his identity to Jane before reaching out.

But never let it be said he stood in the way of a good relationship between Will and his mother's family. Pettiness wasn't in his nature.

Reid twirled a fallen leaf in his hand. "I found a lead to my grandparents, my mom's parents."

"Seriously? Where are they?"

Maybe he shouldn't have mentioned it yet. "They're in a little town in northern Indiana called Wabash."

"Why didn't you try to find them when you left Liberty's Children with me?"

"My dad had said they were dead so I didn't look very hard. And I didn't have the money back then to hire anyone. It was all I could do to keep us both fed and with a roof over our heads. I was working a lot of hours, too, so there wasn't much time. I hired an investigator a couple of weeks ago, and it didn't take long for her to find them."

Will's brown eyes shone above his hopeful smile. "Are you going to call them? Or maybe go see them?"

"I haven't decided what to do yet. Kelly—that's the investigator— seems to think they are in good health. They're in their midseventies and still living at home."

"A-Are there any aunts or uncles? Or cousins?"

"My mom had two younger brothers, and they each have kids. I'm unsure of ages and names yet. Kelly's putting together information for me, and I should have it tomorrow or the next day. Then we can decide what to do."

"I want to go there. Just show up on their doorstep."

"I'm afraid that might be too much of a shock to them."

"Don't you think it would be a good shock, though?"

Reid looked out at the moonlight glittering on the water. "I'm not sure how they parted with my mom and dad."

"And is she still alive? Your mother?"

"I was ten when she went missing. I heard her yelling at my dad that it wasn't right for him to have another wife. When I got up the next morning, she was gone. He said she left, b-but I always thought he had her killed. Or killed her himself." He shuddered, remembering the rages his dad would get into. "Within a month he had two other wives."

"Did Kelly search for her too?"

He probably shouldn't be talking about all this with Will. Sometimes Reid forgot he was only fifteen. The boy had always acted mature and steady.

He nodded. "No sign of her."

"If you haven't talked to them, they probably still think she's out there somewhere."

He needed to change the subject. "You have homework?"

"Yeah, some algebra." Will got up. "I'll do it now. The mosquitoes are zooming in."

"I'm right behind you." Reid listened to the fading sound of Will's flip-flops, then got to his feet. His personal life could wait. Keith McDonald was still missing, and the possibility of an attack on the oil platform loomed large in Reid's mind, even though it was in the hands of Homeland Security now.

He should leave it alone, but as an investigative journalist he had the unique position of being someone people wanted to talk to. Maybe he could find out more than the law. And it wouldn't be a bad thing if he and Jane worked together on this. If anything could get her to put the past behind her, it might be a new case they could solve together.

She'd rather walk through fire than go in there, Jane thought the next day as she pulled up outside her father's prepper compound and sat staring at the gate and the long driveway back to the buildings. All she had to do was punch in the code, but her throat was tight, and she couldn't get her hand to move from the steering wheel. She hadn't talked to her father in several weeks, not since he'd admitted the heinous things he'd done fifteen years ago.

Thanks to his lie, she'd missed out on the first fifteen years of Will's life.

She exhaled and reached for the button to lower her window. Sitting out here wasn't going to get her questions answered about Keith's disappearance. Her father would know more about that oil platform than most. He was part of the environmental group in town that oversaw the marshes and wetlands. He knew all about the impact from Deepwater Horizon and helped oversee safety measures on the platforms.

Her hand shook as she punched in the code. The big gate opened, and she was through both gates in under two minutes. Her pulse was beating like a tom-tom in her chest when she parked in front of her father's porch. She stared at the two-story brick four-square for a long moment. How did she even open the conversation when she hadn't come close to forgiving him yet?

She forced herself to shove open her door and step out into the blazing heat. She opened the back door and let Parker out to run into the shadow of the big trees where he would chase squirrels before taking a nap—though she didn't intend to be here long enough for the squirrels to wear him out.

Her shoulders back, she strode up the steps to the door and pressed the bell. A few weeks ago, she would have opened the door and gone on in. But a few weeks ago she still naively believed everything her father told her.

Footsteps came toward the door, and it opened. Her dad's gaze sharpened on her face. "Jane." His eyebrows rose.

"I need to talk to you about a terrorist threat."

He opened the door wider and stepped aside. "Sure."

Most people thought he was much younger than his early sixties. His biceps were as firm and strong as a twenty-year-old's. Only his bushy white hair matched his age.

She entered into a welcome wash of cool air and shut the door behind her. Coffee aroma drifted toward her, and her stomach rumbled at the scent of beignets. They wouldn't be homemade. With his ex-girlfriend, Elizabeth, in jail, he'd be buying most of his food. For a prepper he was surprisingly unhandy in the kitchen. Until Elizabeth had moved in, he ate fast food, frozen pizza, and cereal. Or the dreadful freeze-dried meals he rotated out of his stockpile in the bunker.

"It's good to see you, Jane."

His cautious tone did nothing to quell the anger rising in her chest. Instead of answering, she dropped onto the sofa and clasped her hands on one knee. "What do you know about Zeus?"

"The Greek god?" His smirk told her he knew exactly what she meant. And that he'd noticed the anger shaking her voice.

She didn't take the bait. "The oil platform."

He settled in the armchair across from the sofa and reached for a coffee mug atop it. "It's the largest oil platform ever constructed in these waters and has more safety stops built into it than any other as well. Before it was approved to be erected, I wanted to make sure we didn't have another Deepwater Horizon on our hands off our own shore. Has something happened?"

She considered how much to tell him. It was likely Homeland Security would contact him anyway. "It might be the target of a terrorist plot."

His eyes widened. "Who would do such a thing?"

"I don't have details yet, just suspicions." She told him about Keith's email and subsequent disappearance. "Reid is doing a documentary on the platform, and he's hoping to find out more. I've called it in to Homeland Security as well."

"You're talking to Reid?"

She wanted to leap to her feet and make for the door, but she drew in a deep breath. "I'm not going to talk to you about Reid or Will."

He banged his cup down hard enough, some coffee sloshed over the lip onto the table. "Oh, get over it, Jane. You're making a mountain out of a molehill. It all turned out okay. You have a relationship with your son now."

It was all she could do not to pummel him with her fists. "I missed out on fifteen years, Dad!"

He leaned forward and pointed a finger at her. "And you're alive. If I hadn't lied to you, you'd be in an unmarked grave in Michigan."

"There would have been time to get him."

"You don't know that! You didn't see all the carnage scattered around us. After the birth, you were weak and shocked from loss of blood. If you think back, I'm sure you don't even remember much about our escape."

"You cheated me, Dad, and you haven't even apologized. You're so sure you were right, and you don't care how much it hurt me. How much it changed me and made me afraid of any kind of normal life." She rose and swept her hand toward the window where the top of his bunker gleamed in the sunshine. "And you're no better! Hiding guns and food for a coming apocalypse. What kind of life is it when you live in fear?"

His narrowed gaze skewered her. "There's nothing wrong with being prepared."

"Was that wall around your heart the real reason Elizabeth betrayed you?"

His hazel eyes blazed under his bushy white brows. "I never want to hear her name again, and I'm surprised you would bring her up. She's a murderer and a liar. If you want to talk about her, you can leave now."

She spun on her heel and stalked to the door, which she slammed behind her. Parker came when she called, and she couldn't wait to get away from her dad and his smug certainty he'd done the right thing. She texted Ruby asking for a meeting at Pelican Brews, then drove off with a plume of dust behind her.

———

Shadows loomed in the dark warehouse. He walked quickly to where the other two waited in the back. His boots clacked along the concrete floor and echoed against the tall ceiling. It sounded like someone was following him, but he knew he was the last to arrive.

He'd made sure of it, before he slid out of his truck and came inside. He wasn't the most important piece of this puzzle to the Boss, but he knew his role would be foundational. He was the cleanup guy, the one who ensured everything happened as it should. It wasn't a role he usually embraced, but this was his quest. He couldn't rest until justice was served.

"There you are." The Boss pointed to an empty metal chair. "Kind of you to join us." He lifted a brow.

He smiled at the Boss's displeasure and slid into the end seat without a reply.

The Boss focused his attention on the IT guy. "We're ready for our event?"

"I am, sir," the blond IT guy said. "It's ready when you are. I can schedule it sooner if you like."

"No, no. I have my reasons for the timing. This meeting is to ensure there are no hiccups."

He was likely the only other person who knew the reason for the date. The other guy was a hired gun, whereas it was very personal for him and the Boss.

The Boss glanced at him. "You're quite sure our lark is dead?"

He fingered the small scar on his upper lip. "Quite sure. I have pictures if you like."

The Boss wiggled his fingers for the phone. He scrolled through the pictures and grunted with satisfaction. "Good work. You do realize there's an ongoing investigation?"

"I assumed there would be, but they have no body."

"That won't stop the chief of police. Don't underestimate her because she's petite. She's very smart and focused, and she doesn't give up. We may need to think outside the box to dissuade her." The Boss tapped the pen against his chin. "She has a son. A threat to him might do the trick."

"I don't hurt kids, Boss."

"This one is fifteen, almost grown. If you can't do what I tell you, I'll find someone who can."

"Fifteen is not a kid. Should I injure him or take him out?"

"I'd rather not kill him because that will have her on our tail like a small tiger. I want to discourage her from looking too hard."

"If she's as smart and focused as you say, a deterrent might spur her into looking harder." He didn't think the Boss was as smart as he thought he was, but he kept his opinion to himself.

"I just need to slow her down until after May 12. See what you can do."

The Boss dismissed them, and he walked back to his truck. He'd have to think of something to deter her, but it might not be easy based on the lady chief's description.

FIVE

Jane's temper hadn't cooled when she jerked open the door to Pelican Brews, but the scent of espresso and pastries took her anger down a notch. She scanned the tables and spotted Ruby. The skin under her eyes was dark enough to be mistaken for a domestic injury. Her red shirt was wrinkled as though she'd slept in it. She probably had.

Jane's gaze went to the figure beside her, and she nearly groaned. Reid again. What was he doing here? Ruby hadn't said anything about him when Jane had texted with a request for a meeting. After confronting Dad yesterday, Jane wasn't in the mood for more drama.

Her idiotic pulse sped up at the sight of his tanned head and the muscular arms showing under his black tee. The smile he sent her way freed a flutter of butterflies in her belly.

Reid held up a coffee in his hand, then slid it along the table to an empty seat. She made her way to the corner and stood looking down at the two of them. "Did I miss a memo?"

The acerbic bite to her tone made her sound like a shrew, but she had a feeling Reid had orchestrated this.

She sat as far away from him as she could, but that meant she was looking him square in the face. To hide the irritation she was struggling to control, she bent her head and picked up the coffee cup. "Thanks for the coffee."

"No problem," Reid said.

Ruby glanced from her to Reid with a frown. "You said you had more questions?"

"Has anyone from Homeland Security or the FBI contacted you?"

Ruby tucked an errant brown curl behind her ear and nodded. "Several people came by yesterday, but I didn't have much more to add than what I'd told you. It was all in the email."

"Did they ask about Keith's friends?"

"Yes, and I told them about his bunkmate and the others he'd mentioned on the rig."

"Who was his bunkmate? I'd like to talk to him."

"His name is Walter. I don't remember his last name."

Jane set down her coffee and leaned forward. "I got to wondering if he would have talked to his friends here on land. And what about a girlfriend? Maybe he's talked about this with people he's comfortable with."

Ruby inclined her head toward the coffee counter. "That red-head there is Bonnie Webb. They dated about a year, but Keith said she didn't like the way he was gone so long at a time and broke up with him. They broke up about a month ago."

Jane swiveled to gaze at Bonnie. She'd worked here several months now and was always cheerful and outgoing. She appeared to be in her early twenties, and while she had a cute build, she always dressed modestly in jeans and a T-shirt that covered her curves. Her vibrant red hair drew anyone's attention. She always noticed Jane in the line and had her black coffee poured and ready to go.

"I think I'll see if she can take a break and join us for a few minutes. There's no line, and three people are behind the counter."

Bonnie looked up with a smile when Jane approached the counter. "Need a refill, Chief?"

"Actually, I wondered if you'd have time to answer a few questions about Keith McDonald?"

Bonnie's brown eyes clouded, and Jane noticed the red rims around them. She'd probably heard of Keith's disappearance.

Bonnie glanced behind her at the two young men. "I'm going to take a break, guys. I'll be at the table with the chief if it gets crazy." She came around the espresso machines and exited the counter area.

"Are you sure Ruby will want me there? She didn't say anything to me when she got here." Bonnie's voice choked off.

"Ruby's having a hard time."

Bonnie paused when they reached the table. "Um, where do you want me to sit?"

Ruby patted the chair Jane had vacated. "Sit here by me, Bonnie. Did you hear about Keith?"

Bonnie sank bonelessly into the chair and burst into tears. Ruby reached over and gripped Bonnie's hands in hers while she cried too. Jane's impulse was to embrace them both, but they weren't close enough for that kind of gesture. Her eyes burned at their pain, and she wished she could ease it somehow. Keith had to be dead by now. Regret resided in Reid's eyes too.

Bonnie reached for a napkin and blotted her eyes. "I wanted to get him back." Her voice wobbled. "I tried calling him and texting him for the past week, but he never answered. I was sure he would have realized it was a mistake by now. He said he wanted me to have time to date around rather than waiting on him, but I already knew I didn't want to date other guys."

Reid handed her another napkin. "Wait a minute. Are you saying *he* broke up with you? You didn't break up with him?"

Bonnie crumpled the napkin in her hand and shook her head. "I loved him. I wanted to marry him."

Ruby let go of Bonnie and sat back in her chair. "Keith told me you broke up with him—that you couldn't handle his long absences."

Bonnie lifted her reddened eyes and locked her gaze on Jane. "That's not true. It wasn't my idea at all. Now that he's missing, I think he was afraid I'd get hurt by whoever is behind all this. He made an excuse to break up to keep me out of it."

Jane pulled out her notepad. "Have you met other men Keith worked with?"

Bonnie glanced at Ruby, then back to Jane. "Um, just that English guy he bunked with. He gave Keith a fat manila envelope and told him not to show it to anyone. We were at my apartment, and when Keith walked him out, he warned Keith to keep an eye on me. It was kind of creepy."

Reid made a sound, but Jane held up her hand to silence him. "Why would he warn Keith like that?"

"Keith was tight-lipped about it, but I think it was to keep Keith from talking about what he'd overheard."

"Do you still have the manila envelope?" Jane asked.

"No, Keith took it with him, and he didn't tell me what was in it."

"Do you remember the guy's name or what he looked like?" Reid's voice was tight, and he shot a warning look at Jane.

"He was Keith's bunkmate. He's a really big guy with a gold tooth and tattoos."

Reid leaned forward. "Dex!"

Jane stared at him. "You know this guy?"

Reid's brown eyes narrowed. "He's a deck pusher on the rig and showed me around yesterday. Let's see if we can find out when he's coming ashore. He knows a lot more than he let on to me. He didn't say a word about being Keith's bunkmate."

And Reid's aggrieved tone indicated he didn't like Dex's subterfuge one bit. Jane was going to have to work with him on this a lot more closely than she'd like.

———

Jane was going to be madder than a wet cat.

Reid rose with his empty cup, then held out his hand for Jane's cup. She handed it to him. Pelican Brews picked up with lunch business, and Bonnie had to get back to work. Ruby excused herself as well to go back to the school.

He let his gaze linger on the beautiful planes of Jane's angular features as he took the coffee cup. The humidity released the curl in her light-brown hair, and her eyes were more green than hazel today. He wanted to linger on those lips he still dreamed of kissing again, but she'd be furious if she knew what he was thinking.

He gestured to the daily menu on the chalkboard. "Any food to take with us? The paninis smell good."

"I'm not hungry, thanks. Go ahead if you want something."

"I'm good." He led the way to the door.

Outside, he turned toward the trash receptacle, and the gulls hanging around gave him arrogant stares from their black eyes. They didn't even fly away when he approached.

He tossed the cups. "We need to find out when Dex is coming ashore. And where he lives."

"I was going to see Steve Price today anyway. He's the shore manager, and he'll know."

He swung back toward her. "Mind if I tag along?" He expected a glare and an emphatic *no*, but she assessed him for a long moment.

"Okay. He might be swayed to be more honest by the fact you're with the media."

He hid his jubilation and followed her and Parker across the street and into the sunshine. A muscle car roared past, and he missed what she'd said. "Sorry?"

Her gaze locked with his. "Let me ask the questions. And don't think this means anything has changed between us."

He gave a jerky nod. "Understood."

He wanted to ask if she'd ever forgive him, but the words got tangled with regret. Before he could say anything else, she swung away from him and stalked toward her SUV in the police station's parking lot. He followed, admiring the strong curves of her legs in the khaki skirt she wore.

The lights flashed with the beep of the vehicle unlocking, and she put Parker in the back before she climbed behind the wheel. Reid slid into the passenger seat. Maybe changing the subject would be the wisest choice about now.

He cleared his throat as she exited the lot and pulled onto the street. "I told Will he could go fishing with your dad."

The glare he'd expected earlier shot his way before she turned her attention back to the road. Her jaw tightened, and her knuckles went white on the steering wheel. "You didn't think to ask for my permission?"

"Uh, no. I assumed you'd want him to spend time with your dad."

"My dad doesn't deserve to be around Will, not after all the lies."

"That's not Will's fault. He's pathetically eager for a relationship with his grandfather. I know the feeling. I've been searching for my grandparents too."

Too personal. He should have kept his mouth shut.

Her grip on the steering wheel relaxed. "Any luck?"

"Actually, yeah. I found my mother's parents living in Indiana. I haven't contacted them yet. I'm not sure if I should."

Shut up, Reid.

"Any aunts and uncles?"

"Two uncles, younger than Mom. I just got the report from Kelly, my investigator. They're both married with kids. One has two girls and the other one has twin boys. The older of the two, Randy, still lives in Wabash. The other one, Rick, lives in Wickenburg, Arizona."

She turned into the parking lot of an industrial complex. "I found an online article this morning about Liberty's Children."

She was actually *talking* to him? "A recent one?"

"Dated last week. According to the article, the group has taken over an abandoned town along the Cumberland River in Kentucky."

"That's about as clear as mud. The Cumberland is nearly seven hundred miles long. Did the article say just where?"

"I don't remember the exact details. It mentioned the headwaters? I don't really know what that means."

"I do. I did a documentary about the Cumberland about five years ago. Its headwaters are three separate rivers that converge near Baxter, Kentucky. The river is wild and turbulent throughout much of the area. Thick vegetation, not many people. Maybe we can find out more details and make a visit. See if your mom is still there."

"I can't see her ever leaving."

Reid nodded. "You think this Price fellow will talk?"

"He won't want any negative publicity." She parked the vehicle near the front of the building and turned it off. "Let's see what we can find out."

She was all business again and would be unlikely to open up to him again. If only he'd had a little more time.

SIX

Reid's presence had her on edge.

Jane led the way and had only to flash her badge before being ushered into Steve Price's office. The room was massive, and windows filled one whole wall that flooded the space with light. His desk was a sleek modern one, and the room was furnished with a sofa and comfortable armchairs on one side plus a long meeting room table with seating at the other end. Her whole studio apartment above the bakery would fit in this one room.

Steve stood from behind his desk and approached them with his hand out. "Jane, nice to see you." He shook her hand, then petted Parker.

Jane had been around Steve at various events in town. He was about forty with wings of gray threaded through his dark hair at his temples. His tall, distinguished air attracted female attention, but since his wife's death, she'd never seen him with another woman.

His gaze went past Jane's shoulder to Reid. "I don't think we've met."

Reid held out his hand. "Reid Dixon, journalist. Your office gave permission for me to board the oil platform for a documentary. I was out there yesterday."

Steve's thousand-watt smile dimmed. "I suppose this is about our man overboard?" He gestured to the seating area to Jane's left. "I have about half an hour before an important meeting, but I'm happy to answer anything I can. It's tragic, just tragic."

Jane waited until they were all seated, then took out her notepad. "Are you aware Keith McDonald feared a terrorist attack on the oil platform?" Might as well go for shock value and see what happened.

Steve shook his head. "Homeland Security contacted me about it, and I told them I've seen no evidence of anything like that. We have top security out there, and cameras all over the place. Our IT department reviewed every feed we have, and there's nothing to indicate Keith was in contact with terrorists. Supposedly he overheard a conversation, but we've found nothing like that in our feeds. I wonder if it might have been an attention stunt. The young man had some, uh, issues."

Jane's ears perked. "Issues?"

Steve nodded and petted Parker, who laid his head on Steve's knee. "He had taken my son under his wing after my wife died. Our families have been friends for years, and Tyler idolized Keith. But he's been strange lately."

"Tyler or Keith?"

Steve frowned. "Keith, of course."

"I heard your son was having some short-term memory loss after a baseball accident."

Steve gave a dismissive wave of his hand. "Minor. The doctors say it will pass. Where'd you hear about that?"

"His ex-girlfriend, Megan."

"I wouldn't exactly call her a girlfriend. He's only fifteen. They 'broke up'"—he put the words in air quotes with his fingers—"over a month ago."

"But Megan says he forgets they've broken up and has been following her. And stalking her on Snapchat."

Steve's brows drew together. "I'm sure it's nothing serious. All she has to do is tell him to quit it."

"She has, but he forgets."

She clenched her fists at his dismissive attitude. "What about Keith? Do you have any idea what was going on with him? His mother said he wasn't on any antidepressants. You think he deliberately jumped off the oil platform?"

"It was my first thought. He'd just been acting strange, paranoid even. He kept looking out the window and asking me if I knew the car going by. The last time he was at the house he insisted on keeping the curtains open, and he sat in the chair where he could see out to the front yard. I thought maybe he was working too many hours and offered to see if I could adjust his schedule, but he brushed that off. Now I wish I had."

Reid leaned forward. "What if he was paranoid for a reason?"

"I just don't buy it. Why would a terrorist want to blow up the oil platform?"

"Major contamination of the beaches," Jane said. "And maybe quite a few dead."

"Even Deepwater Horizon only killed eleven. Now, that's a tragedy. I'm not discounting those lives, but it's not like the attack on the World Trade Center. Most terrorists want at least a few hundred dead to make a point. Blowing up the platform would gain some attention, but not the kind that would make all the cost and planning worth it. At least not in my opinion. It's not something you see much of, even worldwide."

She rose. "Thanks for your time, Steve. We'll let you get back to work. If you think of anything else, please let me know." She passed him a business card with her cell number on it.

He fingered it and put it in the inside pocket of his navy jacket before he rose to escort them to the door. "Will do. Sorry I couldn't be more help."

"I do have one more question," Reid said. "Do you know when Dex, one of your deck pushers, is due to come ashore?"

Steve went to his desk and jiggled his mouse. "I can find out. You know his last name?"

"Sorry, I don't."

"I might still be able to find him." He peered at his screen. "There he is, Walter Dexter, nickname Dex. He's ashore right now."

"Could I get his address?" Jane asked.

"Sure. He lives right here in Pelican Harbor."

The printer whirred to life, and a few moments later, Steve handed her a printout.

"Appreciate your help." She took it and stuffed it in her bag before heading outside.

She squinted when she exited into the bright sunlight and turned to Reid. "What did you think? Keith sounded paranoid."

"Sometimes paranoia is warranted. He appeared to be afraid, and now he's dead."

Heat shimmered off the blacktop of the parking lot, and she paused to think about it. "Maybe we need to talk to Tyler and some of his other friends."

"I'm not so sure Tyler will remember."

"But he might. Steve seems to think he's getting better. How well does Will know Tyler?"

"They've hung out some after baseball practice, and he's often been at the house. We could ask Will if Tyler has said anything about Keith."

"I don't want to pull him into any danger."

"I don't think a few questions will do that. I doubt he knows much." Reid glanced at his watch. "It's nearly lunchtime at school. We could grab him and Tyler a sub sandwich and meet up. I'll text him."

All this camaraderie made her want to take a step back, but she nodded, and they moved toward the vehicle.

───

Jane's manner was still as stiff as a stork's legs.

Reid scanned the kids shooting hoops and lounging in the shade of the water oaks and pecan trees lining the basketball court. He waved at Will and Tyler sitting on a bench under a giant tree near the gurgling creek.

"There they are." Will waved at him, and Reid waved back.

Parker gave a joyous bark and raced to thrust his nose into Will's hand. Jane wore the first genuine smile Reid had seen on her face all morning. Would she ever smile at him like that again? Hope seemed elusive after the hours they'd spent together. How different it might have been if he'd told her who they were as soon as they hit town. They might have been a real family now.

Jane stepped out ahead of him a few feet. Her eagerness to see her son always touched him with her craving to make up for lost time. She might be small, but she was a powerhouse of love and care for others.

Will grinned up at her when she reached them. "How'd you guys know lunch was going to be tuna casserole? I'd rather eat dirt."

Jane started to touch his hair, then drew back with a quick peek at the other kids watching them curiously. "Lucky guess. Your dad got you meatball subs. That okay?"

"He knows it's my jam."

"Mine too." But Tyler blinked and stared at the sack of food as if he couldn't quite remember what a meatball sub was like.

He had a slight build, green eyes, and sandy hair that curled just over his ears. Reid could just make out the name *Megan* on the metal bracelet he wore on his left wrist. Another indication that he still wasn't quite right when it came to his relationship with his ex-girlfriend.

"We had some questions for you both."

Tyler's eyes widened, and he pulled at his lip. "My memory isn't so good right now. I'm not sure what you want, though."

Will took the sack, then opened it and handed a sandwich and a bag of chips to Tyler. "It's okay, Tyler. My parents will be cool with whatever you can remember. What's up, Dad?"

My parents.

The casual pride in Will's voice touched Reid's heart. Family meant everything to a kid who'd had so little of it.

"I'm actually the one with the questions," Jane said. "It's about an investigation."

"What's up?" Will opened his sandwich and took a big bite.

Jane stared at Tyler, who was tearing open his bag of chips. "It's about Keith McDonald, Tyler."

The boy looked up. "Is he in trouble?"

Reid exchanged a glance with Will. Tyler had to have heard Keith was missing. His father would likely have discussed it with him. More of his short-term memory loss problem?

"He's missing." Jane's voice was gentle. "Your dad said you hung out a lot with him, and he mentioned Keith had been acting like he thought someone was following him. Did he say anything to you about it?"

Tyler kept his head down and shrugged. "I don't really remember." He glanced over at Will. "When did we see Keith last?"

"Three weeks ago? He threw some balls for us, remember? You hit a home run."

Reid wished he could comfort him. Kids that age didn't want anyone to think they were vulnerable, though. Three weeks ago would have been before he took the baseball to the head.

"Yeah, sure," Tyler mumbled.

Will took a swig of his Coke. "After practice, we went to the ice-cream store for milkshakes. Keith was all jumpy and huddled in the corner when a white pickup went by real slow. I asked him who it was, and he just shook his head."

"Could you see who was driving?"

"It was a guy, maybe twenty-five or so, but I couldn't tell you much beyond that. I didn't get a good look through the tinted windows. I probably wouldn't have even remembered that much if Keith hadn't been acting so weird."

Parker growled low in this throat, and his ruff stood on end. He stepped away from Will to place his front paws toward the creek.

Jane swiveled with her hand on her gun. "What is it, boy?"

Reid moved to her side. "You see anything?"

The brush rustled, and a large bull alligator charged from the vegetation. Parker lowered his head to charge and uttered a volley of ferocious barks. Jane drew her gun, but the dog had the situation under control. He forced the alligator back to the water, then trotted back with his tail high.

Will petted his head. "Good dog."

COLLEEN COBLE

The school bell rang, and the boys jumped up to toss their trash in the barrel. "Gotta go," Will said.

Reid watched them walk toward the door. Jane touched his arm, and he turned to look at her.

Her eyes were soft. "That's some son we've got. I love the way he was trying to take care of Tyler."

"He's always been that way. Little kids are drawn to him, and I've seen him make the rounds at school functions, making sure any new kids aren't feeling left out. I can't even claim any credit for it. It's just who he is."

He'd take that tender expression in her eyes over the contemptuous one any day, even when the tenderness wasn't directed at him but at Will.

She patted her leg to attract Parker, and the dog whined after Will. "Come on, Parker." With the dog in tow, she walked beside Reid back to the parking lot. "You hear anything from Lauren?"

Was she asking because of Will or because she cared about him? Reid didn't really care which it was—the fact that she was asking something personal was a major win. "Not a thing."

"Good. I hope she stays away from Will."

That put Reid in his place, but at least the ice between them might have thawed a degree or two.

"Let's go talk to Dex. We can eat our subs on the way there."

SEVEN

Jane didn't like having her son in the middle of this investigation. She glanced at Dex's address while they gulped down their sandwiches sitting on a bench in front of Island Bling on Oyster Bay Road. The French Quarter–style building's white facade appeared freshly painted, and it gleamed against the wrought-iron railing.

Her fingers itched to draw Reid's profile as he stared across the street toward the boardwalk, but she didn't have her sketch pad and pencil. She tossed some bread to the gulls. "You replace your boat yet? Never mind. It's not my business."

"I'm looking, but I haven't found the right one yet."

His boat had been destroyed by an explosion a few weeks ago, and she knew Will missed being out on the water.

"You want one the same size?"

"Will wants bigger." He smiled and shook his head. "That boy would live on a boat if we let him." He tossed the last of his bread to the gulls. "I'm ready if you are."

"This way." Dex's apartment was above Island Bling. An iron staircase on the south side of the store ran up to his place, and

Parker whined when she stepped onto it. "He hates open iron stairs. His toenails get caught in the perforated metal treads. My metal steps are solid, but even they took some time to coax him into navigating."

Reid paused. "I can talk to Dex alone if you like. He was comfortable enough with me yesterday."

"I want to be there too." She looked across the street. "Let me see if there's someone who will watch Parker for a few minutes along the water. You can wait here if you like."

"I'll come along."

The heat that flooded her cheeks had nothing to do with the sunshine. He never made her feel she had to hurry to keep up with his long legs, and she allowed herself to slow down and enjoy the walk down the French Quarter alley lined with small shops along the brick pavement leading to the boardwalk. The three-story buildings set at ground level were painted white stucco with black trim and iron details. Charming balconies overlooked the shady alley, and she waved at several people lounging in chairs.

Victor Armstrong's car approached, and his pale-blue eyes skewered her as he drove past. He was a big man in his fifties and had opposed Jane's appointment as chief of police. As a commercial real estate agent, he was well-known in town.

He slowed and stopped beside her. "Good job on the last case, Jane."

He didn't call her *chief*, but he never did. "Thanks, Victor. I appreciate the vote of confidence."

He snorted. "Confidence is the last thing I have in you. I'm just giving credit where credit is due." He accelerated away from her without another word.

She doubted she'd ever win him over.

The scent of the bay wafted toward them, and Pete, the pelican she'd rescued, swooped down to land on the pier. He swallowed down a fish, then peered at her with his black eyes. "Sorry, buddy, I don't have any fish for you today." The pelican seemed to give a derisive squawk before flying into the cloudless sky.

Alfie Smith, an old shrimper who was a fixture around town, lifted his hand from where he sat on a wooden bench by the water.

She waved to him. "Hey, Alfie, you going to be here awhile?"

He stretched out his legs clad in long pants stuffed into rubber boots that used to be white. "Sure thing, Chief. *Seacow* is in dry dock getting the hull fixed. I ain't going nowhere."

"I thought your daughter wanted you to quit shrimping anyway."

He shrugged. "She only *thinks* she's the boss of me. The old ticker is still chugging along. I'd rather keel over on my boat than sitting in my chair in the house."

She smiled and nodded. "I'm with you." She touched Parker's head. "Would you mind if Parker hung out with you for a few minutes? I need to conduct an interview, and he doesn't want to climb the open metal stairs."

His rheumy blue eyes blinked and he gazed past her shoulder. "This about that boy throwing hisself off the oil platform?"

The coconut telegraph at work again. "What have you heard about it?" Sometimes rumors in a small town could lead to a gold nugget of information.

"That boy used to go shrimping with me. I saw him last time he was ashore. He spouted some nonsense about terrorists, but that don't make no sense. What would a terrorist gain by doing that here? I told him to dig deeper, that sabotage could be lots of things."

"Any idea of the identity of the men he overheard?" Reid asked.

"Nope. But you gotta stop it if it's coming. My nephew, he was aboard a platform that caught fire. His lungs still ain't no good. That heat and smoke wrecked his health. And the burns . . ." Alfie winced and shook his head. "It's a terrible thing to be burned."

His gaze went over her shoulder, and she heard shouting. She turned to see Victor waving his arms and yelling at someone getting out of a red sports car.

Victor thrust out his chin aggressively. "I had my blinker on to pull into that space. Back out of there right now."

The woman shook her blonde hair. "I was here first." She stalked past him and disappeared into Island Bling.

Alfie muttered something, and Jane turned back to him. "What did you say?"

"Just that he's always meaner than cat dirt this time of year."

She didn't like Victor enough to waste her time with more questions. "He's always mean."

Alfie nodded toward the alley behind her. "Yonder comes the guy you wanted to talk to."

She swung around and saw a burly guy in knee-length orange trunks headed their way with a paddleboard.

Reid muttered, "That's Dex."

She eyed Alfie. "How'd you know?"

Alfie stuck a toothpick in his mouth. "He's the only one 'round here who works the platform. Had to be him."

"Maybe I should hire you as a detective, Alfie. We're shorthanded." She nudged Reid. "Let's get to him before he enters the water."

Reid stepped out and lifted his hand. "Hey, Dex."

The big guy rested the tip of the paddleboard on the boardwalk and wiped the perspiration from his forehead. "I need to leg it if I want to catch the waves. Whatcha need, guv'nor?"

Reid jutted a thumb toward Jane. "The chief has a few questions about Keith McDonald. We found out you were Keith's bunkmate. You could have told me that on Monday."

Dex scowled. "This is a load of codswallop. I don't know anythin'."

"I'll make it short then," Jane said. "What was in the manila envelope you gave Keith?"

The florid color washed out of the big man's face. "I don't know what you're talkin' about."

"Not true, buddy," Reid said. "We have a witness who saw you give Keith a manila envelope and told him to keep it secret."

Dex's blue eyes narrowed. "You talked to Bonnie. Look, this 'as nothin' to do with Keith's suicide, guv'nor. I want to keep my job." He picked up his paddleboard.

Jane stepped in front of him. "Were you threatening Bonnie?"

"Me? No! Some bloke paid me to deliver the envelope. No big deal."

"What bloke?"

"I don't know 'is name. Never seen 'im before."

"What'd he look like?"

"Muscular like he worked out. In 'is twenties. He 'ad a small scar on 'is lip like maybe he'd 'ad a cleft palate as a child. Like I said, I'd never seen 'im before, but he offered me a thousand bucks to give it to Keith in front of Bonnie. So I did."

Jane put her hand on his arm. "Is Bonnie in danger? You warned Keith to keep an eye on her."

"If she goes blabbin' to the wrong bloke, she's in for a world of hurt. That bloke's brown eyes looked sharp enough to cut you." He ran toward the water and didn't glance back. He dove under the waves, pushing his board under too.

"We have to find that envelope." Jane turned toward the buildings and called Parker to her side. "I'm going to get a court order to search Keith's premises. We have probable cause that he might not have gone over the side willingly."

"You don't have a body."

"But I know the judge, and I think I can convince him. Ruby might let me circumvent all that, though. I'll see if she'll give permission and hand me a key."

Everything about this smelled off, and she'd seen the flash of fear in Dex's eyes when Reid mentioned Bonnie.

Jane's nerves were on high alert.

She inserted Keith's key, obtained from Ruby, into the lock and pushed into his apartment. The space was part of a complex on the edge of town and was a studio with a queen bed occupying a bump out of the minuscule living room and kitchen.

Discarded clothing lay draped on the love seat and armchair, and another pile was heaped on the edge of the bed.

Reid entered behind her with Parker and waved his hand in front of his nose. "Whew, stinks in here. He must not have taken out the garbage before he went to the platform last time."

The dog sniffed the air and went to the overflowing trash. "No, Parker," Jane said. He gave her an offended look and plopped down, resting his head on his paws.

Reid stepped to the thermostat on the wall and kicked down the air. The compressor hummed to life.

54

Jane glanced around. "This place hasn't been tossed. It's just guy-messy."

"Hey, some of us are neat freaks." He went to the small desk along one wall and opened a drawer.

Jane didn't think Keith would have put something sensitive in the most likely place. Hands on hips, she searched for a good hiding place. Not under the mattress, not under the love seat cushions. The kitchen.

She pulled on Nitrile gloves, then went to the kitchen, pulled out drawers, and opened cabinets. The stainless-steel cookie jar held only stale macaroons. She pushed aside a few bowls of moldy leftovers and rummaged through browning fruit in the bottom bin, then opened the freezer door. It was stuffed full of frozen pizzas and other microwavable meals. She pulled them all out and placed them on the counter, then inspected them one by one. They were all sealed tightly except for one large pepperoni pizza that had a loose flap. She opened it.

Bingo.

She pulled out the manila envelope. "Reid, I found it!"

He came into the kitchen and watched as she opened the envelope and pulled out the contents. "Pictures?"

She cleared a spot on the counter and fanned them out. They were pictures of a woman. She gasped when she recognized the red hair. "They're pictures of Bonnie."

"And they were taken with a high-powered lens. Someone was stalking her."

"Several look like they are in her bedroom. She's changing her jeans." At least she was partially clothed. She probably shut her blinds when completely disrobing. "Dex seemed afraid."

"And Bonnie was convinced Keith broke up with her to protect her. She was right. This seems like a warning that he could hurt Bonnie at any time."

Jane nodded and snapped pictures of the photos with her phone, then gathered up the pictures and stuffed them back in the envelope. "Let's see if there's any other evidence in the apartment."

She and Reid spread out to search different areas. She found a stash of money in a cookie jar, his bank records in a box under the bed, and not much else. Reid came up empty-handed too.

She pulled off her gloves with a snap and balled them up. "I need to talk to Bonnie again and see if she has any idea someone was watching her. Or if she's seen these pictures. I'll drop this packet off to Forensics on the way to the coffee shop to see if Nora can find any DNA or prints."

Reid stepped to the thermostat and turned off the air again. "Do you know if Bonnie is working this afternoon?"

"She usually works all day and gets off at five." Jane glanced at her watch. "We'd better hurry. It's already three, and you'll need to pick up Will after practice." She patted her leg. "Come, Parker."

The dog got up and trotted toward her. Reid followed them out into the sunshine.

"The killer was trying to intimidate Keith to back off by threatening his girl. The threat was effective enough that he broke up with Bonnie."

"I don't blame him. I'd do pretty much anything—" He broke off and opened the back door to let in Parker before he climbed into the passenger seat.

Do anything? What did he mean? Had he meant to insinuate threatening her would make him do something?

Maybe she didn't want to know. She got behind the wheel and

headed for the station. Reid glanced at her but didn't continue his thought. She said nothing during the drive and parked in the lot.

"I'll meet you at the coffee shop." She shut off the vehicle and let the dog out.

"I'll take Parker with me," Reid said. "You want a coffee?"

She wiped the perspiration from her forehead. "I'll have an iced one."

She found Olivia at the dispatch station on the way in and stopped to speak to her. Olivia swung around in the chair and nearly toppled out of it.

Jane grabbed hold of her. "Whoa, you okay?"

"A little weak and shaky today." Olivia's smile held a wobble.

Jane squatted beside her. "Go on home, Olivia."

"We're too shorthanded. I'm fine."

"I can call in a temp."

"I'd rather be here than stuck at home wondering what's happening here." She squeezed Jane's hand. "You worry too much. No matter what happens, it's going to be okay."

Jane's eyes burned. "I don't want to lose you."

"Even if I die, it's not over, you know."

Jane wasn't so sure of that. Though she'd been going to the first service at church with Olivia, she wasn't ready to say she believed any of what she'd heard. Olivia's faith was so strong—how did she manage to walk this path without wavering? If Jane were facing a diagnosis like this, she'd be doubting all the so-called love she'd read about in the Bible.

"You still reading *The Screwtape Letters*?" Olivia asked.

Jane nodded. "Nearly finished with it. 'Our cause is never more in danger than when a human, no longer desiring, but still intending, to do our Enemy's will, looks round upon a universe from which every trace of Him seems to have vanished, and asks why he has been forsaken, and still obeys.'"

"I don't feel abandoned. It's not about this life, Jane. God is still with me."

And maybe he was. Jane would give anything if she could help Olivia somehow, but all she could do was helplessly watch it play out.

EIGHT

These pictures would rock Bonnie.

Pelican Brews held teenagers hanging out after school, but most of them lounged in chairs near the windows, so Reid found a quiet corner by the display of mugs and teas near the back. He left Parker at the table and approached the counter. Three baristas were working, and he spotted Bonnie's bright hair.

There was no line, so he ordered their drinks. When Bonnie handed him the order, he leaned over the counter to speak softly. "Chief Hardy is coming over and needs to talk to you. Can you take a break?"

Her smile faltered, and she tucked a red curl behind her ear. "I can ask to get off work early. I'm due a little time anyway. I came in for a friend this morning before my shift started." Her gaze went over his shoulder. "Here she comes now. Let me tell my manager I'm taking off."

He nodded and carried the coffees to the table. A rowdy group of laughing teens shouldered out the door and nearly knocked Jane over. He watched her reprimand them and grinned. She was like a tiny drill sergeant. Underestimating her was never wise.

He lifted his hand when she came through the door, and she

headed his way. She slung her bag over the back of the chair and started to turn toward the counter, but he caught her by the wrist.

"I already spoke to Bonnie. She's about to get off work, and she'll join us."

She didn't pull away from his touch, and the skin-to-skin connection heightened the attraction between them. He knew she felt the tension zinging between them as much as he did.

"Chief Hardy?"

Reid let go of Jane at Bonnie's appearance. "Have a seat."

Bonnie's brown eyes held trepidation as she slung her purse over her chair and settled in. "What's wrong now?" She chewed on her thumbnail.

Jane pulled out her phone and handed it to Bonnie. "I found these pictures in that manila envelope you mentioned. Have you ever seen them before? Do you have any idea who might have taken them?"

Bonnie took the phone and scrolled through the photos. She inhaled and shuddered. "Someone was secretly watching me."

"Looks that way," Jane said.

Bonnie continued to swipe. "I was right. He broke up with me to protect me. That big guy threatened him?"

"Walter says he was just delivering a package. I don't think he was the threat." Jane leaned forward. "Do you know who might have been watching you? Did you see anyone?"

Bonnie handed back the phone, then clutched herself. "This creeps me out. I don't know who could have been watching me. I never saw a thing."

"Tell me exactly what Keith said when he broke up with you."

"He said it wasn't fair to me that he was gone so much. That he wanted me to have a good life, a happy life. He said to be careful when I started to date other guys, that not everyone was who they seemed. That was the comment that made me think he might be trying to protect me."

Tears flooded Bonnie's eyes and trickled down her cheeks. She swiped at them and sniffled. Jane dug in her bag and handed her a tissue. Reid exchanged a glance with her while Bonnie composed herself.

He saw the frustration in Jane's eyes. Where did they go from here? "Can you trace who might have processed these pictures?"

Her eyes lit. "Let me ask Nora if there are any identifying marks." Jane shot off a quick text.

"Am I in danger?" Bonnie asked in a small voice.

"I don't think so. I believe it was used as leverage over Keith. Someone was trying to get him not to report what he knew. Now that he's gone, I doubt they're watching you. But until I solve the case, keep your doors locked and be aware of your surroundings."

Bonnie nodded but seemed even more scared. Her gaze darted to the window. "I think I'll go home unless you have any more questions."

"That's all. If you remember anything else, give me a call." Jane slid a card across the table to her. "And try not to worry, Bonnie. I didn't mean to scare you."

"Someone wanted to shut up Keith awfully bad," Bonnie said. "He tried to save me. I'll never forget that." Her voice choked off, and her throat moved in a convulsive swallow. She rose and grabbed her purse from the back of the chair, then rushed from the building.

Jane exhaled and sank back in her seat. She took a sip of her iced coffee, then set it back on the table. "I scared her half to death. She'll be peeking around every corner."

"Maybe that's for the best. We don't want another casualty."

He reached over and took her hand, which was cool from the iced coffee. "You're a good detective, Jane. I like watching you work."

Her cheeks reddened, and she drew her hand back. "You'd better go get Will. He'll be waiting for you."

She hadn't rebuffed him, not with any real malice.

He rose and grabbed his coffee. "Call me if you need anything."

She nodded but didn't answer. He'd take it. He could have stayed longer if he'd told her Will's coach was dropping him off, but it was better not to push. And he just might surprise his son with a home-cooked meal.

Will sniffed the air when he entered the house. "Whoa, Dad, shrimp and grits." He grabbed a paper towel and mopped his sweaty brow. "Practice was brutal in the heat."

His face was still red from baseball practice, and sweat soaked his tee. The constant sunshine had turned him as brown as a pecan. Pelican Harbor High School had made it into the baseball play-offs.

Reid stirred the cheese into the grits. "Did you thank Coach for dropping you off?"

"It was his girlfriend, but yes, I remembered my manners. I'm not a kid, Dad! I wish you'd quit treating me like one."

"Sorry. I'll try to do better."

Will snagged a piece of shrimp from the plate and popped it into his mouth. "I'm starved. When will it be ready?"

"Right now." Reid mixed everything together and slid the skillet contents into a bowl. "Grab the plates and we can eat." He glanced at the clock. "You're a little late."

Will got down two plates, then hesitated. "I don't suppose you invited Mom to join us? I was surprised to see the two of you together at lunch."

"I think she was ready to kick me to the curb by the time the day was over."

Will winced. "That bad?"

"Kind of. Don't get your hopes up for normalcy." He followed Will to the table by the window and set down the food, but someone pounded on the front door. Hard enough to make the window rattle.

Reid pointed. "Upstairs."

Oh wait. Maybe it was Lauren back for another round, which was another good reason to get Will out of the way. Lauren was a wild card in every way.

Will was heading for the stairs, but he swung back to face Reid, who was nearly to the door. "It's Mom."

Reid frowned as he got close enough to see out the door panes. Sure enough, Jane's narrowed eyes peered through the glass. What could have her in such a state?

He threw open the door. "What's going on?"

She had to have been home long enough to change because she wore khaki shorts and a red tee that set off her tanned skin and hazel eyes.

She waved a sheet of paper in the air. "This was on the windshield of my vehicle." Her voice shook and tears hung on her lashes.

He caught a light scent of vanilla as she pushed past him into the living room with Parker on her heels. She thrust the paper into his hand, and he stared down at the block words.

STOP OR WILL DIES.

A spasm seized his chest. "Stop the investigation? Is that what this means?"

"What else could it be? The guy threatened Bonnie to get Keith to back off. Same tactics."

She raked her shaking hand through her brown hair and went to pull Will into an embrace. He didn't resist and melted into a close hug with her face tucked into the crook of his neck.

"You're okay," she muttered.

"Sure. I'm fine." Will peered over his mother's shoulder. "What's the note say?"

No sense in trying to hide it from him. They'd have to make sure Will took extra precautions. Reid held it up so Will could read it.

Will's mouth drew down, and he pulled away from Jane. "I'm not afraid of a coward who would write something like that."

"Well, I am!" Jane pressed her lips together and snatched the note from Reid's hand. "I'll turn the investigation over to Augusta."

She practically fell onto the sofa and lowered her head between her legs. "I'm going to be sick." Parker whined and nudged her hand, but she drew in a shuddering breath.

Reid leaped forward and pushed her head farther down. "Take a deep breath. Will, grab a wet paper towel for the back of her neck." He patted her back as Will ran for the kitchen. "That's it, deep breaths. Will is fine. We'll make sure he stays that way."

But could they? And watching her extreme reaction to the threat sent a tsunami of emotion through him. What must it be like for her to realize she'd missed out on so much and then be faced with a threat of losing future days as well? He itched to put his fist through the face of whoever had been cowardly enough to threaten a kid.

What were they going to do?

Will returned with a wet paper towel and plopped onto the sofa beside her. He pressed it against the back of her neck. "It's okay, Mom. I'm not going anywhere. I'm fine."

She took several more deep breaths, then sat back and took the paper towel from her neck. Swiping it over her face, she managed a smile. "I panicked when I read that. I was so afraid I'd get here and find the place enveloped in flames or maybe discover you were missing."

Everything in Reid wanted to sit by her and pull her onto his lap, but she'd push him away. "I'll get you some juice." Reid left Will to comfort her and grabbed orange juice from the fridge. He poured it into a glass and carried it back to the living room.

Her fingers curled around the glass, and she took a big slug of juice. "Thanks." She stared into the glass as if it held the answer to all her questions. "I can ask the state police for help."

"I'm not sure that will satisfy the killer. He wants the investigation stopped altogether. I could send Will to stay with friends in New Orleans."

"Not far enough," she said.

Will stood and braced his hands on his hips. "Hey, I'm right here. I'm not going to New Orleans. I've got a big game this Saturday. No way would I desert my teammates."

Jane stared up at him. "Dad would take him. No one will get past the gates easily, and Dad could beef up the security with more cameras."

"But school is going to be a problem. And baseball. You're short-handed and wouldn't be able to provide security."

"Dad could call in some favors."

A thousand thoughts raced through Reid's brain. He had to protect his son somehow, but it wouldn't be easy. The fact Jane was willing to turn over the investigation to the state showed how much she loved Will. She wouldn't walk away from her duties easily.

He became aware of both Jane's and Will's intent stares, and he nodded. "Talk to your dad. We need to figure out who's behind this and fast. We won't be able to rest until we get the killer behind bars."

NINE

No lights illuminated the perimeter around her dad's house, probably to deter a shooter.

Tremors shuddered down Jane's spine at the thought. She turned off the SUV and exhaled before she climbed out of the vehicle into the night sounds of katydids and cicadas. The mossy scent from the woods blew toward her on the breeze.

Reid got out and went around to raise the lift gate. "Good of your dad to suggest we all stay."

Somehow Jane would bear being around Reid if it meant safety for Will. They could take turns keeping an eye on the perimeter cameras, though Dad assured her an alarm would sound if anyone attempted to breach the fencing. And if they needed to, they could head to the bunker. Not even a tank could get through the steel enclosure.

This was the safest place for Will.

Reid took his suitcase in one hand and Jane's in the other as Will and Parker joined him. Will grabbed his suitcase and headed for the porch with an eager smile. Parker ran for the woods like usual.

Jane waved away the mosquitoes buzzing around her face. "I can take my own suitcase."

"I'll carry it. You can open the door and direct me on where to put them."

She didn't bother arguing and rushed ahead to hold the door.

Her dad met her on the top step. "Your old room is ready, and Will can share with Reid in the guest room on the attic floor. I thought that might be safest. An intruder would have to go through the whole house to get to him."

"But it's also farthest from the bunker."

"Not really. I installed a secret staircase from up there. I'll show you all later. There's one in your bedroom too." He waggled shaggy white eyebrows. "You know how I like to be prepared."

She brushed past him into the entry and headed for the stairs. "Third floor," she called to Reid. "I'll join you as soon as I drop off my luggage."

Her bedroom was the first one on the right at the top of the stairs. She dumped her suitcase just inside the door and turned to follow the guys up the back staircase to the third floor. She used to curl up and read here as a teenager. It had been a magical place full of trunks and hidden treasures in the drawers of old furniture. She hadn't realized her dad had turned it into bedroom space.

The steps were narrow and steep, but the ceilings were high. She exited onto the hardwood floors in the bright light cast from modern can lights in the newly finished walls. Two queen beds and dressers barely took up a fraction of the huge square footage. There would be plenty of room for both Reid and Will up here. They could even move the beds around and have space for a seating area with a TV. Not that they'd be here long enough for redecorating. At least, she hoped to have the perp behind bars soon.

She went to the big windows overlooking the drive and pulled back the blackout curtains to peer into the dark night. "Any disturbances since I called?"

"Nope." Her dad twitched the curtain back into place. "But let's don't tempt fate. Come with me, all of you." He led them to a wall of bookshelves along the opposite wall tucked into a nook to the left of the stairway. "Here's the stairway to the bunker. See that?" He pointed out what appeared to be a copy of Orwell's *1984*. "Just pull it toward you."

He pulled on the top of the "book" and the bookcase slid back into the wall. The first few feet of a small staircase barely big enough for Reid's shoulders came into view. The darkness swallowed up the rest from their sight.

"Is there a light?" Jane asked.

Her dad nodded and reached inside to flip a switch that revealed the way down. "And you close it behind you by pressing this button of the wall beside the light. Make sure to close it if you have to use it, to delay any attacker."

She shivered at the thought of having to race down those stairs with a killer on their heels. "Will, you try it. You too, Reid. Make sure you know how it works."

The guys opened and closed the door several times, and when it worked perfectly, she began to relax. "I'll leave you to unpack, and I'll do the same. See you downstairs in a bit."

Her father grunted and followed her down the steps to the second floor. He put his hand on her arm when she turned toward her room. "How credible is this threat to the boy?"

"Pretty high on the scale. Someone knows I've been asking questions and doesn't like it. He's already killed once. If it would hide his plan, I doubt he'd hesitate to do it again."

Her dad's hazel eyes, so like her own, studied her face. "You really think it's terrorists?"

"I don't know. Something's off about the whole thing. All I know is that I can't lose Will. Thank you for taking him in."

"He's my grandson. I don't want to lose him either." He withdrew his hand. "I'll put out some beignets and milk. Come to the kitchen when you're unpacked."

Maybe in the meantime she could steel herself to keep from staring at Reid. Being around him had proved challenging today, and it wasn't likely to get any better.

———

The dark outside the window felt like it hid a thousand dangers.

Reid washed the beignets' powdered sugar from his hands in the kitchen sink. Charles and Will were playing chess, a game Reid had never understood. His son was eating up the attention from his grandfather, and the sight caused war to rage in Reid's heart. He wanted the best for his boy, but Charles had walked away from Will without a second thought.

At least it appeared that way.

He felt Jane enter the kitchen. Her light vanilla scent wafted toward him, and he dried his hands on the towel before he faced her. "Which watch shift do you want to take?"

She had taken a shower, and the heat and moisture left vibrant color in her cheeks. She'd pulled her hair back in a headband that made her look like a teenager, and her yoga pants and tee showed off her toned yet curvy figure. He glimpsed the girl she'd been fifteen years ago. That girl had been timid and compliant, though, and this woman was strong and focused.

Her hazel eyes narrowed. "What?"

"You're a warrior," he blurted out. "I never would have guessed that Button would throw off the mantle of servitude and become so resourceful. You're amazing."

More color washed up her neck, probably from hearing that unfamiliar nickname from the cult she'd left so long ago. It was hard to believe they'd once been "married" by his dad, though hardly legal. She'd been a mere fourteen to his eighteen. Kids, really, both of them.

"I don't think I made the transformation until I went to college. My dad would have kept me under his thumb forever, but I knew I'd die there like a slug never allowed to see the light of day. But even still, I doubt myself. Tonight especially. Can I keep my own son safe?" She blinked and turned to grab a glass of lemonade from the fridge.

"We'll do everything we can, but Jane, it's out of our control. Any semblance of control we have is false. Life happens. Bad things happen. The good thing is that happiness is not about this life."

She pressed her lips together. "See, that's what I don't get about people like you and Olivia. How can you face evil and death with such peace? Wouldn't Will's death devastate you?"

His stomach cramped in a painful grip. "Beyond devastation. I'd never be the same. But Will is a believer, and I know I would see him again. There's comfort and peace in that."

She shook her head. "I could never live with myself if I let anything happen to him."

The condemnation in her voice stung a little. "I understand where you're coming from. We parents all struggle with that same thing. We want nothing to ever trouble our kids, nothing bad to ever touch them. You're wrong if you think I don't wrestle with that.

I'd take a bullet for him. In the early days after we left the cult, I second-guessed what I'd done. How could I keep this little guy safe and even fed? How did I believe I had anything to offer him but hardship?"

She set her glass on the counter. "How did you make it, Reid? You were what, eighteen or nineteen?"

"Not quite nineteen. I don't talk about it." Not even Will knew the story of how he'd escaped and survived. "It was a hard time."

"Would it be easier to talk about in the dark? We can go to the screened back porch."

He could stare into those hazel eyes with their golden flecks for hours. It wasn't her—it was him. He'd failed so often in the early years that talking about it was like struggling in quicksand that would try to suck him under again.

He tore his gaze away. "Sure, let's go outside."

He followed her out a door off the dining area. The moonlight cast long shadows around the furniture, which was cushioned and smelled new. He waited until she settled onto a love seat before taking a rocker on the other side. The crickets and katydids harmonized in a raucous noise that masked the way his pulse thundered in his ears.

His mouth was dry, and he cleared his throat. "Uh, what do you want to know?"

"What was the catalyst to leave?"

The truth hovered behind his teeth. He tugged on the neck of his tee and wished he'd brought out something to drink. The sweltering night pressed in on his chest. "I wanted to find you. For Will."

He heard her light gasp but didn't look at her. Couldn't.

"Yet it took you fourteen years."

The hard note in her voice struck him, but he still didn't dare look at her. "It wasn't as easy back then, and I was working two jobs to try to feed and house us. Once I had enough money, I started searching. Charles Hardy isn't an uncommon name. And don't even get me started on Jane Hardy."

"What jobs? And how did you escape?"

"Will and I slipped out of the compound at midnight and I started hitchhiking. I made it to Chicago, where a trucker named John, with more tattoos than Justin Bieber, picked us up. He was on his way to Vegas. He was a family guy with four kids and couldn't drive past a guy with a kid thumbing it down the road. He took us to his house in Vegas, and his wife, Geena, took one look at Will and opened the door wide. They let us stay with them for several weeks, and he helped me find my first job flipping burgers at a local café. It didn't pay much—not enough to get my own place—but I kept plugging away.

"A guy came into the café for lunch and asked me if I knew anyone who wanted a part-time job. He was a reporter, and the job was basically to be a gofer for him. Running errands, making sure he was where he was supposed to be, that kind of thing."

"And where was Will while you worked?"

At her soft tone he glanced her way. "With Geena and John at first. When I got our first apartment, a fleabag studio I scrubbed up, I made friends with an elderly lady across the hall. She took a shine to Will and offered to keep him. I wasn't sure at first, but she took us both to her church, and I could see she was good people. Really good. We still go visit her in Vegas as often as we can, and Will calls her Nana."

"And the job with the reporter eventually led to your profession?"

He nodded. "Took a few years, of course. But I had a natural aptitude for the screen, and I started giving him ideas for documentaries. One day he told me to do it myself, and I was off and running."

"Where did Lauren fit in?"

He winced. Lauren was an even unhappier memory. "She was Nana's niece. I was vulnerable and right across the hall. An easy target. It didn't last long though. We bought a small house, which she thought was a stepping-stone to a mansion soon. She thought I was going to start making money much faster than I did."

"When did you start looking for me? Before Lauren or after?"

"After. Every Saturday I'd take Will to the library, and I'd search around on the computer. Then when several of my documentaries hit big five years ago, I hired an investigator. But I knew so little information. She's not even the one who found you—I did."

"That news story you mentioned."

"Yes."

His chair squeaked as he rocked back and forth, more to soothe his agitation than anything.

She rose and touched his shoulder. "I'm glad you found me. Get some sleep. I'll take the first watch."

Before he could answer, she slipped through the door back inside the house. He exhaled and put his face in his hands. Those years seemed an eternity ago—and yet also seemed like just yesterday. He was beginning to understand he hadn't escaped his past any more than she had.

TEN

She would never be able to sleep after what Reid had told her.

The blue light from the security screens flickered in the small control room on the first floor. Jane glanced at the time on the one nearest to her. One o'clock. His emotionless recitation of escaping the compound left out so many nights where he must've second-guessed himself, and she'd sat in here filling in the gaps and sketching his face.

She flipped to the last picture she'd drawn and stared into the slight smile in his eyes. He was a handsome guy, and everything about him drew her.

Had he really tried to find her? His silence when he first came here seemed to indicate it was a lie. But then again, he *did* finally tell her. And he'd come here after he found out she lived in Pelican Harbor. Maybe he was just being careful.

She rubbed her forehead and surveyed the backyard screen. A movement caught her eye, and she leaned forward to peer into the shadows in the woods. It could have been a deer. A lot of them roamed her dad's property.

The room plunged into darkness. She shot to her feet and drew her gun. "Reid, Dad!" she shouted up. Her dad had security speakers linking all the rooms even during a power outage, so they'd hear her instantly. "Will, take the stairway to the bunker!"

Her dad's feet hit the floor and ran down the hallway to the steps as she advanced through the living room and toward the back door. Reid came thundering down the steps from the third floor. When she reached the door to the screened porch, she paused at the right side, then peered into the dark yard. Nothing moved but leaves. Parker, who'd been sleeping with Will, reached her side before the men.

His ears flattened, and a low growl emanated from his throat. Someone was definitely out there. She touched his head. "Easy, boy."

How had the intruder managed to cut the power without triggering the alarm? They should have been warned if someone managed to get through the fence.

Someone touched her arm, and she glanced back to see her dad with an AK-47 in his hands. "No alarm," she whispered. "I saw movement in the backyard just before the power went out."

Reid, handgun at his side, came into view. "Will should be in the bunker by now. I sent him down the secret passageway."

"Good." She turned back to survey the yard again. Parker still bristled at her side. "My dog's sure someone's out there."

Reid turned. "I'll go out the front and circle around."

Her father followed. "I'll go the other direction."

What she wouldn't give for a couple of officers with her too. Reid was a good shot, but he wasn't a cop. Dad was, too, but she had no idea what she was facing out there. It could be a terrorist army for all she knew. Her dad had an armory in the bunker, and maybe she should have grabbed a rifle with an infrared scope instead of her Glock.

Almost as if he'd heard her thoughts, her dad reappeared with night-vision goggles. He thrust one at her. "You'll need this." Two more pairs dangled on his wrist.

"Good idea." She took it and slipped it on.

Details jumped out at her, and she could see nearly as well as if it were twilight. In a crouched position, she eased out the door onto the screened porch and moved toward the exit. The door opened noiselessly, and she stepped to the exterior door that opened to the deck with Parker on her heels.

A bullet slammed into the door casing by her head, and splinters stung her cheek. She hit the ground as a figure darted around the corner of the house to her left. Reid. He fired toward the woods lining the back of the property, and she heard twigs and debris snapping under someone's feet. She caught sight of a figure fleeing farther into the tree cover.

She sprang to her feet and ran after the intruder. Parker barked and gave chase as well, and she caught sight of Reid and her father circling around from either flank.

The guy had vanished, and though they searched for another half an hour, they found no sign of him.

Her dad signaled to her and Reid, and they convened under a large tree. "I want to get the power back on. I think it's safest if Will sleeps in the bunker the rest of the night."

"I don't think he should go to school tomorrow," Reid said.

She called Parker to her side. "Me neither. This guy brazenly waltzed in here without triggering the alarm and managed to cut our power."

Will wouldn't like it, but they had no choice.

Reid's every nerve was alert, and he couldn't think about what might have happened.

He propped a foot on a fence rail and frowned at the destruction the intruder had left. "He came through here, but why didn't an alarm trigger when he cut through the fence?" He didn't know that much about Charles's protection system, but he knew it was top of the line.

The Thursday morning dawn pinked the eastern sky and lit the trees with orange, purple, and red. Charles was back at the house guarding Will while Reid and Jane scoured the perimeter for clues about the attack.

Jane frowned at her phone. "Just got a text from Dad. He found evidence of a system intrusion that turned off the alarm system. And the intruder turned off the power the same way. Sophisticated stuff. I need to find out who might have had the password to get into his Wi-Fi." Her voice wobbled, and panic flared in her hazel eyes when she locked gazes with him. "How are we going to keep Will safe with someone like this?"

He stepped closer and gripped her shoulders. "You're going to find out who's behind this, Jane. If Will needs to live in the bunker for a few weeks, that's what we'll do. Let's call in all the help we can get and finish this. This guy has no idea who he's dealing with."

Her eyes filled with tears and she swallowed. "I don't know if I'm up to this, Reid."

"But I know you are." He infused as much confidence in his gaze as he could. "Let's arrange a meeting with Homeland Security and whomever else we need to talk to. Find out what they know. The state guys and the FBI too. Surely they are all on it."

She nodded. "You're right—I know you're right. I'm feeling overwhelmed from lack of sleep. I can do this."

He dropped his hands back to his side before she objected—which he knew was coming by the way she stiffened. "Let's find your dog, make any calls you need to, and get on this."

"I'm going to leave Parker to help guard Will. We'd better tell Will he can't go to school. He'll be up by now."

The sun was already getting hot, and it was only seven. They walked toward the house, and Will sat on the porch with the dog. "What's he doing out of the bunker?" Reid broke into a jog, and Jane ran with him.

Will smiled when they reached him. "I wondered where everyone was. I heard Gramps in the shower, but you two were nowhere to be found."

Which explained why Charles hadn't kept him in the bunker. Reid mounted the steps. "You need to go back to the bunker."

Will's smile vanished. "I need to leave for school in half an hour."

Jane squatted in front of him. "Will, you're nearly an adult, so I'm going to give it to you straight. Whoever broke in here last night had very sophisticated equipment. There's no way we can keep you safe at school. We'll need you to stay in the bunker until we apprehend him."

Will's dark eyes flashed. "And how long will that take? Weeks? Months? I've only got another two weeks left of school, and I don't want to miss it. We play the final baseball game of the tournament on Saturday. Our relief pitcher pulled a muscle in his shoulder, so it's all up to me. I can't let everyone down."

Reid set his hand on his son's shoulder. "Your life is more important than school or baseball."

Will shrugged off Reid's grip and leaped to his feet with his hands fisted. "No one will try to take me out with everyone around!

And there will be a ton of people at the baseball game. Who would be stupid enough to shoot me in front of hundreds of witnesses? It doesn't make sense."

Reid winced and knew he and Jane sounded unreasonable to their son. "Who would have guessed someone could bypass your grandpa's security system and come after you? He shot at your mom. The bullet only missed her brain by inches."

Will's eyes widened. "Mom?"

Jane shot a glare at Reid. "I'm fine, honey. I'm a trained law enforcement officer. I can take care of myself, so don't worry about me. We want to keep you safe."

"I'm not a kid! I need to be at that game."

Reid's chest squeezed at the panic in his son's voice, but he couldn't back down. "You're old enough to man up, Will. Adulting can be hard, and this is one of those times when you have to do the right thing to protect others. What if bullets started flying at school and some of your friends were hit? Or teachers? If the killer doesn't care about collateral damage, being around you could be dangerous."

"But what idiot would think Mom would leave off an investigation because of a threat? She's not that kind of officer."

Jane swiped at her eyes. "I'd like to abandon the investigation to protect you, but you're right. I have a sworn duty to my town and the people who live there." She rose with her head up. "You reminded me of all the reasons I have this job."

Will's hands curled into fists. "I want to help—not be holed up in the bunker like I'm scared."

"The best way you can help is to let your grandpa guard you here in the bunker." Jane swept her hand to the right. "And there's a lot to do down there. Tons of electronic games, a treadmill, weights, even an indoor golf net. Books too. Your dad can pick up your assignments, and you can keep up. I'll call in other agencies so we can crack this sooner. Please, just be patient, Will."

He heaved a sigh and hung his head. "You're asking a lot."

Reid embraced him in a one-armed side hug. "I know we are. We need to pull together with this. Okay?"

At least he didn't shrug off Reid's hug, and he relaxed in the embrace. "Okay, but figure this out before Saturday."

Reid's gaze met Jane's over the top of Will's head. That was going to be a tough request.

ELEVEN

Jane couldn't believe what she was hearing.

She paced her office while Reid went to pick up coffee across the street. "How can you drop the case? Someone tried to shoot me last night!"

The guy on the other end from Homeland Security—she'd already forgotten his name—sounded distracted. "Chief Hardy, as I said, we've found no corroborating evidence a terrorist cell is planning to attack the oil platform. The attack on you could have been anyone, correct? You didn't identify the intruder."

"That's true, but I got a warning to stop or they would hurt my son." She wished she had Parker here to help calm her agitation, but Will had begged to keep him.

"Stop what? The copy you sent over makes no mention of what you're supposed to stop. I'm sure you have other investigations going on."

True enough. Attempted burglary at the bank, a rape case on the outskirts of town, and an assault charge in one of the bars. "Nothing worth trying to kill me over."

"But the shot might have been more of a warning. And we've combed through the McDonald man's emails and contacts and have found nothing. Sorry."

"What about Keith's death?"

"It's presumed an accident or suicide. Not foul play."

"We haven't recovered his body. What if we find it and discover he was murdered?"

"Then let us know and we'll revisit it. Look, I have to go. Sorry." The call clicked off.

Jane plopped into her chair and huffed. The threat had to be related to Keith's death. Had to be. There was no other explanation. Ruby would be devastated if the investigation was being abandoned.

Reid came through the door carrying two cups from Pelican Brews. His smile fell when he saw her face. "What's wrong? Is it Will?" He started to wheel to the door before she stopped him.

"No, no. I talked to Dad fifteen minutes ago, and he and Will are playing a video game in the bunker." She told him about the call with Homeland Security. "And with them discounting what we've learned, I doubt I can get the state police or the FBI to pick up the case. The FBI will investigate violent crimes, but we have no evidence yet that there *is* a murder."

He handed her a coffee, then sank into a chair opposite her desk. "So there's no one but you to investigate."

"And without a body, I can't even say for sure Keith was murdered. DHS thinks it was likely suicide or an accident."

"Is the Coast Guard still searching?"

She shook her head. "They called off the search this morning. If we find him, it will be an accident."

Reid stared at her. "Did anyone dive down to see if they could find a body, or has it been an air-only search?"

"No divers. Just boats and helicopters."

"I dive. How about I go down and see if we can find any clues to what happened?"

She took a sip of her coffee. "You need a buddy to dive. I haven't gone down in a while, so I'm a little rusty, but let me get my gear checked out. We could go down tomorrow. It's very deep there, though. It's doubtful we'll find anything. The bottom is over two thousand feet down. I'm certified for a hundred and thirty feet."

"Yeah, we won't be able to reach the bottom, but there might be something floating around there. It's worth a shot. You sure you're up to it? I could always get Will . . ." He stopped and shook his head. "I keep forgetting he has to stay in the bunker. It seems wrong."

"It *is* wrong. We've got to fix it. No one else is going to do it." Coffee in hand, she headed for the door. "I'll drop my gear at the dive shop and make sure everything is ready to go."

"I'll come with you."

Though his tone was casual, she stopped and stared at him. "I'm a trained law enforcement agent, Reid. I can take care of myself."

"I don't doubt it for a minute, but we might be dealing with more than one person. I'd feel better if I had your back until your new officers are up to speed. When are they starting?"

"Monday."

His concern touched her, but she didn't want him to know. "I'm just going to my place to get my dive gear. You can come along if you want. I need to get Parker's dog food and a few other things as well since it appears we'll be out at the compound for a while. Do you need anything from your house?"

"Wouldn't hurt. We threw things into bags so fast, I'm not sure I got everything."

He followed her out into a light rain. "Hey, I just thought of something. I did a documentary with NOAA. There are some deep-sea robotic submarines in use out there. If we don't find anything tomorrow, I'll call my contact and see if she can come take a look."

She? Jane jerked her gaze away so he couldn't read her expression. She was afraid the green monster she'd stuffed back down might have been visible for half a second.

Had Jane stepped closer emotionally just a bit? Reid couldn't quite tell.

Sunlight glimmered on the Bon Secour River as he got out of Jane's SUV. "You want to wait here while I take a walk-through?"

She sure was pretty with the sun glowing on her light-brown hair. Her hazel eyes were tired though, and he knew her duties weighed heavily on her shoulders. He wished he could lift the burden in some way, but all he could do was pray for her and make sure Will stayed safe. The rest of it was all hers.

She shook her head and shoved open her door. "I should sweep the house before you go in and make sure there are no intruders."

She held out her hand for the key, and he passed it over. It felt wrong to let her step into danger instead of him, but she was more than competent, and she'd be offended by any hint that he felt a need to protect her. He stuffed his hands in his pants pocket and forced himself to stand back while she unlocked the back door and pushed it open.

Gun out, she disappeared inside, and it seemed an eternity before she reappeared in the doorway to motion him inside. "All clear."

He moved through the rooms to the office off the hallway, where he grabbed his laptop and files. "I really need to circle back to Elliot and see how the editing is going on the footage we shot on the platform. I want to review it and see if anyone seemed to be taking an unusual interest in the search for Keith."

She followed as he deposited the items in the living room before he went upstairs to grab more clothing from the bedrooms. "Should I call Will and ask if he wants anything special?"

"Wouldn't hurt." Reid listened as she placed the call and chatted with their son.

She ended the call. "He beat his grandpa in the video game and they're fixing dinner—Cajun chicken Alfredo, my dad's specialty."

"Sounds good. Does he want anything?"

Her frown deepened. "His baseball jersey. When I asked why he wanted it, he said just in case things cleared up in time for him to join the final tournament game."

"The boy always likes to be prepared."

"You don't suppose he's thinking of sneaking out, do you?"

"He's never done anything like that. Will has always been obedient."

"But he's a teenager," she pointed out. "They're apt to be unpredictable. And they think they're invincible too."

"I'll keep a close eye on him. And who knows—maybe we'll figure this out in time."

He ducked into Will's room and retrieved the baseball uniform along with baseball cleats and glove. While he was there he grabbed more jeans, tees, underwear, and socks. He took Will's Nintendo and games too. It was new, and there were several games his boy hadn't played much yet.

When he stepped back out into the hallway, he didn't see Jane, but he found her standing in his bedroom with a framed picture from his nightstand in her hands. It was of him and Will in front of their first real house in Nevada.

A flush ran up her neck, and she set it back. "Sorry. I saw this from the doorway and couldn't resist. You still had hair in this. Will was what—maybe five?"

Warmth curled in his belly at her gentle tone. "It was the first day of kindergarten."

"The two of you look so much alike." Her gaze lingered on him. "When did you shave off your hair?"

If he laid out the bare facts of *when*, maybe she wouldn't ask *why*. "About ten years ago." He rubbed his head. "You don't like it."

The color in her cheeks intensified, and she averted her gaze. "It looks good on you."

Though the compliment sounded grudging, he had to fight to keep a grin from spreading. "I guess I'll grab a few more items of clothing." He removed a duffel bag from the closet and stuffed Will's things inside before he put more of his own clothing in it.

Jane still examined his room. Was she trying to cipher more about him or what? Her manner had thawed slightly over the past two days, and he could only pray that the defrosting continued.

He slung the duffel bag over his shoulder and turned toward the door. "I'm ready."

She followed him downstairs and toward the back door.

He paused as they passed through the utility room. "I need to give you back the bolt cutters Will borrowed to work on that science project." He picked them up and carried them out the door to where the SUV sat at the end of the curving driveway. He stopped short when another vehicle pulled in behind Jane's vehicle.

With one smooth draw, she had her gun out. "Get down!" She grabbed his arm and pulled him down with her, using the SUV's engine block as a shield.

The door to the gray car opened, and he gritted his teeth when he recognized the shapely legs emerging from the vehicle. Lauren.

The bolt cutters dangling from his hand, he advanced to block her. "What do you want? I thought you were out of town by now."

She tipped her blonde head to smile up at him, but when he didn't respond, she tossed her cigarette to the ground and scowled over his shoulder at Jane. "I see what's happening here. You've found someone new, haven't you?"

Jane holstered her weapon and came to stand by Reid. "I can wait in the vehicle."

He put his hand on her arm. "I have nothing to say to Lauren."

"I'm the mother of your child! There will always be something to discuss. You might talk to your attorney. There's new information on the case." Her green eyes gleamed with triumph.

Nothing was attractive about her twisted expression.

Jane straightened. "Actually, I'm Will's mother. His *real* mother."

Lauren gasped. "That's impossible."

"I'm surprised you haven't heard the news around town." Reid found himself enjoying this moment way too much. "Jane is the underlying reason I came to Pelican Harbor. And why I'm still here. Will is thrilled to have found his real mother."

Lauren's eyes widened, and she got back into her car without another word. She slammed the door behind her and peeled out with a glare their way.

Jane grinned up at Reid. "That was so much fun I'd like to do it again."

He smiled at her, and the moment between them stretched into something charged with attraction. If he could keep his hands at his sides, he might be able to resist the compulsion to kiss her until they

TWO REASONS TO RUN

were both breathless. He moved his right hand toward her shoulder, but her phone rang and he dropped it back to his side.

His only consolation was the glimpse of regret in her eyes. *It's Megan*, she mouthed to him.

He nodded and put the bolt cutters in the back of her SUV. It was always something, wasn't it?

TWELVE

Jane and Reid jumped out of the SUV and ran to the school. Olivia was already there on a bench with Megan in front of the building when Jane and Reid arrived, breathless and sweating in the heat.

Tears ran down Megan's face, and Olivia held her. Jane didn't like the way Olivia's legs trembled.

"Where's the text?" Jane asked.

Olivia handed Megan's phone to Jane. "It's all there."

Jane glanced at the screen to see a picture of Tyler holding a knife. He wore a menacing expression, and she took it the same way Olivia and Megan had—as a warning. "Did you see him at school?"

Megan nodded and wiped her wet cheeks with her palms. "He acted fine in French class."

"When did you get this?"

"When I called you. I know he doesn't mean it, but it scared me. He's not himself."

"These messages disappear, don't they?"

Megan nodded. "I took a screenshot though so it's saved. I emailed it to you."

Jane gazed at Olivia, who was straightening her left arm, which was twitching. "You okay?"

"Just a muscle spasm."

Her slurred speech was difficult to understand, but she'd been talking fine this morning.

Jane forced her attention back to Megan. "Did you talk to Tyler today?"

"After school he kept trying to give me his ring back, but I reminded him we'd broken up. He rushed off, and I went to the coffee shop. He showed up and came toward me, and I ran off. I probably shouldn't have. A few minutes later I got that message."

Megan was sounding stronger and less panicked. Was Tyler really a danger? Jane didn't want to believe the nice kid would hurt anyone, but with that head injury, she wasn't sure. He needed to be assessed.

"How'd he know you were there? Did you tell him you were headed for coffee?"

Megan shook her head and punched the screen on her phone. "There's a map where your friends can track you."

"And where a stalker can find you. Megan, you should know better than to use that app. Your mom has seen and heard every horror story possible in her years in dispatch. Can you disable that feature?"

"I don't think so."

Jane read the mutiny in Megan's hard expression. "I want to keep you safe, Megan."

"I'm fine. All my friends are on here. I can't stop using it."

"You can if you want to."

Olivia reached for the phone, but her fingers wouldn't curl around it. "Honey, listen to Jane. Tyler might be dangerous."

Megan rose and stuffed her phone into her book bag. "I'm sorry I called you, Jane. It was nothing. He's just a little weird since his accident."

Jane grabbed her arm. "It's disturbing, and I can't let this go, Megan."

"Whatever."

"How about you and your mom come for dinner tonight at my dad's? Will and Dad are making chicken Alfredo, and it's going to be good. Will could use some company and school news."

Megan tightened her ponytail. "Really?" She glanced at her mother. "Mom?"

"Sure, we'd love to, Jane." The slurring had improved a bit.

"I'll drive you out and bring you back later. Wait here, and I'll get my vehicle."

Should Olivia even be driving? It appeared these symptoms could intensify at a moment's notice. Jane walked back toward her SUV with Reid beside her with nothing to say. He seemed lost in thought.

She paused and called up her email, shot off the picture to Augusta with instructions, then sent it to Steve. "I'm going to have Augusta get Tyler assessed. I'd like to believe he's not dangerous, but a doctor should make that call."

"You going to give Steve a heads-up?"

"I already sent him the picture." She called the number she had for Steve.

His voice was wary when he answered. "Chief."

"I just sent you a picture Tyler sent Megan. I'm sorry, but a doctor will have to assess him. I know it's upsetting, but that picture was threatening."

"That's ridiculous! Tyler wouldn't hurt Megan."

"If you're at your computer, check out the photo."

He paused and papers rustled. "I know it looks bad, but I'm sure it's a prank."

"I can't take that chance, Steve. Augusta will pick him up, and you'll need to accompany him. Where is he now?"

"Home, I think. I got a text from him. Can we meet Augusta rather than have her take him in a police car that will get the neighbors talking?"

"Augusta can meet you at the hospital."

"Thank you." He hung up.

She texted Augusta the new instructions, and she and Reid climbed into the SUV. It was a sauna inside, and her forehead instantly beaded with perspiration.

She started the car to get the air revved up. "I don't like to see Olivia that shaky."

"I noticed. She's not good, Jane. ALS can move so fast."

"I don't want to believe it's really ALS. She's going to see a Lyme disease specialist next week."

He said nothing, and she knew he thought she was grasping at straws. Maybe she was, but the thought of Olivia's light being snuffed out of her world nearly made her heart seize.

"Did you see Megan's face light up when she heard Will would be there?" Jane smiled. "She has it bad."

"I noticed." He chuckled. "I'm not sure Will has noticed there's another gender yet. Baseball is the most important thing in his life right now."

"Megan wants to make him notice."

Jane parked in front of Olivia and Megan, then got out to open the door for Olivia. Megan helped her mother up and put her arm around her waist to support her as she staggered to the car. Her gaze caught Jane's, and the sorrow in her eyes broke Jane's heart. Especially since she felt the same way.

She had to do something. Being helpless didn't sit well with her.

———

Jane hadn't brought up Lauren's visit, and Reid wasn't about to open that can of worms.

Would the shock of discovering Jane was present in Will's life be enough to send Lauren away for good? He hoped so, but she'd proven him wrong by coming back this time. Her persistence seemed to have no bounds.

The garlic and cheese aroma of the chicken Alfredo and bread wafting from the kitchen made his mouth water as he watched Elliot ready the footage they'd captured aboard the oil platform. Will tinkered with the electronics alongside the young videographer, and Megan sat close beside him. So far, his son hadn't acted like it was anything special to have a pretty girl show up out of the blue.

Jane had gone to take a shower while her dad finished food preparation. After being with Will all day, Parker had followed her as if he didn't want her out of his sight. Olivia lay sleeping in the recliner. Good. Maybe she'd wake up feeling better.

"Dank place here," Elliot said. "Can I move in too?"

Though Reid had only been around him three weeks, he'd already figured out some of Elliot's slang. *Dank* didn't mean dark and wet but really cool. The bunker's living room had high ceilings, a nice rug, comfortable furnishings. It would have looked nice in Reid's house.

Will rolled his eyes. "It looks cool when you first check it out, but the walls start closing in when you know you can't leave."

Elliot nodded. "Gotcha. Lots of time for video games or reading." He squirted sanitizer into his palm and rubbed his hands together.

Reid plugged in the monitor. "Speaking of video games, I brought your Nintendo and the games you got for your birthday."

"Good. Any progress on finding the guy after me?"

Reid put his hand on his son's shoulder and shook his head. "Sorry, buddy. You know your mom though—she'll ferret him out of whatever hole he's hiding in."

He pursed his lips. "I really want her to get him by Saturday morning."

"She'll do her best."

Blasted baseball game. Reid didn't want to tell him the chances of her finding the guy by then were slim to none. Better to take it a day at a time. It would crush Will to miss the game, but it couldn't be helped.

"Here we go." Elliot leaned forward and jiggled the mouse. "I brought all the footage, even what I've edited out for the documentary. You sure you want to watch all of it? I've got about five hours' worth."

"I need to see people's expressions. Is there a way to fast-forward and only look at people?"

"Sure." Elliot did his magic, and the video sped up, then paused as people came into view.

Reid pulled up a chair and settled in to watch the people parade across the screen. He didn't remember most of the names, though Elliot had gotten permission notices signed and logged. He could check those later if he found something interesting here.

Jane appeared in the doorway. Wet tendrils of hair escaped from her bun. She wore yoga pants and a red sleeveless top that showed off her toned arms. Reid tore his gaze away before he started drooling. Reid's neck went hot at the knowing expression in Elliot's eyes and shook his head when the videographer started to say something.

Reid nearly knocked the chair over scrambling to his feet. "Smells great. I'm starved."

"I watched Gramps make all of it so I could recreate it at home," Will said. "He uses cream cheese in it. Wait until you taste it."

"You'll make some lucky woman a good husband," Megan said.

Will gave her a sidelong glance and a slight smile lifted his lips.

"Can't wait to taste it." Reid clapped an arm around Will's shoulder and walked into the kitchen with him.

Jane made a detour to wake Olivia. Reid heard them talking, and Olivia wasn't slurring her words now.

White cabinets went all the way to the nine-foot ceiling, and the smooth white counters reflected the light of gleaming stainless-steel appliances and small kitchen gadgets. Coffee brewed, and blue stoneware mugs had been set out on the large farmhouse table. Like being at home.

"You've done a good job with this bunker, Charles. Getting stuck here for a while wouldn't be a hardship."

Charles carried a steaming bowl of chicken Alfredo to the table. "The day is coming, Reid, and you're always welcome here when the apocalypse strikes."

Reid wanted to ask the older man's views on all that, but now wasn't the time. Jane walked in with Olivia, who was moving by herself. She had more color in her cheeks too. Reid couldn't decide if he wanted to sit by Jane so he could catch a whiff of her luscious skin or sit across from her so he could see her face.

She took the decision out of his hands by pointing to the seat across from her. "Have a seat, Reid. Will, you can sit by me. Olivia, you want to sit by Megan?"

"I do." Olivia moved over to drop beside her daughter, who looked crushed that she was across the table from Will and not beside him.

Reid sat in the assigned seat and realized his videographer hadn't followed them. "Hey, Elliot, you're invited to dinner."

When Elliot didn't answer, Reid went to see what was holding him up. The young man was hunched over the screen. He turned when Reid neared. "I knew we'd find something." Elliot pumped his hand in the air. "Check it out."

He had paused the screen, and a face peered around the corner at them. Reid couldn't make out much detail about the face, but the clothing revealed an important detail. "Is that a woman?"

"Sure looks like one to me. There can't be many women on the platform. It's a hard job physically. If you can get the list of workers, we can narrow it down."

Reid studied the image. "She appears like she's eavesdropping and trying not to be seen." It was in every line of her body and the way she tilted her head.

"That's what I thought." Elliot hit a key. "I'm printing it out, and we'll see where this takes us."

THIRTEEN

If only she could get Homeland Security to listen.

Jane put the last of the dishes away while Olivia wiped off the counters in the bunker's kitchen. In the living room the guys yelled and hooted with laughter over a video game. While she wasn't up on titles, she'd heard mention of Mario. That had been around forever, but she gathered this was a new version. Megan sat right beside Will.

Olivia rinsed out the sponge. "My daughter is smitten with your son, but he doesn't seem to notice."

"Give it time. When a girl as pretty as Megan fawns over a guy, he has to pay attention sooner or later."

Olivia's dark-blue eyes sparkled. "Too true. I think I'll go watch the game for a few minutes. Sounds like fun. Then I'll need to get Megan home kicking and screaming. She has school tomorrow."

"I'll be along shortly to run you home."

Her dad entered the kitchen. "Done already? That bottomless pit of a grandson is calling for a snack already. I think he had three plates of pasta and two slices of pie, but he must have found some corner of his stomach not filled with food." He beamed with pride as if he were the one who could eat the refrigerator.

Jane smiled. "The first weekend he stayed with me we went

through four family-size bags of cheese puffs, three boxes of Kind bars, four dozen homemade chocolate chip cookies, and countless beignets. Did he say what he's in the mood for?"

"Probably more chocolate pie." Her dad opened the fridge and peered inside. "Only two pieces. It'll probably be a bloody fight to the death for them."

"There are beignets." She opened the cupboard and pulled out a covered plate of them. "They can be the consolation prize."

"They'll console me." He reached for the plate she slid across the counter to him.

"Um, Dad, before you go, there's something I wanted to talk to you about."

"Okay."

"It's about Elizabeth."

His longtime girlfriend was in jail for accessory to murder after she helped Brian Boulter, Jane's former deputy, plot to take down her dad with false charges. The plot included murdering two people. She was also up on second-degree homicide charges due to her vigilante efforts. As far as Jane knew, her father hadn't been to see her since the arrest, but the topic was a landmine of emotion.

The events had aged her dad. His hair and eyebrows had gotten even whiter over the past few weeks, and his hazel eyes looked weary as he studied Jane's face. "What about her?"

His calm manner and voice didn't soothe the twitch in his cheek. After Elizabeth's arrest, he'd told Jane he didn't want to talk about Elizabeth—not ever—but they had to.

"Look, Dad, I know you don't want to talk about her, but there's evidence that someone was able to get into your Wi-Fi system. Of course it could have been a hacker, but what if Elizabeth gave the password to someone?"

He gave a slow blink and exhaled. "She's the one who set it up, so yes, she knows what it is."

"That's what I needed to know. I'll talk to her and maybe she'll tell me the truth."

He lifted a bushy white brow. "Haven't you learned anything yet, Jane? She hates me and, by extension, you too. If you want to waste your time, fine, go see her. But don't expect honesty. She hasn't given us that virtue in the last ten years, so she's not going to start now."

"I think she cares more than you think. She got caught up in trying to hide her vigilantism. Step-by-step, she dug herself into a deep hole, and she didn't know how to escape."

"Believe what you want, but whatever you do, don't trust a thing she says." He scooped up the plates of beignets and pies, then stalked back to the living room.

Jane rubbed her forehead. Maybe he was right, but she had to search under every rock.

Her phone dinged with a text from Augusta. Tyler was being assessed by a psychiatrist. He'd likely be there overnight, and Steve was making a ruckus. It was nothing Augusta couldn't handle though. Jane sent a thank-you text and turned toward the doorway.

"Hey." Reid stepped into the kitchen. "Our son is beating me, and I might need rescuing."

She managed a smile. "Don't come to me to save you. I'm not a gamer."

"You look like someone just kicked your dog. What's wrong?"

She told him about her chat with her dad. "And maybe he's right and Elizabeth won't know anything, but I'm not sure where else to look."

"We can contact Steve Price and see if he will give us a list of women working the platform. That might lead to something."

She nodded. "And I still need to interview Keith's friends. One of them might know something."

"Our dive tomorrow could be helpful."

"Maybe."

"But you're not holding your breath."

"Nope." She opened the drawer and got out a handful of forks. "Y'all might need forks to eat that pie."

"I'll bet Will has it half devoured by now." A fresh burst of groans erupted from the living room. "And I'd guess he just won the game."

His gaze wrapped her in warmth, and she smiled. "I don't know how you do it, but you always manage to make me feel ten feet tall instead of five two."

He fell into step beside her and dropped an arm around her shoulders as they moved to the living room. "You're an Amazon in my opinion. Never underestimate the short girls. Their smarts make up for their lack of stature."

A chuckle bubbled up her throat. "I've spent most of my life being underestimated."

She liked the weight of his muscular arm around her shoulders and the scent of his aftershave. It was dangerous, but she couldn't bring herself to shrug him off.

The morning was too beautiful to be searching for a body.

Reid watched Jane a few feet below the surface until he was sure she was competent, then kicked down through the water along the massive pylons and beams holding up the oil platform. Algae, barnacles, coral, and oysters coated the surfaces in the bright colors of an artificial reef. The oil rigs had proven to be perfect habitats for the invertebrates.

A pod of dolphins swam near, and Jane paused to watch them. He swam over beside her and floated in the current as a curious sea turtle cruised by under their feet. Reid pointed down, and Jane nodded before following him into deeper water. He was certified to 130 feet, though he didn't want to go that deep because Jane would insist on following him, and her diving skills were rusty.

He shot a glance upward to see the hull of their boat bobbing in the waves where he'd anchored it to a pylon, then glanced at his dive computer. A hundred feet. He shouldn't take Jane much deeper. Squinting toward what seemed to be a limitless depth, he saw something floating close to a girder. He kicked his fins to take him down to examine the scrap of red. His dive computer read 120 feet.

He was three feet away when he realized what he'd spotted—a body with a rope wrapped around his ankle. The rope secured him to the girder to make sure he didn't float to the surface. Reid flailed back away from the grisly sight and bumped into Jane, who had followed him.

Her eyes widened, and a flurry of bubbles escaped her mouth as she bit back the same scream that wanted to erupt from his throat. Keith McDonald? The body would be tough to identify since the fish had nibbled at the poor guy's flesh. Even his mother wouldn't recognize the mangled remains.

Bile rose in Reid's throat, and he forced it down as Jane circled the body and examined it. He pulled out his waterproof camera and snapped off a few pictures as she pointed to various spots on the body like the head and chest. He couldn't see a clear cause of death.

He glanced at his computer. They'd been at this depth for twenty minutes, and he blinked to clear his vision as the numbers for his nitrogen intake wavered. That couldn't be right. They had to start up and make at least one safety stop. Jane glanced at her computer and jabbed her thumb upward.

He nodded and kicked his fins. They paused for a decompression stop, and impatience radiated from Jane's eyes. When the time was up, she nodded and they ascended the final fifteen feet to the boat.

A wave broke over his head as he tore off his mask and let Jane climb the ladder first into the boat. She shook her head and pushed him toward the ladder. "Get aboard."

He obeyed her terse command and climbed the ladder. Jane clambered aboard and ripped off her mask, then threw it down before rushing to his side as he came onto the boat. "You okay? You look a little green."

He nodded. "I'm fine. Hard to look at though. That poor guy."

She grabbed for the phone she'd left on the console and made a call. He listened as she gave a pointed request for forensic divers out at the rig.

She ended the call and turned to face him. "His mother was right. It wasn't an accident, and he didn't commit suicide."

"If it's Keith. It might take a while for a positive ID. How long for the forensic team to get here?"

"An hour or so." She held out her hand. "Let me see the pictures."

He stood silently as she flipped through the photos on the camera's screen.

She gave it back. "They're good, but I was hoping the pictures would show what I couldn't see. I have no idea how he died."

"It's not obvious. Could have drowned, but it's hard to say. It's possible he was killed and tied to the girder to conceal the body. How will you ID him?"

"DNA maybe. Unless we find something definitive on the body." Her phone dinged, and she reached for it. "It's Augusta." She frowned as she read the text. "The doctor released Tyler this morning. He put him on some medication he thinks will help until Tyler's memory issues clear."

"So he's not a danger to Megan?"

"He doesn't think so." She dropped the phone back on the console and reached for a sandwich from the cooler. "I'm starved." She offered him a turkey and cheese sandwich.

He took it. "Diving always makes me hungry too."

The oil platform high above their heads clanged with noise and activity. Reid had an hour before people showed up. How did he bring up the topic of their past again?

FOURTEEN

Jane couldn't get the image of the body out of her head. At least Ruby hadn't been faced with it.

When they finished their sandwiches, she handed Reid a banana and a packet of almonds from the basket. "Still hungry?"

He nodded and peeled his banana and took a bite.

His somber expression took her aback, and she frowned. "What?"

He swallowed his bite of banana. "Just thinking about . . . us."

She wanted to tell him there wasn't an *us*, but it would be a lie, and they both knew it. The story of their past would likely haunt them both until they talked about it.

He cleared his throat. "Are you ever going to forgive me, Jane?"

She tore open her bag of nuts and didn't look at him.

"Jane?"

She risked raising her gaze to meet his. "Why are you so different now? Why didn't I recognize you?"

"I'm not the same person. I worked hard to overcome what I did—what my dad did." He rubbed his shaved head. "I shaved it all off to become a new person, to leave the old behind. To show my true face to the world."

She clenched her left hand into a fist. "That didn't work well, did it? You hid your true face from me for way too long."

"I know, and I'm sorry."

"Sorry doesn't cut it when you should have told me immediately."

"What would you have done if the situation were reversed? Would you have trusted me and believed that I wouldn't do anything to hurt Will?"

She opened her mouth to assert she'd have been brutally honest, but the words died on her tongue. She didn't trust easily after the way she'd been hurt as a child. If she'd come to town with Will in tow, she would have checked out Reid carefully.

"You can't say it, can you?"

She shook her head. "Maybe I wouldn't have told you either. But by the time you k-kissed me, you already knew what kind of person I was. You let me begin to care about you, and all the time you were hiding something so vital from me. If you'd told me as soon as you knew you could trust me, I could have taken it better."

His gaze fell, and he ripped open the bag of almonds. He lifted his eyes again to hers. "You're right. Even when I was beginning to care for you, I knew I should tell you. I didn't want to spoil what was starting between us. I was wrong. I don't know how to fix what I did though. I wish I could."

No excuses, no rationalizations. His naked sorrow over his behavior touched the sore places of her heart with a soothing balm.

She popped a handful of almonds into her mouth so she didn't have to answer him while she thought about a response. The bite of the wasabi powder made her nose run. At least that's what she told herself. She grabbed a tissue from a storage compartment and sniffled as she willed the tears away.

Why would she cry now? She had Will in her life, which was

incredible. Maybe she wanted more. Maybe she wanted Reid too. But that sounded crazy after what he'd done.

She balled up the tissue in her fist. "I'll try. That's all I can say."

"That's enough. I-I care about you, Jane."

What did that mean? She couldn't look in his face because she wasn't sure she was ready to find out. "Any texts from Will?"

He cleared his throat. "Nope. He's probably helping your dad load ammunition."

"Just make sure he's okay."

Reid tapped on his phone, and it dinged moments later. "He's working on homework. Megan came over after school, and she's hanging out."

"Uh-oh, it's starting. He'd have to have been a concrete post not to notice her flirting last night. Did he say anything after she left?"

"We talked a little. He asked what I liked about you."

She grinned. "So he asked for love advice? That's so cute. What did you say?"

"I put him off. It didn't seem the time to discuss things. I didn't want to talk about you behind your back."

"She's the first girl I've seen him interested in."

"I tried to probe a little after his question, but he clammed up."

"I suppose it's all too new. And she was Tyler's girl. That has to feel wrong somehow too."

"He probably doesn't know how she feels yet. I remember the first time I—" He broke off and looked down.

"You what?"

"After my dad made us a couple. I-I didn't have any idea how you felt about me."

Her hands went as clammy as the first night he'd come to her. "I was terrified."

"Me too. But I liked you. I always liked you."

"You didn't know me."

She didn't want to talk about this. Those nights were memories she'd worked hard to bury, but it appeared he hadn't dug a hole as deep as she had.

The sound of a boat motor grew louder in the distance, and a small motorboat sped toward them. "There's the forensic divers. We might get some answers now."

"And you might get to avoid talking about the past, right?"

Had he really whispered those words, or had they come from her own heart? She wasn't sure she wanted to know.

A rock lodged in Jane's stomach at the coming interview.

The fireball in the west plunged into the dark sea, and Jane switched on the boat's headlights. The lights of Gulf Shores beckoned across the water, and she headed for Bon Secour Bay. Every muscle in her body ached from the dive, and her spirit hurt as well from what faced her.

The forensic team had found a necklace on the body—a distinctive platinum pelican Ruby had mentioned he never took off. She'd given it to him on his sixteenth birthday. Jane had Reid take a picture of it to show Ruby. The body had to be Keith.

Reid shifted in the seat next to her to face her. "You sure you want to tell her tonight?"

"Wouldn't you want to know as soon as possible?"

Reid sighed. "Yeah, I would. I'm worried about you. It's been a rough day."

"It's my job, and Ruby is a friend."

Silence fell until she navigated the boat to the Pelican Harbor dock. Strains of "Stolen Moments" carried to them from one of the jazz bars along the waterfront. The aroma of grilled shrimp and fish wafted to her nose from Billy's Seafood. She should have been hungry, but the smells turned her stomach after what she'd seen today.

Reid hopped onto the pier and tied off the boat, then held out his hand to help her out. His fingers warmed hers, and he didn't release her hand once both feet were ashore.

She took strength from the clasp of their hands, then pulled away and gazed up into his chocolate eyes. "You don't have to go with me. Go home and check on Will."

"He's fine. Megan stayed for dinner. I guess Olivia isn't back from her doctor's appointment in Mobile yet."

Jane glanced at her watch. "It's eight o'clock. She should be back by now. Her appointment was at four."

"Will said there'd been an accident, and the traffic was backed up, so she stopped for dinner until it cleared out."

Jane exhaled. "Scared me for a second. I tried to arrange a ride for her, but she's so stubborn. I wondered yesterday if she should still be driving." She squared her shoulders. "Let's go see Ruby before she hears a rumor."

The school principal lived about four blocks west of the harbor. On the sidewalk Jane broke into a jog to stretch out her aching muscles and to feel the sea wind in her hair. She felt soiled by the horror of finding that poor young man's body.

Why did people do such horrible things to other people? She'd never understand it, and sometimes she wondered why she'd chosen a field in law enforcement that highlighted the evil in men's hearts.

Reid jogged beside her in an easy lope. He didn't even seem

to be breathing hard, but then she wasn't either. The exertion felt good and reminded her they were alive. She would find out who did this to Keith, and the killer would pay. Keith and Ruby would have justice.

Light shone through the front windows at Ruby's house, and Jane slowed to a walk as they approached the front door. Her heart was trying to jump out of her chest, and she swallowed hard before she pressed the doorbell.

Steps came toward the door, and the porch light came on. Ruby opened the door and peered out. Her gaze landed on Jane's face, and after a few moments, tears filled her eyes. "You found him, didn't you?"

"Can we come in?"

Ruby stood aside, then shut the door behind them. Her miniature dachshund sniffed at Jane and wagged her tail. More to delay the inevitable, Jane knelt and rubbed the dog's belly. She stood and wished she felt comfortable enough to embrace Ruby, who stood with her hands clenched in front of her.

Ruby exhaled in a harsh sound. "Tell me."

"Reid is a diver and decided to go down to search for a body since we hadn't found one. We found a male lashed to the girder." She pulled out her phone and showed the picture of the necklace to Ruby. "Do you recognize this?"

Ruby uttered a sob. "It's Keith's. He was lashed to a girder?"

Jane didn't want to tell her how they'd found the body, but Ruby needed closure so she gave the details about what they'd found. "He didn't kill himself, Ruby. He was murdered."

Ruby sagged against the foyer wall and put her hands over her face. A ragged sob made her shoulders shudder. "I knew he wouldn't kill himself."

Jane brushed her fingers across the woman's shoulder. "I'm so sorry, Ruby."

Ruby put her hands down and revealed a pale, tear-streaked face. "Thank you for finding him. Who did this, Jane?"

"I don't know yet, but I'm going to find out."

"What about the terrorist attack?"

"Homeland Security has found no evidence pointing to something like that. Maybe Keith misunderstood what he heard."

Ruby swiped the moisture from her face. "He was a smart guy. I think Homeland Security needs to look harder."

"I'll talk to them again. In the meantime, do you know who this woman is?" She pulled out her phone and showed Ruby the picture of the woman lurking nearby when Reid had been on the platform. "You can't see her face well, but I thought she might seem familiar to you."

Ruby took the phone and enlarged the photo, then nodded. "She came here with Keith last Thanksgiving because her family is on the West Coast. Her name is Sara, but I can't remember her last name right now. Let me think on it."

"Even that much is helpful. If you can't remember, I can go see Steve again and find out."

Ruby handed back the phone. "I'm sure it will come to me." She took a step toward the door. "Thanks for telling me before I heard rumors about it. It will probably be all over town by morning." Her eyes welled again. "I might stay home tomorrow. Please, please keep me in the loop, Jane."

Ruby opened the door, and Jane took her hand on the way out. "I'll find out who did this, Ruby."

Ruby shut the door behind them without answering, but Jane had seen the hopelessness in her eyes. Wouldn't she feel the same

COLLEEN COBLE

way if she'd lost Will? Love made you vulnerable—any kind of love.
And it was too late now. Her love for Will knew no bounds.

She slid a sideways glance at Reid. Was it really a lot more risk
to open her heart a bit to him?

He focused his gun sight on the kid's head.

The boy was out of the bunker and on the porch with a girl.
An older woman and man sat in rockers talking. An idyllic scene
he could shatter if he wanted to. One twitch of his finger and
there would be bloody confetti around. He imagined the horrified
screams of the girl with him.

He lay on a grassy knoll hidden by shrubs and vegetation. Gnats
and flying bugs swarmed around his head, but he ignored them as
he refocused the gun sight on the kid's head. Dusk was falling, and
he was well hidden here. He put down the gun and picked up a cigarette. Nothing was happening now, and he couldn't bring himself
to pull the trigger. Not yet.

Young love.

He didn't think he'd ever felt it. Luckily, a passing stab of lust
or attraction was all he'd experienced. He'd seen too many stupid
actions committed by lovesick people.

He stubbed out his cigarette and picked up the binoculars. He
let his gaze sweep over the teenagers. The girl with Will was hot.
Long, dark hair, big blue eyes. His gaze dropped lower. Luscious.
No wonder the kid was smitten. How would he feel if a bullet came
zinging out of nowhere and plowed straight into that beauty?

The man shook his head. Who was he kidding? For all his fan-
tasies, he still had misgivings about this job. These two would soon

be adults so that wasn't the problem. The real issue was his boss was an idiot. He might think he was smart, but he was letting emotion dictate his behavior. That was a good way to get caught, and jail was no place to be.

He'd even broken into Dixon's house in New Orleans in case there were traces of the videos there, but he'd found nothing. As far as he knew, no one had noticed the break-in yet. Or seen the message he'd left, which was a shame.

He didn't consider what he'd done with the McDonald man murder. Someone else had tipped him over the edge. He would never have survived for long in the water since no one knew he'd gone overboard. He had hidden the evidence. That was all.

And he wanted to keep it that way. If he had to take out the kid, he'd do it to attain his goals.

An SUV turned in the drive, and he ducked down. That pesky police chief. It would be a lot easier to take her out than to try to scare her. She didn't seem to frighten easily. But the Boss said no. It would bring in the state police and more scrutiny of her cases. Including this one.

He picked up his rifle and sighted it again. Maybe a slug into the doorjamb would send them all scurrying like rats.

FIFTEEN

Reid's pulse kicked at the sight of his son out in clear sight of a potential shooter. "Will shouldn't be out of the bunker."

He stared off to his left for a moment. Had there been a flash of movement? He didn't see anything, but a shudder ran up his back. Maybe it was his imagination. Olivia's car was parked outside the farmhouse, and Megan and Will were under the porch light beside Olivia.

"No, he shouldn't." Jane shoved open her door and got out.

Reid jumped out and grabbed her arm before she could stalk to the porch. "Don't embarrass him in front of Megan. He wouldn't want her to think he's weak."

She started to pull away from his grasp before she relaxed. She stared up at him. "I have a lot to learn, don't I?"

"You're making leaps and bounds, but teenage guys hate to be made to look small in the eyes of a girl they're interested in. I remember . . ." He released her arm. "Let's go see what's shaking here."

At least she didn't ask him what he was about to say. He let her go ahead of him up the steps.

She hugged her friend. "Olivia, what did you find out at the doctor's?"

Olivia stared down at her hands. "He tested me for Lyme disease, but I could tell he doesn't think that's it." She spoke softly with a glance at the two teenagers who were deep in a discussion about a science project.

Jane hoped they weren't listening. She didn't want Megan to hear the sadness in Olivia's voice.

She clasped her hands together and tried not to show her dismay. "When will you get the results?"

"Several weeks, but he suggested I see an ALS doctor. I already burned my bridges with the one, so I'll find another."

"This is my fault. I shouldn't have said anything."

Olivia took her hand. "It was worth a try, Jane. I love your fierce determination to change my circumstances, but really, I'm at peace. I don't want to leave Megan or you, of course. But I-I think I'm getting worse. It was all I could do to drive the car here. I nearly steered it off the road several times."

Jane fought the tears burning her eyes. "Do you need to quit work?"

"I-I hate to do that. It's been such a big part of my life. Mornings seem to be good for me, at least so far. I can have Megan drop me, and if someone could run me home at lunchtime, I could try working for a while. But if that's too much, if you don't think I'm doing a good job, please tell me."

"You're a wonderful dispatcher, Olivia. People trust you. I want you to work as long as you're able."

"Let's stumble along a little longer for now then." She turned and held out her hand to Megan. "We need to get you home for school tomorrow. I'm sorry it's so late. That accident shut down the road forever."

Megan made a face but moved slowly away from Will to her mother's side. "I'm not tired."

"You will be at six in the morning."

Megan glanced back at Will. "See you, Will."

He nodded and smiled. "See you."

Jane's dad came down off the porch. "I'll run you home. I'll catch an Uber back."

"I can come get you," Reid said.

"Think I'll grab a beer at Pelican Pizza so don't bother. I'll be home later." Charles offered his arm to Olivia, and she took it with a smile. The three of them descended the steps to the car.

Jane's smile faded as the car pulled away and Reid returned. She punched Will lightly on the arm. "Inside, mister. You shouldn't have been out of the bunker." She pushed him toward the door.

"Aw, Mom, I couldn't look like I was scared when I'm not. You guys are freaking out over nothing."

Reid bit back a chuckle at the exchange between the two of them. Will's grousing wasn't directed at him this time, and he liked the way Jane handled him. Firm but loving. She was a fast learner.

He followed them into the house and snatched a still-warm chocolate chip cookie on his way through the kitchen to the tunnel down to the bunker. "Good."

"Megan made them." Will said it as if he'd just won the Nobel Prize.

This relationship had moved along quickly. The boy was smitten—about like his old man was with his mother.

Jane held up her hand. "Wait, are you telling me you were out of the bunker long enough to make cookies?"

Will scowled. "So what? Nothing happened. I didn't want her to see me cowering in the bunker like some kid."

"You're not taking this seriously!" She waved her hands and took a step closer. "We found Keith's body today—murdered and strapped to an iron girder under the oil platform. The killer has targeted *you*, and I couldn't bear to find you in the same condition." She choked on the words and a sob escaped.

Will started toward her, then stopped and braced his hands on his hips. "I'm not a kid!" He spun on his heels and stalked off.

Jane exchanged a glance with Reid as their son vanished through the door to the bunker stairs. She shook her head. "I didn't know parenting would involve girlfriends so soon."

"You like Megan, right?"

He followed her into the dimly lit stairwell, and they descended toward the sound of canned laughter on TV.

"I love her. She's a great girl. I don't want him hurt though, and relationships at this age can be a flash in the pan."

"Like either of us would know." He nearly ran into her when she stopped abruptly. "What's wrong?"

"Neither of us is going to be any good at parenting a teenager."

He chuckled at the panic in her voice. "It takes the same love and boundaries as any other age. I think we'll stumble through just fine."

"You might, but I'm not so sure I will. I feel very inadequate."

"I think it's something every parent feels. He's mad now, but Will knows we love him, and everything will turn out in the end."

She started back down, and he grinned in the dim light. Their joint love for Will just might draw them together.

———

What was she missing?

Jane tossed and turned in the bamboo sheets and sighed when she caught sight of the clock. After one on Saturday morning, and she hadn't slept a wink yet.

Even though Homeland Security had taken over the case now that she'd found Keith's body, she couldn't let go of the murder. She tried to tell herself it was the case, but it was more than that. The more she was around Reid, the more she wanted to be around him.

She rolled over again. At this rate she would still be awake when it was time to take over the watch from her dad, who had come back around ten.

She might have been able to sleep with Parker in here, but the dog was enamored with Will. The last she'd seen of him had been him padding off to Will's room.

She flipped on the light and reached for her Kindle. Getting to know her son the past few weeks had pushed reading aside, and she hadn't gotten any further with *The Screwtape Letters*. She read several pages before getting to a sentence that made her stop and think.

"Gratitude looks to the Past and love to the Present; fear, avarice, lust, and ambition look ahead."

Love looks to the present. That's what she needed to focus on. Not what she'd missed or what might come in the future, but today. The minute-by-minute experience with Will. Maybe even with Reid. Too often she focused on the future and found her ambition was what drove her on. It wasn't pretty.

She closed the cover on her e-reader and swung her legs out of bed. What would Reid think if she went to his door and told him she wanted to talk? He might assume more than she was willing to admit. A snack would be safer.

She tiptoed to the door and eased it open, then stepped into the hall. Reid's door was open when she went past, and somehow she managed not to peek in on him sleeping, though it took every ounce of her strength.

A light shone around the closed door to the control room where her dad was keeping watch. She didn't bother him and went on toward the kitchen. She turned on the light and blinked at the figure turning toward her from the refrigerator. On autopilot, she reached for her gun. She didn't have it—and she didn't need it because Reid was the man smiling at her.

She put her hand to her heart. "You scared the daylights out of me."

"Sorry."

He didn't seem sorry—he looked inordinately pleased to see her. She resisted the impulse to flee back to her room. "What are you doing in the dark?"

"The refrigerator light comes on, you know." He held up a plate of cold chicken. "Neither of us got dinner, and I'm famished."

Her stomach rumbled. "Maybe that's why I couldn't sleep either. Anything in there but cold chicken? Like maybe chocolate?"

He grinned. "That's dessert, not dinner. There's some gumbo. Want me to warm it up?"

"I need carbs. It's been a stressful day." She brushed past him to peer into the fridge, but his nearness made her vision glaze over, and she found it hard to concentrate on her mission. Carbs, that's what she was here for.

He reached past her, his arm brushing hers. Her skin tingled at the contact, and she stepped back.

He withdrew a half-eaten pie. "How about chocolate pie? Somehow that human garbage disposal we call Will didn't eat it all."

"He probably didn't want Megan to see him wolfing it down. You want half?"

"Let's just share it in the pie plate." He slid out a drawer and took out two spoons, then carried the pie to the island and set it down.

She hopped onto a bar stool and grabbed a spoon. The chocolaty goodness cheered her. "Yum, that's good. My dad makes the best chocolate pie in the state."

"Where'd he get the recipe?"

"He said it was my mom's. If it was, she never made it at Mount Sinai. We never got dessert. Did you?"

He shook his head. "When I'd go to town, I sometimes bought a Snickers bar on the sly."

They were talking about the cult without it being awkward. How did that happen? Maybe those few meetings at the cult recovery group had helped.

She licked the last of the chocolate from her spoon. "I've been thinking about what you said about Liberty's Children, about taking me to check out the place in Kentucky. My new officers are getting up to speed, and Homeland Security has told me to butt out of the McDonald case. Maybe I can take a few days off soon. I've accrued a ton of overtime, and the mayor likes me to take it off rather than pay me when that's possible. Maybe we could go next weekend?"

"We could take Will and get him out of jail for a while. Make it a family camping trip. You ever go camping?"

She wrinkled her nose. "You mean other than what we endured in cabins with no running water? No, and I can't say the idea is appealing. A tent? A camper? Sleeping bags unfurled on the ground?"

He laughed, a deep sound that reached into her core, and she found herself leaning toward him and wishing she had the nerve to kiss that last smear of chocolate filling from the corner of his mouth. The intimacy of this moment alone in the kitchen connected them as if they'd been holding hands.

"How about a motor home? Would that be modern enough? Satellite TV, Wi-Fi in the campground, and a comfortable bed?"

Somehow he'd leaned closer, and she wasn't sure if she'd moved or he had. She shifted on her stool. "That sounds wonderful. You own a motor home?"

"I have a friend in New Orleans who loans it to me whenever I want. I'll pick it up, and we'll travel in comfort."

He reached out and brushed a stray strand of hair from her cheek. "I wish you knew how special you are. Maybe someday you'll let me tell you."

A chill swept over her when he withdrew his hand, and she wanted to tell him she was ready to listen, but before she could muster the courage, he said good night, slipped off his stool, and headed for his room.

She touched her cheek and could have sworn it was warmer from his touch. Maybe going on a trip with him wasn't the smartest thing, but having Will along would keep her heart safe. Wouldn't it?

SIXTEEN

Traffic on the outskirts of town was at a complete standstill, an occurrence Reid had never seen before in Pelican Harbor.

He glanced at the time on Jane's dash. "What's going on? We'll be late."

Jane had a meeting with her new officers in the war room, and they were still fifteen minutes away.

From the time they'd all taken to get around this morning, you'd have thought they were wearing chains. He'd gotten up late, Jane had been engrossed in something on her computer, and Will had taken forever in the shower before getting to work on his homework.

Jane's radio blared to life with a male voice. "Ongoing protest has spawned an attack right in front of the oil company headquarters and city hall. Jane, you copy?"

She reached over and flipped on the lights and siren, then grabbed the mic. "I'm on it, Jackson."

"One of your new officers?" Reid asked.

She nodded. "Jackson Brown."

Reid ran his window down and leaned out but saw no way through the crowd. "We're only three blocks away. Maybe we should hoof it."

"I don't think I have a choice." She pulled the SUV into a parking lot and turned it off.

He got out and opened the back door for Parker, who jumped out and went to stand beside Jane at the back of the vehicle. She hauled out three extra sets of handcuffs. She locked the vehicle, and Reid fell into step beside her as she jogged toward city hall. Their fast pace had them on the edge of the main body of people in a few minutes.

"Any idea what's going on?" he asked. "Was there a demonstration scheduled for today?"

"Nothing came across my desk."

The crowd ahead of them churned with angry shouts. People began to step back from whatever confrontation was ongoing, and Reid ran into a man who wasn't looking where he was going. The guy glared and fingered a small scar on his upper lip before he shouldered past.

The thump of blows being landed joined the shouts and curses. It sounded like more than two people sparring.

Victor Armstrong, jaw tense and mouth tight, stepped through the crowd to block Jane's way. "This is on your watch, Jane, and you're doing nothing about it."

Her hazel eyes flashed, and her chin came up. "I'm handling it, Victor. Get out of my way."

She shouldered her way through the crowd with Parker following. Reid went, too, and they broke through the circle of spectators to find at least ten people in an all-out brawl. A young woman slung the sign in her hand at a man's head and shouted expletives, while an older man landed a punch on a young man's jaw. The man had an oil company logo on his shirt, and the young woman's sign read *Stop Polluting Our Oceans*.

Seemingly with no fear, Jane grabbed hold of the woman's arm and pulled it behind her back. "Police! Stand down!"

The woman fought her, screaming, "Pig," in her face with spittle flying.

Jane tightened her grip until the woman collapsed onto her knees. Jane brought the woman's other arm behind her back and clapped her in handcuffs. "Watch her," she told Reid before she plunged into the melee again.

Reid itched to help her, but Jane had the fight broken up in minutes. By the time she was through, four people were in cuffs, and the others stood off to the side with hangdog expressions. It seemed to be a battle between those against the oil platforms and those who supported them, probably workers and their families.

He spotted a familiar head of bushy white hair. Charles? He nudged Jane. "Your dad is with the protestors."

Her brows drew together, and she stared his direction until someone called out, "Chief Hardy."

An older man in a suit with a sign in his hand stepped out of the crowd. He was a small guy, probably not even five six, and his thick black hair was carefully combed. He seemed vaguely familiar, but it wasn't until he spoke in a modulated deep voice that Reid recognized him as Congressman Henry Williamson, Speaker of the House. He'd been on the news lately with his bill restricting offshore drilling, and Reid had met him a few months ago when he first started working on the documentary about the oil platforms. A sign dangled from his hand, so he was with the protesters.

He approached Jane with a genial smile. "Chief, I'm sorry things got out of hand. That's not what the group wanted at all." His gaze cut over the top of the crowd to her dad.

Jane's grim expression didn't change. "I'm not sure who threw the first punch, but your people resisted me when I tried to break up the fight."

Reid noticed a red spot on her jaw. He stared at the four in hand-cuffs and frowned. Which one of them had punched Jane?

A young man lifted his chin in a contemptuous gesture and stared back. Probably that guy. Reid wanted to jerk him to his feet and show him what a blow felt like, but he managed to keep his cool.

"I'm sure they didn't realize you were law enforcement," Williamson said. "Those of us with a smaller stature are often dismissed. I'm sorry you were injured. Let me pay for a doctor to check you over."

Jane managed a smile at his self-deprecating tone. "I'm fine."

She stared down at the four on the ground, and Reid could almost see the wheels turning. She'd have to delay her investigation into the murder to book them. It would take hours.

She pulled out a key and approached the closest protester, a young man in a tie-dyed T-shirt. "I'm going to release these guys into your custody, Congressman Williamson. Get them out of here and don't let me see them making a ruckus on my streets again. I don't mind peaceful assembly, but I won't allow a riot."

"Thank you, Chief. I give you my word I'll have a talk with them. Young hotheads. They care so much about the planet."

She unlocked the first set of cuffs. "So do I, but there are peaceful ways to go about helping. You're a prime example yourself, sir."

She released the remaining protesters, and Reid stepped closer in case one of them made a move toward her, but they rubbed their wrists and followed Williamson to a small bus on the corner. Others in the protest filed after them, too, but Reid didn't relax until the bus pulled away with all of them.

He touched the spot on Jane's jaw. "It's swelling. I hope it doesn't bruise."

She didn't move away, and for a moment, he thought she was going to melt against him. Until she stepped back and turned away. "I'd better go to the office and get to work. My new hires should be there, and I want to arrange a call to Elizabeth."

The tender moments from last night in the kitchen seemed a lifetime ago.

———

This was starting out to be a lousy day.

The new officers were already in her office when Jane and Reid made it to the station. Jackson shot to his feet when Jane glanced toward the handsome young black man. His uniform was crisp, and his black hair was cut close to his head.

He took a couple of steps toward her with his muscular hand outstretched. "Good morning, Chief."

His eagerness made Jane hide a smile. She'd been the same way fresh out of the police academy. She'd been impressed with him from the first interview. He was from Mobile, twenty-four, and unmarried. His work so far this week had been exemplary.

She shook his hand. "You settling in, Officer Brown?" She noted the way he squared his shoulders at the title.

"Yes, ma'am. Getting to know the ways of the townspeople." He had a soft-spoken Southern drawl.

She turned her attention to the woman standing behind him. "You've been kept busy, Detective Richards?"

Augusta Richards was a seasoned veteran of ten years in the Mobile department. She'd been a detective for five years and had applied for a job to bring her two school-age kids to a quieter area. Her husband was opening a sporting goods store downtown. Tall and lanky with kind brown eyes, she towered over Jane by a good eight inches. Her unruffled demeanor and quiet manner would be an asset to the department.

Augusta smiled. "I love the slower pace here, Chief."

"It's not always so slow, and we have our hands full with a murder investigation. Not to mention that unexpected protest this morning."

Jackson brightened at the word *murder*, but Augusta went wide-eyed. She'd probably expected Pelican Harbor to deal mostly with minor theft and vandalism. She would learn people were the same in every community. Greed, revenge, and hatred made people do crazy things.

She stood with Reid and Parker while the officers got coffee from the front break room.

Reid glanced out the window. "You want me to wait in the lobby while you have your meeting?"

"Or you can take your computer to the conference room if you need to get some work done."

"I do need to go over Elliot's video from the oil rig. I might spot something important."

Now that she had help in the station, there was no need to use Reid as a backup or sounding board. The realization wasn't a welcome one.

The officers rejoined her with coffee and beignets in their hands. It felt good to have a team again. She went around to her desk and logged in to her computer. Parker plopped at her feet. She handed them the files she'd prepared. "Homeland Security is taking the lead on this now, but I want us to help all we can. You have a complete report to date. Maybe you'll see something you want to follow up on."

Jackson stooped and petted the dog. "We've even got a canine unit. Parker, right?"

"Yes. He's a good officer."

"He stays with you?"

"He belongs to me, and I trained him. After you're finished reading the report, we'll reconvene in the war room with what forensics we have and brainstorm next steps."

Augusta took the folder and caught Jane's eye. "You've been hard at work, Chief. Any time off?"

"Not in weeks. Probably about a month."

Augusta grimaced. "Sorry, Chief. We've got this, don't we, Jackson?"

"We sure do." He was as eager as a new puppy.

"You can work more regular hours now, maybe even have a weekend off."

It was a rare day when she got home before nine at night. Now she might have a normal life.

"You guys can take the files to your offices. Jot down anything you think might help. I'll see you in the war room at ten."

There was a final report from forensics from Keith's apartment, and she sent it to her officers, then printed it out. She leaned back in her chair and began to read with a fresh eye.

Whoa. She sat up and stared at the forensic report, which included documents recovered from Keith's laptop on the platform. One was a copy of an email sent from Keith to an unnamed person.

I don't believe Steve Price had anything to do with the death of your daughter. And even if he did, an attack on the oil platform would kill innocent people. Are you willing to have that on your conscience? I'm going to report what I know to the police so this plan is dead.

Steve Price and murder didn't go together. Jane had known Steve for years, and she'd always had the greatest respect for him. She couldn't discount this email though, so she would have to see if he had any idea what Keith was talking about.

SEVENTEEN

Steve Price. Jane couldn't stop mulling over his name popping up in an email.

When she entered the war room, her team was already there. Nora Craft, her forensic tech, had arrived as well. All three sat in the front row near the whiteboard. Her new officers straightened when she entered.

"You've all had a chance to get up to speed on the case?"

Nora pushed her glasses up on her nose and nodded. The brunette had been with the department about five years and was in her late twenties. Her forensic and computer knowledge had been a great asset to Jane. She had a steady boyfriend, also a computer nerd, and she was always willing to put in extra effort even when there was no overtime pay.

"You've all read Nora's report? I sent it over half an hour ago. The pictures of Bonnie are a dead end."

Both Jackson and Augusta nodded at Jane, and she went to the whiteboard and picked up the marker. She wrote down what they knew. "Neither of you have met Steve Price, but I'd guess seeing him accused of murder was as much of a surprise to Nora as it was to me." She glanced at Nora but saw her wrinkle her forehead. "No? You weren't surprised?"

Nora hesitated, then shook her head. "I went to the University of South Alabama. Steve lectured a few times when I was in college, and I was warned before I went not to be alone with him. Supposedly, he had wandering hands. I made the mistake of ignoring that information after the lecture I attended, and he got me up against a wall. I had to get a little rough to get away."

Jane bit back a gasp. "This is a surprise. I've never felt endangered around him."

"He's hardly likely to assault a police officer," Augusta said. "Since you know him, I should interrogate him about this."

"I agree." Jane shoved away her shock and moved on to the next item. "We have two unknown fingerprints on Keith's laptop. Nora, are you still running fingerprint ID on them?"

"I am. It's going to take a few days to run a complete report, but I've had no hits yet."

She glanced at Augusta and then to Jackson. "Okay, anything else you want to discuss?"

Augusta nodded. "I started to mention it in your office earlier but decided to wait for our official meeting. To say I'm concerned about the threat to you and your son would be an understatement. If we put out a press release about the new hires in the department, maybe whoever shot at you will realize the investigation isn't going to be stopped. They might back off."

"You have children too—smaller than Will. I'd be concerned he might turn his attention to your family."

Augusta chewed on her lower lip. "I can't understand why the guy would think he could stop a full-blown investigation. It takes on a life of its own. We could also let the coconut telegraph have its way and tell a few people that Homeland Security has told us to back off. They are the lead investigators."

"Not a bad idea," Jane said.

Jackson frowned. "What if the attack on you and Will isn't really about this investigation? What if it's a cover for something else?"

"What else could it be? The note read STOP OR WILL DIES."

"What else are you working on?"

Jane twirled the marker between her fingers as she thought it through. "Nothing but the minor things I handed over to you last week. Shooting at me and my son would be overkill on a breaking and entering."

"I'll spend some time going over the cases and see if I can find anything else the attacker might have meant," Augusta said.

"I appreciate that, but I think it has to be this investigation." Jane turned back to the whiteboard. "We need to speak to Keith's coworker on the rig, Sara Wells. We found some video of her eavesdropping on Reid Dixon's documentary when he was asking about Keith. She's the only female, and her address is in the file. Jackson, you and I will tackle her while Augusta talks to Steve."

Augusta shook her head. "It might not hurt if you were with me on that interrogation. You might detect signs in his demeanor since you know him. But I would handle the questions."

"Good cop, bad cop strategy."

"Exactly."

"Okay. You can do a little more digging here at the office while I go with Jackson to see if Sara Wells is at home. We'll connect back here at the station when we're done and go talk to Steve." Jane put down the marker and motioned for Jackson to follow her.

What did she do about Reid, who was still in the conference room? She probably wouldn't be gone long, so she texted him and let him know she'd be gone for an hour or so. They could grab lunch afterward.

She poked her head into the conference room and found him staring at his computer screen. "Hey, I have to run out for a bit."

"Okay. I have that appointment with my lawyer anyway."

"Good luck. I'll be back in an hour or so."

"Sounds good."

A pain hit her heart that she was leaving him. What was wrong with her?

The last thing Reid wanted to do on a Saturday morning was talk about Lauren.

Though Scott Foster's office was designed to put people at ease with its comfortable seating and tasteful ocean art, Reid shifted restlessly in the armchair by the fireplace. The vanilla-scented candle was overly sweet and cloying, and it felt wrong that he had to be dealing with more of Lauren's ridiculous behavior.

The door opened and Scott entered. In his sixties he was as thin as a stork. According to Jane his reddish-brown hair had once been as bright as a cardinal, and his golden-brown eyes were intelligent and alert. Reid's anxiety faded as Scott moved to his desk and had a seat.

Scott turned on his computer. "How are you holding up, Reid? Any more demands from Lauren?"

"She's still around. I saw her two days ago. I really thought she'd disappear when she found out she can't get anything from me."

Scott leaned forward. "Well, that's the thing, Reid. I don't think you're going to get out of this totally unscathed."

"What do you mean?"

"I did some digging, and you owned a house together when

she disappeared. Her name was on the title. She also owned life insurance that you collected. Is that correct?"

"Well, yes, but what's that got to do with anything? She's been declared dead. I think she disappeared on purpose and hid her tracks."

"You were residents in the state of Nevada, correct?"

Reid nodded. "Yes."

"Nevada has an interesting law about death in absentia. If the person who's declared dead turns up within a year of the declaration, he or she is entitled to have their property restored. According to my records she showed up just under the wire. She owned half the equity in the house at the time of her disappearance."

Reid tried to take in a breath and couldn't find any oxygen. "You have to be kidding."

"I'm afraid not. As near as I can tell, the house was worth a hundred thousand dollars eight years ago."

"Fifty thousand. I owe her fifty thousand dollars." It took his breath away. "What about the insurance?"

"The insurance companies don't often go after the money when the death in absentia was done in good faith. If they do go after it, they might target her instead of you since she vanished of her free will."

"At least I don't have to pay that back. And it might deter her from pursuing this. I collected fifty thousand dollars from insurance."

"What is in dispute here now is her access to Will. He doesn't want to see her, but she is his legal mother."

"She mistreated him."

"Your word against hers. You have anyone else who saw her shove him away or neglect him?"

"No." He forced the answer out. This was a catastrophe. "Do you think she knows about this?"

"I'm sure her attorney has told her."

"I'm surprised she hasn't brought it up." He stopped and re- membered the gleam in her eyes when he saw her last. "She did say there was new information in the case. This is probably what she meant."

He felt sick. Just as he and Jane seemed to be getting past what he'd done, he was going to have to deal with this. And coming up with fifty thousand dollars would wipe out his savings, money he'd been squirreling away as a cushion for travel to the location of his documentaries. It would make things tight, very tight.

"If I give her the money, does that mean all this is over?"

"I doubt it. There's still the custody issue."

"Does the fact that she cleaned out every bit of our money before she took off matter at all?"

Scott frowned. "It might mitigate the amount you owe her if we take it in front of a judge. The insurance company could sue her for fraud. How much did she take?"

"Twenty thousand dollars."

And how much would attorney and court fees cost? It might quickly eat up any savings he might get from taking it to court. He wanted this over so Will wasn't constantly faced with the pain of Lauren's behavior.

He leaned back in the chair. "What about the fact that Will's real mother is in the picture now? Jane is very involved."

Scott rubbed his chin. "I'm sure the court will take that into account. Will doesn't want to see Lauren, and I doubt they will make him. Her attorney has certainly told her that. And I'll be honest. Trying to get that twenty grand she took deducted from what you owe would probably cost more than that."

"She will want more than she's due from the sale of the house.

She's trying to say she helped me establish the business and wants part of it too. Can she get it?" It would be a nightmare to separate that.

"Maybe. How much was it worth eight years ago?"

"Not much. I was in debt to my eyeballs."

Scott straightened and smiled. "She should have to assume half the debt if her name was on the business papers too. Was it?"

"No. I formed a corporation only in my name."

"Then I'm sorry to say that won't mitigate your obligation."

"What's the next step?"

"We could draw up paperwork to pay it back in installments," Scott offered. "But if you have the money and offer it in one lump sum, she'd be more apt to sign off on the custody issue."

"She's vindictive. I'm not sure what she'll do."

"I've spoken with her attorney. He's a good guy, and while he can't tell me outright, he let it slip that she is most concerned about the money. I think she'll go for it."

Reid sighed and rubbed his head. "Then I'll get the money together. You write up something for her to sign, and maybe this can be over."

EIGHTEEN

For an hour they'd circled the house Sara Wells rented. Jane had gone to the door each time, even though there was never a vehicle in the driveway.

"We'll try one more time before we give up." She slowed her SUV as they turned the corner. "There's a car in the drive now. She must be here."

Parking behind Sara's vehicle would prevent her from jumping into it and running. Jane had a feeling the woman wouldn't be pleased to see them. Jackson leaped from the passenger seat and started around the front of the SUV.

"Stay behind me," Jane said.

He looked chastened but fell back behind her. "I'm a good shot."

"And a little overeager. I hope there's no need to draw a gun today."

"Sorry," he muttered.

He'd learn. The first time he had to shoot his gun, he'd find out how awful it was.

She pressed her finger to the doorbell. When there was no answer, she rapped her knuckles on the door. Hard.

"I'm coming. I'm coming." Footsteps sounded on hard floors from inside, and the door opened.

Jane immediately recognized the shape of her head from the video. Sara's wet hair was piled on top of her head with a clip as if she was getting ready to blow-dry it. She wore a terry cloth robe, and her feet were bare. Jane guessed her to be in her midtwenties. One eyelid had taupe shadow on it, and the other was bare.

Jane smiled. "Sara Wells? I'm Chief of Police Jane Hardy. I'd like to ask you a few questions about Keith McDonald."

Wariness sprang into the woman's brown eyes. "I don't know anything about his murder."

"How did you know he was murdered?"

Sara's eyes shifted to the left. "I-I heard something about it in town. And I mean, you show up here on my doorstep asking about him, so I assume what I heard was the truth."

Small-town life. "Can we come in? We have just a few questions."

"I guess, but you'll have to make it snappy. I have a date with a sexy fireman." Sara stepped out of the way, leaving behind the aroma of herbal shampoo.

Her house was a small ranch built in the seventies. The carpet was probably new at that time. The small living room held a worn tweed sofa and one end table. There wasn't enough room for all of them to sit, so Jane stood near the sofa and took out her notepad.

"Did you know Keith well?"

Sara chewed on a thumbnail, then shrugged and dropped her hand back to her side. "As well as anyone else. We workers are tight. You can't escape from the platform, so you might as well make the most of it."

"You and Keith date at all? I heard he'd broken up with his girlfriend."

"A time or two. Just some laughs and drinks. It wasn't serious. We weren't exclusive or anything."

"Did he ever talk to you about his suspicions about an attack on the oil platform?"

"A little, just one night, when he'd had too much to drink." Sara put her hand over her mouth, then jerked it away. "I mean, he was concerned, of course. I was, too, but I didn't think it was a real threat."

"What did he say about it?"

"He said a terrorist attack was planned."

"Terrorists as in jihadists?"

"I don't think it was religious. He seemed to think it might be a group wanting to shut down the oil platform."

"Do you know who he overheard?"

Sara shook her head. "He never said, but it was two guys who'd been paid to lower cybersecurity. Keith didn't think they knew more than that."

"You were there when Reid Dixon was filming his documentary. The video caught you eavesdropping on him. What did you want to find out?"

Sara shrugged. "I cared about Keith. I wanted to know if anyone was going to mention him. He was supposed to meet me at noon on Sunday, and he never showed. He was the kind of guy who never broke a date or his word, you know? One of the good ones." Tears pooled in her eyes. "I hope you find out what happened to him."

Her answers were too pat, and Jane didn't like the way she didn't make eye contact. "I think you know something you're not telling me, Sara. Why don't you get it off your chest and help me find out who did this to Keith? I found his body. He'd been tied to the girders under the platform and left to drown."

Sara flinched at the brutal words, and the tears flowed down her cheeks. "I'm afraid."

"You think someone will come after you?"

Sara met Jane's gaze for the first time. "Yes. I don't want to end up at the bottom of the ocean like Keith."

"Then tell me! I can arrest him."

"I don't think you can. He's too powerful."

"Give me a name."

A wall came down in Sara's eyes. "I want you to go now. I have to finish getting ready for my date."

Jane pulled out a card and tried to give it to Sara, but she pulled her hands back. "Call me if you want to talk. It's the only way to be safe, Sara." Jane set it on the end table and motioned for Jackson to follow her.

As they reached her SUV, a pickup truck pulled into her drive. Finn Presley, a local firefighter. His muscles would fall into the hunky category. Jane waved at him as they got into her SUV.

She glanced at Jackson. "Too powerful. Could she be talking about Steve?"

"Guess we'd better find out, Boss."

Reid glanced at Jane's set face as they stepped into the pub. The interview must not have gone well.

Either that or she was *really* regretting the way they'd talked last night. Patience was hard when he wanted to take her in his arms and tell her how he felt about her—how he'd always felt.

But did he even have that right? When this was over with Lauren, any money he'd saved would be gone. He wouldn't even have enough left for a wedding and decent honeymoon. Sheesh, was he dreaming or what? Like she'd ever agree to marry him. He was letting a few gentle words go to his head.

Mac's Irish Pub wasn't busy yet at eleven thirty. They settled at a small table in the corner and put in their order. He studied the dollar bills attached to the walls and ceiling. "A lot of money stuck up here."

"Over a hundred thousand dollars. Or at least that's what rumors say."

"How'd it go this morning?"

Her hazel eyes traveled back to his face. "Okay."

"I think I'll get the motor home after lunch. You still want to drive to Kentucky tomorrow?"

She nodded, and the wariness in her expression eased. "You can put the motor home in Dad's barn, and when we're ready to go next weekend, we can hustle Will into it without anyone knowing he's left the compound. I think he's starting to get a little stir-crazy."

Just the three of them off on an adventure together like a real family. It sounded idyllic, so why did she seem so far away?

He took a sip of his homemade root beer as the server brought their shepherd's pie. The aroma of garlic, potatoes, and beef wafting off the cheesy top made his mouth water.

His gaze wandered to the window. "Hey, there's Henry Williamson again. Looks like he's coming in for lunch." He watched the congressional representative's entourage of two women and a man follow like ducklings. "Does he live here?"

"His son is with him too. He's his aide." She scooped up a bite of shepherd's pie and blew on it. "No, he's from Mobile. I've seen him around quite a few times though. I think he has a vacation home out on Fort Morgan Road. He's contributed a lot to the community. When the Deepwater Horizon disaster happened, he was right out there helping clean up wildlife and estuaries. For weeks. His daughter too. She drowned off Fort Morgan a few years ago, and the congressman has been even more devoted to environmental issues in her memory."

Williamson followed the hostess through the restaurant. He stopped a couple of times to say hello to other diners.

His face lit when he saw Jane. "Chief, I want to apologize again for what happened this morning. All we wanted to do was bring understanding to how serious a threat the oil platforms pose to our area. We never want another Deepwater Horizon, but I never expected violence to start."

Jane smiled up at him. "It wasn't your fault, Congressman. Thanks for your help in calming things down."

He bent down a bit. "Listen, Chief, I heard through the grapevine that a terrorist attack was suspected on the Zeus oil platform, and a young man might have been killed over it. What can you tell me about that?"

"Through the grapevine? Did my dad tell you?" He shrugged, but the glint in his eye told her all she needed to know. "I don't discuss ongoing cases with the public."

"I'm not the public." He went around her and pulled out a chair to join them, then motioned for his staff to go on to their designated table. "I might be able to help."

Reid gave a slight nod toward Jane. The congressman would have access to other resources at the federal level she didn't have.

Jane took a sip of her root beer. "Keith McDonald sent his mother an email telling her if he came up missing or dead to contact Homeland Security because a terrorist attack was planned."

"Yet Homeland Security hasn't found any credible threat," Williamson said.

"You spoke with them?"

"I did. I'm not so convinced they're right. Even if they've heard no chatter, it doesn't mean there's no threat. How credible do you think it is? I'll do everything in my power to prevent another catastrophe. Ever since 9/11, I've been worried about this kind of thing. That's why I'm so passionate about shutting them down. We're vulnerable here."

"We found Keith's body. He'd been attached to a steel girder under the oil platform. We're waiting on the autopsy, but it was clearly murder."

Williamson winced. "Any leads who might be behind this?"

Jane bit her lip, and Reid knew she hated to speak until she had proof. "I'm working on figuring that out."

"If you have no concrete evidence, why are you so sure the threat is credible?"

"Someone wants to squelch this investigation so badly they're willing to threaten a fifteen-year-old boy. Our son." Jane told him about the threat and the attacks.

"I could put some pressure on Homeland Security and the FBI to get it off your plate."

"They're already overseeing the investigation now that we have a body, Congressman, but I'm working it too. I'm not one to shirk my duties."

"Your reputation proves that, Chief Hardy. I didn't mean to insinuate you wanted to pass off your duty, but surely you're concerned for your boy."

"We both are," Reid said. "And our son is in a safe place."

Williamson's blue eyes assessed him. "You're the boy's father?"

"Yes."

The congressman's shrewd gaze returned to Jane. "Let me at least poke around and see if I can find out more information that might help you crack this sooner and put the guy behind bars. I'm sure your son is eager to get back to normal life. I have a son that age, and he's all about sports and girls."

Jane smiled. "That about sums it up. And thank you. Any information you can acquire would be very welcome."

Williamson rose and pushed his chair back under the table. "I'll leave you to your lunch. I think I'll have what you're having. I'll be in touch."

Reid watched him rejoin his staff. "You think he can get anywhere with more information?"

"Probably. I'm sure Will is ready for this to be over. So are we." She glanced at her watch. "I'm sure he's upset. His big game started a few minutes ago."

Reid winced, hating that his boy was hurting. Sometimes parenting was too hard.

He dug into his shepherd's pie. Once this was over and he was home with Will, Reid was going to miss being with her. He intended to make use of every opportunity he had in Jane's presence.

NINETEEN

Would Brian really try to hurt her dad from in jail?

Jane entered her office after lunch and shut the blinds in the big window by her desk to block out the brutal heat of the sun. The whining AC thanked her by changing its pitch. Reid and Parker trailed in behind her, and the dog came around the desk to plop at her feet.

She reached for her phone. "I set up a call with Elizabeth to see if she can think of anyone who would know the code to my dad's Wi-Fi."

"I'll grab us coffee while you talk." Reid exited and shut the door behind him.

She placed the call to the correction facility where Elizabeth was being held pending trial. After last night's chat with Reid, she felt unsettled and distant, something she hadn't expected. And it was all on her. He'd been staring at her with confusion and hurt in his dark eyes, but she had no answers for the way she'd taken a step back this morning.

Even though the call had been prearranged, it seemed an eternity before Elizabeth came on the line. "Elizabeth, it's Jane."

"What do you want?" Her tone was more weary than truculent.

Jane hadn't been sure if Elizabeth would talk or hang up. "We had an intruder the other night, and I wanted to talk to you about it. The guy threatened Will, and while you might be angry at Dad and me, I hoped you might be willing to help me for Will's sake."

"For a second I thought you were saying I had something to do with it, which would be a trick since I'm stuck in here."

"The guy somehow got past our security on the Wi-Fi and turned off the electricity. Dad said you set up the Wi-Fi. Have you mentioned the password to anyone?"

Elizabeth let out a harsh bark of something that sounded like a cross between a laugh and a snort. "Your dad's Wi-Fi password is the least of my concerns."

"It might have been something you mentioned long ago when you installed it."

Elizabeth went so quiet Jane thought she might have lost the connection until she heard a door slam. "Can you think back? Maybe even the tech who installed the fiber-optic line for you."

"Well, yes. I was having trouble getting it set up, and the tech was still there. He did some fiddling, then asked what password I wanted. I told him, and he got it working."

"Do you remember his name?"

"That was two years ago, so no."

"Did he mention anything that might help me identify him?"

"He worked for the cable company. Maybe they would have records."

"Young, middle-aged, older? Do you remember anything about him?"

"In his twenties. Red hair, muscular."

That should help. Redheads weren't as common. "Thanks, Elizabeth. I appreciate the help." She hesitated. "How are you doing?"

"How do you think I'm doing? I'm back in the one place I feared. It's awful, just awful." Elizabeth sounded near tears.

Jane wanted to point out all that Elizabeth had done to land back in jail, but it would fire her up more. "I'm sorry, Elizabeth. I miss seeing you."

"So much that you come for a weekly visit, right? Good-bye, Jane. Don't contact me again."

The line clicked, and Jane put down her handset and sighed. That was a bust.

Reid entered with two cups of coffee in a cardboard tray.

He set the tray on her desk and handed her a coffee. "Was she any help?"

"The tech putting in the line knew the password, but that was two years ago. I doubt it's him."

"Could be a hacker then."

"That seems more likely. It was something I had to check." She sipped her coffee and set it on her desk, then called up her email. "Whoa, there's an email about the autopsy already. They must have gotten right on it. I thought they'd call me."

She opened the document and scanned it. "Cause of death was drowning, so Keith was alive when he went in the water. Toxicology isn't back yet though to make a certain determination."

"Any clues to his killer?"

She was still studying the autopsy and scanned the items found in or on the body. "His clothing appeared to be shore attire—sandals, shorts, and a T-shirt. He must have been killed after he changed to fly home."

"Any estimate on time of death?"

"Likely sometime Saturday."

"Makes sense with what Ruby said about him supposedly coming home then and not showing up."

Back in her usual domain, Jane was relaxing around Reid again. As long as they didn't discuss anything personal.

Parker rose and stretched, then ambled over to sniff at Jane's shoes.

Reid hadn't mentioned his visit with Scott Foster.

She knew Scott well since he'd been her father's best friend for years, but she wasn't sure how he would get all the wrinkles out of Lauren's crazy lawsuit. Did she dare ask? Would he think it was too personal?

She leaned back in her chair. "You want to talk about what you found out from Scott?"

He ran his hand over his forehead. "It wasn't good, Jane. Nevada has a crazy law where if the so-called deceased shows up within a year of being declared dead in absentia, she can even get her property back. That means I owe her fifty thousand dollars."

The amount took her breath away. "Can't Scott fix it?"

"Apparently not. I have to come up with the money."

"Can you do it? I-I have a little in savings. About ten thousand."

His face went soft, and the heat in the room seemed to shoot up. "It means a lot that you'd offer, but I have the money. It will wipe out my savings, but I hope it will put an end to the situation."

She hesitated to bring up her other question since he was already dealing with so much, but it was something she had to know. "Does this mean you're still married to her?"

His eyes went wide. "I never asked Scott. I don't think so. I believe having her declared dead nullified the marriage."

"I think you'd better check for sure," she said softly.

He gave a jerky nod, and she hated to see the fear in his face. "A friend is going to fly me to New Orleans to pick up the motor home. Want to go along?"

"I can't. I've got to talk to Steve again."

"Wish I could be there, but you don't need me any longer."

She had the same regret, but she didn't want to admit it. "See you tonight."

Whoa. He grinned as he stared through the binoculars. The kid was sneaking out. He'd known it would happen sooner or later. The teen wore a game jersey and carried a baseball glove. Now that he thought about it, he'd heard the final championship game was today. Will was their star pitcher.

The kid darted from tree to tree and crept through the thick brush and high weeds. Surely he didn't intend to walk to town. It was five miles. The man followed at a decent distance and watched Will climb into a blue Corolla. The Price kid was picking him up.

Surprising that the old man hadn't seen him leave. But kids were sneaky. The man had done his share of slipping away from his parents in the dead of night. His objective had never been something as innocent as a ball game though.

He thrashed through the brush to his truck and climbed in. Should he force the Price kid's car off the road and take Will? That would shake up the chief. But maybe there was a better way to play this game.

What would the town do if he opened fire and shot an unsuspecting spectator at the game? Would they cry for the chief's head on a platter for letting her son bring danger into town? It might be fun to see, and he'd like it more than firing at a teenager.

TWENTY

It was three o'clock when Reid paid the cabbie and got out in front of the home he'd shared with Will for most of his young life. He'd bought the two-story brick home after they'd moved to New Orleans seven years ago, and it held many happy memories. Once things settled down in Pelican Harbor, he planned to pack up everything and take it to the new place. He'd rent this out or maybe sell it.

Selling it would be the smart decision. He had no time to manage a rental. He dug out his keys and approached the front porch. He was still four feet away when he saw the door standing ajar a couple of inches. Splintered wood showed its raw edges around the lock's faceplate. A shoe print marred the part of the door near the lock.

A hard dose of sanity made him reach for his phone and dial 911 instead of going inside. He texted Jane, too, but it was hard to say when she'd see it. It was his need to be close to her that made him do it. Pathetic.

Minutes later the scream of a siren grew louder from around the corner. He waited by the sidewalk. When the officers parked their car and joined him, he explained what'd he'd seen.

The two had him wait a few minutes while they went inside and checked the place out. The minutes seemed to tick by slowly as he waited for them to reappear. After fifteen minutes, the door opened and they came toward him.

"It's a mess in there, sir," the younger officer said. "I'm not sure what they were searching for, but there's no one inside now. We'll fill out a police report on it, so go ahead and see if you can determine what was taken."

"Can I go in now?"

The other officer was already heading for the squad car, and the younger man nodded. "Yeah, go ahead. Call us if you see or hear anything. We'll be here filling out the report, and we'll take any documentation you have before we leave."

Reid nodded and strode up the porch steps and into the house. Stale air rushed him. He entered the living room, then stopped and stared at the damage. The contents from every drawer in the end tables had been dumped on the floor. The TV was missing as well as the home theater equipment. He trailed into his office. All his extra equipment was gone: video cameras, tripods, extra computers, everything. The desk had been emptied as well. He checked the safe in the closet and discovered the burglar hadn't found it. He opened it to be sure and found passports and other items still inside.

In a daze he snapped pictures of the destruction here and in the living room. The kitchen seemed untouched, and he went upstairs to the bedrooms, where he found more chaos in his bedroom. Will's room was worse. His boy's clothing was slashed and ripped. He sniffed and smelled the stench of urine. The source seemed to be a pile of Will's underwear heaped on the bed.

His gut clenched, and a wave of nausea knocked into him. What craziness was this? It was almost as if someone hated Will, but that wasn't possible.

He snapped pictures and left as quickly as he could. In the bathroom he pushed open the door. A slash of red at the double mirrors made his heart stutter. The words STOP NOW was on the first mirror and OR WILL DIES was on the second mirror. *Stop now*, just like the note warning Jane.

The intruder was clearly targeting Will.

Reid shot for the stairs and rushed for the front door to have the police look at the warning. He barely made sense as he babbled out what he'd found. The two officers hurried back into the house.

He would have to go back to that bathroom and snap pictures of that obscene message. Jane would want to see everything. Taking a deep breath, he forced himself back inside and up the stairs. The two officers were notating the mirror's warning, and Reid averted his gaze.

He couldn't look at that threat again, not with the letters dripping red as if they were written in blood.

"Will's your son?" the older officer asked.

"Yes. He's fifteen years old. Fifteen! Why would someone threaten him?"

"He have any enemies at school?"

"He doesn't even attend here and hasn't for two months. But to answer your question, no. Not to my knowledge. I think this ties in to a murder investigation in Alabama." He told the officers about the previous warning and their decision to put Will under protection.

"We'll send what we have here to the chief of police in Pelican Harbor."

And that promise was supposed to make him feel better? Reid struggled to control his impotent rage over whoever wanted to harm his boy. He couldn't get out of here and back to Pelican Harbor fast enough. Disappearing for a few days into the backwoods sounded like the right thing to do.

He had to hear Will's voice, make sure he was all right. The phone rang four times before Will's cheery message started. "Call me, son. It's important."

Reid paced back and forth. Should he call Jane? No, he was over-reacting. Charles could assure him everything was okay.

He called up the number and didn't bother with niceties when the older man answered. "Is Will all right?"

"He took a nap." There was a pause. "Actually he's been asleep a couple of hours. I should wake him or he won't sleep tonight. You need to talk to him?"

"Please." Reid's pulse settled.

The boy had just been asleep. He was fine.

Reid listened as Charles knocked on the door. "Will? Time to wake up. Your dad wants to talk to you."

The door squeaked open, and the phone went silent, then Charles's grim voice was in Reid's ear. "He's gone, Reid. He put some pillows under the sheet. His baseball jersey and glove are missing. I'll bet he's gone to the game."

"Call Jane! I'm on my way."

It would be an excruciatingly long drive in the motor home, but his friend had already taken off in the plane that had brought him. He had no choice but to head out in that behemoth.

———

Steve wasn't going to take this interrogation well.

The receptionist had ushered Jane and Augusta in and told them to wait a few minutes until his meeting was over. Glowering clouds made his massive office seem dark and claustrophobic. Jane wandered over to the pictures on the mantel over the fireplace. If what she'd learned was true, the idyllic family portrait was a lie. His daughter was a beautiful brunette with Steve's smile and dark eyes. His son, who appeared a couple of years younger than his sister, was blond like Steve's deceased wife. Steve seemed much the same, though he'd lost his wife in the meantime. The kids appeared to be about eighteen and fifteen.

But she needed to keep an open mind even though she believed Nora's account of Steve's behavior. Augusta had spent several hours poring over the deaths of young women to find a connection, but it was a daunting task without knowing when and where the supposed victim died.

The door opened and Steve stepped in. Wearing khakis and an open-collared shirt, he looked more approachable today than when they'd found him in his suit. His dark hair was a little ruffled. Maybe that "meeting" was over a ball and tee.

He walked over to greet her with an extended hand. "Sorry to keep you waiting."

"We've only been here a few minutes." Jane introduced Augusta as her new detective. "We had a few more questions, but this shouldn't take long. Detective Richards will be handling the case, so I'll let her take over."

"Have a seat." Steve strode to his desk and settled in. "How can I help you?"

Jane perched on the edge of a chair and Augusta did the same. Her back was erect, and her chin held a challenging tilt. She was a formidable detective.

Augusta took out her small notebook. "Do you know why anyone would want to destroy the oil platform in revenge against you?"

Steve blinked. "Revenge? That's preposterous! I don't have any enemies—well, at least not rabid ones like that. A few disgruntled employees maybe. Nothing more than that. Where'd you hear something so outrageous?"

Augusta held his gaze. "We're in possession of an email from Keith McDonald talking about you to some unknown person. In the email Keith appeared to believe the plot against the platform was to punish you for killing the person's daughter. He was trying to talk the person out of it. The state cyberteam is trying to track down the recipient's identity."

"What?" A tide of red washed up Steve's neck and marred his face with blotches. "I've never killed anyone."

"Caused a young girl to commit suicide, maybe? Maybe even someone you fired?"

"No, there's nothing like that." He glanced at his Rolex. "I have an important meeting in a few minutes, so I think we're done here."

Augusta rose. "I have a witness who says you make a habit of manhandling female college students when you teach. Maybe it was a girl you assaulted."

The ugly color on his face deepened. "Out! I'm not speaking to you again unless you're here to charge me with something. This is the most insulting conversation I've ever had, and it's over." He stalked to the door and threw it open.

His accusatory glare at Jane told her he blamed her for the interrogation. Yesterday she would have been chastened, but she'd seen a glimpse of panic and guilt before he refuted the charges.

Jane waited to speak until they were in the parking lot, a light rain misting them. "I like the way you handle yourself, Augusta. Good job."

"Thank you. He's guilty, you know. I'm not sure of what yet, but there was no mistaking his fear."

"I saw it too. We need to find out who the girl is and what happened. That might lead us to the murderer."

They hurried toward the vehicle as a hard rain began to pelt them. Jane slung herself under the steering wheel and reached for her phone. She had several texts, but she didn't get a chance to read them before a call from Reid came through.

"Hey, did you get the motor home?"

"Have you seen Will?"

The strain in his voice tightened her chest. "No. What's wrong?"

"Someone broke into my house in New Orleans. There's another threat against Will. Check out the picture I texted you. But even worse, Will sneaked out of the house. I'm sure he's at the baseball game. Your dad said his jersey and glove are gone too. I'm on my way back, but go find him and let me know he's okay."

Her panic was a thundering drumbeat in her chest. "I'll find him and call you."

"I should have known he'd do this. That game is important to him. I have to get going. Let me know when you find him."

"I will." She ended the call and went to her messages. She clicked on the picture he'd sent. The dripping red letters on the mirrors leaped out at her from the phone screen.

"What is it?" Augusta asked.

Jane passed the phone to the detective. "We have to make sure Will is all right. And we need to find out who's threatening my son."

TWENTY-ONE

Jane couldn't get the ugly word *die* written in red on the mirror out of her head.

A roar of approval from the crowd washed over Jane as she approached the bleachers with Augusta and Parker. A disgruntled player approached the dugout after striking out. And there was Will, face set, on the pitcher's mound ready to strike out another batter.

She nudged Augusta. "That's Will."

"He came to the game just like you thought." Augusta studied the crowd and the area surrounding the diamond. "I don't see anyone lurking. I'll walk around for a closer look though."

"Thanks."

Part of her wanted to march to the pitcher's mound and drag him off the field and back to the bunker, but for the first time, she realized he was almost an adult. He was smart and thoughtful. His team mattered to him, and wasn't that the way it should be? She wanted a kid who cared about other people, who took his responsibilities seriously. A young man who kept his word and thought through consequences to other people even when it came with a cost to himself.

Her vision blurred with pride. Reid had done a remarkable job raising Will by himself, but she wanted to be part of it now too. She couldn't tell him he'd done the wrong thing because he hadn't. He'd lived up to his personal code of conduct and honor.

A glint or flash caught her eye near the tree line on the back side of the ball diamond. She shaded her eyes with her hand and stared at the location. There. It came again. She skirted the spectators lining the field and hurried that way. Augusta was striding toward the same area.

Before Jane could decide if the danger was real, a man carrying a rifle burst from the bushes and ran for the street.

She gave chase and Augusta broke into a run as well. The man kept his head down and sprinted down an alley. Jane picked up the pace, her breathing quickening. She exited the alley onto Bay Road by Petit Charms in time to hear a vehicle roar away. The taillights in the white pickup flashed before speeding off too quickly for her to catch even one letter of the license plate number.

White pickups were as plentiful as shrimp here, and she hadn't been able to make out the year. Her SUV was back in the lot, and she had no chance of catching the guy.

She whipped out her phone and called Jackson. "Possible shooter by the school. White pickup, Caucasian male suspect, maybe in his twenties." The age was a guess based on how fast he moved.

"On it, Chief. I'm patrolling the other side of town, but I'm on my way."

Too far to be much help. She ended the call as Augusta reached her. "I called Jackson to search for him."

"Did you see he had a rifle?"

"I saw it. Under normal circumstances I might have thought he was hunting, but it's safe to assume he was watching Will." A shudder ran down her back at the thought of what might have happened.

She called Reid's number and turned to go back to the school. "I'd better let Reid know Will is all right."

He answered on the first ring. "Did you find him?"

"He's pitching a no-hitter at the moment. That's some kid you raised."

"He's all right?"

Should she tell him about the possible shooter? No, it would only worry him more. "He's fine. What's your ETA?"

"Maybe an hour. I've got the speedometer pegged as far as I dare. You didn't interrupt his game, did you?"

"What kind of mom do you think I am? When I saw him on that pitcher's mound, I realized how remarkable he is. He doesn't want to let anyone down. He's got strong ethics and a conscience."

"Yes, he does. Is the game about over?" His voice held a thread of worry.

"Two more innings."

"Maybe I'll make it in time for the celebration."

"See you soon." She signed off before she said something she would regret.

The motor home had probably never been driven that fast.

The door to the barn was up when Reid drove the RV onto Charles's property. He spotted Jane's SUV parked in front of the house as he drove past.

Reid scanned for any obvious threats but didn't see anyone as he parked inside and closed the door. The bright LED lights overhead illuminated the sleek interior of the barn. Charles had drywalled the walls and painted them a cream color, and the concrete floor was spotless.

The door from the bunker flew open, and Will barreled inside. "Dad, you got it!" He wore an ear-to-ear grin. "I can't wait to go." He caught Reid in a bear hug. "I pitched a no-hitter, Dad! A no-hitter!"

Reid clung to him. "I'm so proud of you, Will. I wish I could have seen it." He released him and pulled Will back to stare into this face. "What you did was wrong. You could have died over a baseball game. You can't do it again, you hear me?"

Color flooded Will's cheeks. "Sorry. I couldn't let my friends down. It wouldn't have been right. They needed me."

"How do you think your mother would have felt if you'd been shot? Or me? Baseball is fun, but it's just a game. It's not worth dying over."

"I know. I know. I'm sorry."

When his boy hung his head, Reid relaxed. "Should I go join the party?"

"In a minute. I want to see this bad boy!"

Reid opened the side door of the motor home and pulled down the metal steps. "Come take a look. It's been updated since we took it out last. Sleeps six, and it's got all new appliances, furnishings, and flooring. What do you think?"

Will started toward the vehicle as Jane stepped into the barn with Parker at her side. Her eyes widened when she saw the motor home. "That thing is huge."

"My friend had it specially built. There are bunk beds and two queens. Gets terrible mileage, but it's terrific to handle, and it can go anywhere. Have a peek inside."

He entered behind Will and Jane and watched them exclaim over the RV. Unlike most RVs, the interior was white and bright—no wood paneling here. The furniture was white leather, and the light bounced off the stainless-steel appliances.

Jane's smile grew bigger by the minute. Parker nosed around, then jumped into the front passenger seat.

Reid nudged Jane. "I've got a copilot."

"The best kind."

"There are two bathrooms," Will said.

Jane went back to look, and Reid followed. The bedroom was large with luxury furnishings. The light-gray, wood-grained vinyl tiles continued from the rest of the RV.

Jane bounced a bit on the bed. "Nice. I think Will should take this room. It's more protected in case of an intrusion in the front."

"I agree."

"Could we leave tonight?" Will asked. "I can't go to school anyway."

Jane frowned. "I have an investigation to run."

"You have officers now. You haven't had time off in weeks, Mom. It's only for two days. You weren't going to work tomorrow anyway."

Reid read the indecision on her face. "You're at a dead end right now, right? This would be a good time to get Will out of town while Homeland Security and your officers work the case."

She glanced at her watch. "It's nearly six. I can probably pack in a few minutes. We could wait until it's fully dark. I'd like to have a decoy of some kind when we leave so anyone watching will think Will is still here."

"I could call Elliot over. He's about Will's size. What do you have in mind?"

"Will is always wearing his Eagle's hat. We could make sure

Elliot is dressed like Will and wearing his hat. Have him out where he can be seen."

Will headed for the door. "I'm going to pack before he gets here."

Jane clasped her hands together. "That message on the mirrors—it scared the life out of me."

"Me too. How did the investigation go today?"

"Okay." She told him about the interview with Steve. "I think he's hiding something, but I don't know what. Not yet. Augusta is on it though. She'll ask Nora if she knew the names of any other girls he harassed. We need the name of the girl he supposedly killed."

"Maybe the first place to start is to find out which universities he's been at. And what years. Any way to acquire that information?"

"Maybe there would be a mention in the newspaper of him speaking. It's a place to start." Jane's phone rang. "What's up, Olivia?"

Her face fell as she listened. Reid walked a few feet away to give her privacy, but he couldn't help overhearing a few remarks. It sounded like Olivia was asking Jane to take Megan for the weekend.

Reid stepped back in front of Jane and mouthed, *We can take her with us.*

Jane nodded. "Reid got a motor home, and we're going on a camping trip near the last known location of Liberty's Children. Do you mind if we take her with us? And what about you driving? Can you even do that?" She paused to listen. "Okay, we'll pick her up around ten if that's okay. We're sneaking out in the night."

They chatted a few more minutes before Jane hung up. "Olivia's mom fell and broke her hip. Megan doesn't want to spend the weekend at the hospital in Pensacola, and Olivia is okay with our taking her with us."

"What about Olivia driving?"

"Her aunt is going to drive her around. She's younger than Olivia's mother and in good health."

"Will is going to be happy."

About as happy as Reid would be having Jane around all weekend.

TWENTY-TWO

Were they doing the right thing?

The boys and Parker had vanished into the game room in the bunker, and Jane heard thumps and shouts as they played a video game. The email she'd just gotten from the sheriff in McCreary County excited her. She sneaked out to the RV while they were distracted and found Reid stashing his things in one of the cabinets.

Reid saw her and closed the cabinet door. "I think Will already brought his things out. He didn't argue about taking the bedroom."

"Who would? The thing is gorgeous. I've never traveled like this before, but I plan to take the copilot seat. Parker can hang out with Will and Megan."

His dark eyes lit and a slow smile grew. "Sounds good to me."

"I sent an email to the McCreary County sheriff. He sent me a map of the area Liberty's Children bought. It's just under three hundred acres, so it appears they'd come to stay. They aren't squatting."

"Did he say anything else about them?"

"Just that they haven't caused any trouble. They keep to themselves, and the members who have come to town are friendly. They don't seem to be in recruitment mode yet." She pulled up the map on her phone to show him. "I thought we could stay at the Cumberland Falls campground."

"It's about where I thought it was so probably a ten-hour drive in this behemoth." He patted the side of their RV tank.

"Where should I bunk?" She eyed the available beds.

"I'm going to sleep with Will so I'll be there to protect him. It's a queen bed, so plenty of room. The sofa bed is bigger. We can put Megan on the bunk bed. She can take the upper or lower, her choice."

"Sounds good." Jane stashed her belongings in the cabinet closest to the sofa, then hesitated. "We should both be armed."

He patted the holster at his waist. "I'm ready."

She searched his gaze. "Do you feel good about taking Will out of the bunker? I'll admit I'm worried. If he were shot . . ."

"I know. I know. I'm struggling with it too. But God doesn't want us to live in fear, honey. At some point you have to have some faith in God's provision."

A vision of the flames consuming her tiny cabin at Mount Sinai flooded her mind. "Bad things happen."

"They do. Will is young. He'll have to resume life at some point. Not just yet, but if this isn't solved soon, we'll have to figure out how to let life go on."

While she knew he was right, the fear for the son she'd just found raged as hot as that fire so many years ago. Was this what most parents went through—the terror that something might happen to take the child you loved with all your heart?

She turned toward the door. "We should take some food as well. The fridge is full-size, so we can stock it with whatever we want."

"Meats to grill, canned stuff to reheat. Let's plan to be easy. And we can eat out some too."

The thought of a leisurely weekend felt unreal after how hard she'd been working. She couldn't let herself think of whether or not she'd find her mother. The disappointment had been too keen every time she thought she'd found her. If nothing else, this would be three days to remember.

The metal stairs creaked as Reid came down behind her. "If we leave by ten, we can be there by morning."

"I thought we'd stop at midnight and get some rest."

"I'm used to this kind of trek without sleep. I'd like to get to Kentucky and see if your mom is still there."

He took her arm, and she turned to face him. "What?" His eyes held compassion that made her want to linger.

"What if she's not, Jane? She could have left."

"I know. I keep telling myself if she had left, she would have contacted me. That's the hope I cling to. But she let Dad take me away, so that belief might be as empty as air."

His warm fingers lifted her chin. "I have a good feeling about this trip. It might be life-changing."

"All in good ways, I hope." Her voice trembled, and she stepped back. It would be way too easy to fall into his arms.

She headed for the house. "I'll pack up some food, and you can bring it out to the fridge."

"While you do that, I'll check on the boys. I'm not so sure of our plan. How do we make Elliot resemble Will? Seems tricky."

She thought it through. "I have an idea."

———

This was going to be tricky.

The night pressed in with humidity and darkness laden with the sharp scent of pine. Reid gave a slight nod to Jane. It was all ready, and they were about to get out of here. Elliot had quickly agreed to wear the disguise, and he and Charles were playing cornhole under the wash of a security light.

"Let's have some beignets," Jane said in a loud voice. "I don't have on any insect repellant, and the mosquitoes are awful. Want some, Elliot?"

Will was in Elliot's clothes. "Sure." He went after her.

Reid followed Jane inside, and they ran for the passageway to the barn.

"You think it will work?" Will said as he ran ahead of Reid and Jane.

They exited into the barn and stopped to catch their breath.

Reid stopped Will from turning on the lights. "Let's just get inside."

They stepped closer to the RV, and Parker's happy bark from inside the motor home greeted them. Reid opened the door and ushered Jane and Will inside. "Will, go back to the bedroom and sit on the floor. The blinds are shut. Jane, you do the same. I don't want anyone seen but me. Take Parker with you."

Jane hustled Will to the back of the RV. She shut the door behind them, and Reid climbed behind the wheel. The big engine roared to life. He hit the garage door opener Charles had given him and pulled the vehicle out before he punched the button again.

He drove the RV to the front of the house and paused to run down the window. "Hey, Charles, thanks for fixing this thing. I'm going to put it back in storage. Seems to be running fine."

Charles looked up and nodded. "Glad to do it, Reid."

Reid ran his window back up and exited the compound.

Perfect. He hoped.

He drove away from the ranch and into Pelican Harbor. The little town was buzzing with Saturday night activity. Jazz music played from one of the bars, and the scent of seafood made its way through the air-conditioning system. He took his time navigating the beast down the narrow streets to Olivia's house.

He parked across the street from Olivia's house in a dark parking lot, then walked back to the bedroom and slid the door open a crack. "Can you text Olivia and have her send Megan down? Tell her where we are and have her hurry. This thing is bound to attract attention."

"On it," came the muffled reply from Jane.

He went to the side door and waited. When a soft knock came, he opened it and let Megan inside, then pointed to the bedroom. "Slide in there and try not to be seen."

She tossed her backpack onto the captain's chair and went that way. His phone dinged with a message. Jane had gotten a text from her dad. Elliot was on his way home, and everything had gone as planned.

A weight lifted from his shoulders as he drove out of town. Once the harbor lights were behind him and only moonlight lit the road in front of him, he called back to Jane. "Come out, come out, wherever you are."

A few moments later, he saw the three of them in the rearview mirror. The kids plopped onto the sofa, and Will pulled out a Yahtzee game.

"I'm getting Cokes from the fridge," Megan called. "You want anything?"

Jane slid into the passenger seat. "I'll have a root beer."

"Same for me," Reid said.

The mantle of a real family slipped onto Reid's shoulder like a custom-made jacket. If only he could keep it.

TWENTY-THREE

A sudden jolt awakened Jane, and she sat up rubbing her eyes. The black road spread before them, and the massive tires hummed on the highway. "Where are we?"

"In Tennessee."

Her gaze went to the clock on the dash. Three o'clock. They'd been driving for five hours. "About halfway there."

"About that. The kids crashed about midnight. Will went back to the bedroom, and Megan claimed the bottom bunk. I made them clean up their mess before they went to sleep."

She yawned. "I didn't hear a thing."

"We haven't been sleeping more than a few hours a night with all the standing watch."

"No. And too much to worry about. It's amazing what having a team behind me has done for my peace of mind." She checked her phone. "Nothing more from Dad, so everything must be quiet. Any sign we've been followed?"

"Nope. There hasn't been a single vehicle behind us for about an hour."

She studied his face in the wash of light from the dash. His eyelids drooped, and he looked tired. "Want me to drive for a while?"

He slid a sideways smile at her. "Think you could handle one of these things?"

"Well, no."

"Then you're proposing to crash us in the ditch, Chief."

"Well, there's that. I wouldn't know the first thing about driving a rig like this. How about some caffeine? I could make coffee or get you a Coke."

"Coffee would be amazing."

"We could stop for a few hours, let you grab a few winks."

"We could, but I really want to get there. I can catnap at the campground. Two hours, and I'll be good."

She nodded and went back to the small kitchen. It had one of those fancy coffeepots built into a cabinet. The carafe wouldn't slide all around while it was brewing. She put in the Captain Davy's Coffee Roasters Guatemalan coffee she'd brought along and got it started. The aroma perked her right up.

She opened the fridge and studied the contents. "I'm starved. How about a cheese and turkey sandwich?"

"I wouldn't say no."

She got out two paper plates, and by the time she'd fixed the sandwiches and heaped corn chips on both plates, the coffeepot beeped. He liked his coffee black, too, so she poured him a cup and carried it to him with the plate of food. When she returned for her food and coffee, she noticed Will was sprawled out across his bed.

A wave of love hit her, and she watched him sleep for a few minutes before she returned to her seat in the front. "Will is totally out."

"He's almost giddy with relief on being out of the bunker. This was the right thing to do."

"I hope you're right." She glanced in the side mirror. "No lights behind us."

"Nope. We'll take two days in Kentucky, then head back on Tuesday. You sure you can take three days?"

"I have a lot more hours than that coming to me, but I do need to get back to work then. I can relax knowing Augusta's working the case as well as I could. But I won't truly relax until Keith's killer is behind bars and Will is safe."

The darkness made her feel safer with her feelings hidden. Reid couldn't read her thoughts and peek inside to see how much she enjoyed being around him. They ate in companionable silence with the tires eating up the miles to their destination. What was at the end of this road? Her mother or more heartbreak?

It could be both.

What if her mother was there but refused to see her? It could happen. She choked a bit as she swallowed the bite of chip.

It is going to happen.

Her panic was so real, it rapped against her ribs like a bird trying to escape its cage.

"Jane, what's wrong?"

Reid's voice was like a lifeline. All she had to do was touch him, and she'd be all right. She reached across the console and grasped his hand. It was warm and real, just like Reid. His fingers took hers in a firm grasp that promised he'd never let her go. She clung to it and took deep breaths.

"Jane?"

His concern broke the panic, and she opened her eyes to see the lights of a town approaching. "I'm okay. Just for a minute, I couldn't breathe."

He pulled into the far shadows of a truck stop and turned off the engine, then climbed across the console and landed beside her in the wide seat.

He pulled her into his arms and stroked her hair. "I've got you. Tell me what scared you."

"She might not want me," she murmured against his chest. "What if she's there and she hates me for leaving? I don't know how I'll handle it."

"No one could hate you, least of all your mother. Let's take it one step at a time. So what if she doesn't want to see you? You still have Will, a-and you still have . . . me. It's her loss. Your life will still be great. You have a job you love, a son who adores you, and a guy who, well, let's just say I'm not going anywhere."

The words enveloped her with warmth. She should probe exactly what he meant, but it was too terrifying right now. She wasn't ready to risk her heart again. Maybe soon, but not right here and now.

She raised her head away from the steady beat of his heart under her ear to gaze up into his face. "You're right. It'll be okay no matter what happens."

His fingers cupped her chin, and his lids went to half-mast as he lowered his head. She raised her lips to meet his, and that same sense of homecoming she'd felt the first time returned in force. She wrapped her arms around his neck and didn't want the kiss to end.

Until her son coughed behind her. "Um, what are you guys doing?"

She straightened and scooted off Reid's lap. "Not a thing. You hungry?"

Reid's eyes were laughing, and he whispered, "Busted," before moving into the back.

The endless trip was finally over.

Reid yawned and rubbed scratchy, dry eyes as he navigated the last of the narrow road to the campground. At his insistence Jane had finally gone back and lay down on the sofa a couple of hours ago. He hadn't been able to resist sneaking glances at her in the rearview mirror.

He parked the RV in the lot by the office and went in to rent a space. At the desk he noticed they rented four-wheelers, too, so he paid for one. It would be perfect to take out to the compound. Five minutes later he pulled into the marked spot under massive trees and sighed. They'd made it.

His stomach rumbled again, and his mouth felt like an oil slick. He swiveled his seat and got into the back, where he found a root beer and a beignet. Not a great combination, but he didn't want to wake the rest of the group.

Jane lay curled in a ball on the sofa with one hand under her cheek. He drank in the sight of her and remembered that amazing kiss. Would she pull away again this morning?

She stirred and her eyes opened, meeting his gaze. The sunlight streamed into her face, and even with smeared mascara, she was beautiful.

"Good morning."

"Good morning." She sat up and rubbed her eyes. "Where are we?"

"At the campsite. There aren't many people here, which is good."

She stretched and yawned. "You need to sleep."

"Strangely enough, I'm not sleepy. I want to get out to that site and see what we find. It's eight so not too early to rouse people. You ready?"

Her hazel eyes flickered, but she nodded. "As ready as I'll ever be." She rose. "How far to Liberty's Children?"

"Fifteen minutes. I'm going to take a quick shower to get presentable and feel human."

"I'll do the same."

"Ladies first then."

She grabbed her clothes and toiletries and vanished into the bathroom. He listened to the backdrop of water running and her humming "This Kiss." He grinned idiotically as he made more coffee. So far she hadn't smacked him across the face either.

When she came back out, her hair was damp and her color was high. Fresh jeans hugged her curves in all the right places, and her toned arms gleamed with fresh moisturizer. She looked too good for his peace of mind.

"My turn. Coffee's almost ready." He grabbed his stuff and stepped under the hot shower. Should he sing "This Kiss" at the top of his lungs? Too much maybe? He grinned and lathered up.

It was going to be a good day. He could feel it.

The kids were awake when he exited the bathroom. Megan mumbled something and dashed past him with a bag of stuff. She probably wanted to get prettied up before Will saw her, though she could be dressed like a Goth and Will wouldn't care.

"Breakfast." Jane slid a plate of food his way. "The bacon is the precooked kind, but I warmed it up. The eggs are fresh."

"I buy precooked all the time."

He settled at the table with Will, who was wolfing down his food. Reid couldn't imagine a better life than the chance to look at Jane over the breakfast table every day. She moved in quick, economical movements as she cleaned up the kitchen and put everything away. She'd look even better in his house by the river. They'd sit out on the back deck and listen to the gators bellow. They'd fish off the dock and take sunset boat rides.

Once he got another boat. He still hadn't replaced the one that burned a few weeks ago.

"I'm going to shower," Will said. "What are we going to do today?"

"First, we'll see if we can find your mom's mother."

"My grandmother. That'll be totally lit, but do we have to come? You don't even know if she's there, right?"

"You have to come. We can't leave you alone."

Will's eyes widened. "Dad, I'm not a kid. Don't lock me up here like you did in the bunker. I want to get out and have fun."

Reid exchanged a glance with Jane. They'd talked about how unfair this all was, but he felt helpless to pull all restrictions off Will. A killer was still out there.

Had he seen anyone following them? No. Had he sensed any danger? No, again. Will was fifteen and Megan was fourteen. They were plenty old enough not to be on leashes like three-year-olds.

He started to suggest they go rafting to the falls, then stopped. "Let me talk to your mother a minute." He motioned for Jane to follow him. The scent of the water and roar of the waterfall a hundred yards away enveloped him as he stepped out of the RV.

He pulled her into the shade of a big tree. "They could go rafting or do something else fun. They might be safer here than at the Liberty's Children compound."

"I don't like it, Reid. Will could tip over and drown. Anything could happen."

He took her by the shoulders. "Jane, we can't do this. *You* can't do this. Living in perpetual fear is no life. Will's been kayaking since he was five. He's an expert. We can't give him a glimpse of blue sky, then slap him back into a box."

She chewed on her lip. "You're right—I know you're right. But it's so hard."

"He's nearly a man, honey. Three more years and he'll be off to college. We have to loosen the strings and let him soar."

"But that guy—"

"Is back in Pelican Harbor."

"You can't know that."

"It feels safe here, and no one followed us, Jane."

To his surprise she stepped forward and put her head on her chest, her arms encircling his waist. He embraced her and rested his chin on the top of her head. "Okay?"

"Okay." Her voice was muffled against his shirt.

She stepped away and he followed to tell Will the good news. What had just happened? She was thawing.

TWENTY-FOUR

He'd been snookered.

Gnats and mosquitoes buzzed his head in the early morning moisture, and he swatted at them as he went over the clues he'd seen. Jane's SUV was still parked in front of her dad's house, but he'd seen no sign of her, the boy, or Dixon since that RV left last night. Not a hint of movement other than the old man's puttering in his garden.

How did they get away without being seen? He dropped the binoculars to let them dangle from his neck, then climbed down from the tree stand and thrashed through the brush to his truck. The Boss wouldn't be happy at this news.

How did he locate them? If they were out in the open, now would be the time to act.

His truck was parked in a clearing surrounded by thick trees and brush back near the road. Hunters often used it, and his pickup sported a gun rack in the back window to further confuse anyone looking. It took a while to hike back where he could see, but his spot had been perfect.

He fired up his truck engine and drove to town, driving slowly past the school. The kids might provide some information. Even though it was early on Sunday, several kids were out shooting hoops while others smacked a tennis ball around on the court. He parked in the lot and grabbed a shirt emblazoned with a Pelican Harbor city employee logo and a small bag of chips, then put on a genial grin and walked back to the basketball court.

He sat on a park bench and opened a lunch box as if he were an employee on break. He tore open the chips and ate them slowly so the kids would get used to his presence. He recognized Tyler as one of the kids who stopped by to see Will.

A loose ball rolled his way with Tyler hot on its trail, and he grabbed it, then stood to hand it back. "I think this is yours. Tyler, isn't it? I'm a friend of Will's dad, and I've seen you around."

Tyler looped his arm around the ball and eyed him with a perplexed expression. "Sorry, I don't remember you. I-I have some memory issues with things from a few weeks ago."

"It's okay you don't remember me, son. I was trying to track Reid down, but he's not answering his phone. Any idea where he scooted off to?" Though if the kid's memory was shot, this was a lesson in futility.

Tyler wrinkled his forehead and pulled out his phone. "I've been writing stuff down." He scrolled through his phone. "Will was talking about going on a camping trip to the Cumberland Falls area. They were going to go this weekend, so I'll bet they've left."

That's why Dixon had brought the mammoth motor home last night! He'd marked down the license number to be on the safe side. Kentucky was too far to drive, but he could take his small plane up there in a few hours.

He clapped the kid on the shoulder. "Thanks, I'll just wait until he gets back then. No wonder he's not answering his phone.

Have fun." Strolling off, he kept his pace leisurely and didn't look back.

Cumberland Falls. Great, just great. But that big RV would not be hard to find. He should be there by ten or even a little before.

He considered calling the Boss before he left to tell him what had happened, but he was in no mood for a chewing out. He drove to the Jack Edwards Airport and filled out a flight plan, checked out his plane, and was in the air sooner than he'd thought.

This should be a piece of cake.

Fear was a bitter taste in her mouth.

The ride to the parcel of land owned by Liberty's Children had been glorious, but Jane was in no mood to enjoy it. The wind in her hair and the scent of wildflowers in her nose had tried to lift her spirits, but what if her mother wouldn't talk to her?

"You think Parker will be all right in the RV by himself?" Reid asked.

"He'll just sleep."

A chain-link fence lay across the narrow track, barely wide enough for a vehicle to pass through the scrubby vegetation crowding in. Jane stared at the heavy forest covering the terrain off Rock Branch Road.

"Pretty place." She sniffed the air, fragrant with pine and wildflowers. "I can hear a waterfall in the distance. This has to be it. Friendly sorts, aren't they?"

"Like always."

"How are we going to get in?"

He started forward again and drove slowly past the front of

the property. "Where there's a will, there's a way. I doubt the whole thing is fenced, and the four-wheeler can go where most cars can't."

Jane squinted in the sunshine and watched for an opening. She spotted one between two oak trees and pointed it out. "Think we can get through there?"

He jammed on the brakes and backed up. "Let's see."

The vehicle barely rolled along as he nudged it toward the opening between the trees. They passed close enough on Jane's side that she had to pull her arm tight against her to avoid having her skin scraped off by the tree bark.

Then they were on the other side, and she released her breath. "Good driving, Captain America. I think you're ready for the next Daytona race."

Reid wore a triumphant grin, and he fist-bumped her. "You still have that map loaded on your phone? I want to see where we are."

She leaned closer to peruse the map with him. Close enough to feel the heat of his body and to smell the faint tang of his aftershave. Close enough that it was hard to keep her thoughts from scattering in unwelcome directions.

She cleared her throat. "Um, I think we're here." She pointed out a spot on the west side of the property, then ran her finger toward the clearing in the middle. "We have to keep going east and north until we run into the buildings."

"Got it."

She swallowed and slid back over onto her own side. "Let's get this over with."

"You're still scared?"

"Yep. Wouldn't you be if you thought your dad might be on the end of this journey?"

"Oh yeah. He'd give me a whupping."

It didn't seem right to laugh, but one bubbled up anyway at the mental image. "You'd stomp him into the ground."

"I never did before." His voice went serious.

She glanced at him, and his eyes were downcast. "He roughed you up?"

"Beatings might be a better word." He looked up with a forced smile. "But hey, he's dead. He can't hurt either of us anymore."

But others could.

She couldn't discount the fact that she'd asked him to take them both into danger. Mount Sinai men had often kidnapped and murdered people—especially women. Liberty's Children were an offshoot from them, so chances were they were snipped from the same coil of wire. Reid knew the facts even better than she did—his mom had probably been murdered by his dad. That was a hard fact to get past.

Reid's jaw muscles flexed. "Let's go."

Moving to the north and east, they meandered through groves and thick brush, through heavy forest and across small streams until they broke through into what appeared to be a larger clearing.

Jane heard them before she saw them. Children squealing and splashing in a body of water somewhere. Hammering and banging from men building something.

She shaded her eyes with her hand and made out several cabins in the distance. There were other buildings, too, bigger and longer. Probably barns and the meetinghouse. Her pulse was erratic, and she struggled to catch her breath.

Finally, after all these years, she was here. She'd come face-to-face with her mother. What should she say? *Hey, Mom, it's Jane?*

She shook her head to clear the thousand jumbled thoughts.

Reid took her hand and squeezed it. "Courage, Jane. No matter what happens, it's going to be okay."

She clutched his hand and nodded before she released it. "I'm ready."

She kept her gaze on the buildings as he drove slowly forward. As they approached she saw naked children splashing in a small, clean pond. Women washed clothes on washboards from the same body of water, and she spotted men working on the roof of a barn. The place was cleaner and more well kept than Mount Sinai had been.

A woman washing clothes was the first to spot them. She rose and turned to yell at the men working on the barn. A burly guy swiveled at her shout, then grabbed a rifle and rushed toward them.

"He's armed." Jane's hand was resting on her pistol before she realized it.

"I see him." Reid stopped the four-wheeler and shut it off, then got off with his hands held up in a placating gesture.

Jane stayed put so she could grab her gun if necessary. She didn't recognize the man approaching, though he was clearly the leader. He appeared to be in his forties, and he was built like a tank. He was balding on top, but his curly blond hair spilled out on his collar on the sides.

Reid dropped his hands to his sides. "Gabriel. I didn't expect to see you here."

The guy's eyes stayed narrowed for a long moment. Then his mouth dropped. "Moose? It can't be."

"It's me, all right." Reid held out his hand, but when Gabriel ignored it, he dropped it back to his side.

"What do you want? You skipped out in the middle of the night like the coward you are. We wouldn't take you back if you asked." Gabriel's gaze went to Jane. "I'd take her though."

His leer stiffened Jane's spine. She tipped up her chin and glared at him. "You'd soon regret it."

Gabriel laughed, a burst of surprise and delight. "I like a spunky woman." His grin dropped. "What do you want?"

"This is Jane Hardy, Kim's daughter. I think she'll want to see her."

Gabriel stared for a long minute. "If wishes were horses, pigs would fly. Get out of here."

"We've come too far to turn back now. We're not leaving until we talk to Kim."

"You'll have to go to hell to do that." He raised his rifle. "I'm happy to send you there."

There was no mistaking the intent in the man's face, and Jane didn't want this to descend into violence. "Are you saying my mom's dead?"

Gabriel shrugged. "Smart lady. Now get out of here."

Jane fought back tears. Of all the outcomes, she hadn't expected to find out her mother had died.

Time to swat a mosquito.

To blend in with other tourists, he'd changed to shorts and a T-shirt before settling at a picnic table with a beer. He watched the RV for a few minutes. Because of its location and size, it was going to be hard to break in to without someone noticing. He'd have to wait for the vacationers to clear out to their various activities.

And he had no idea when Dixon and Jane would be back, so

he needed to get in there and scope it out before they did. He'd assumed when they bugged out like that, Dixon would have brought his laptop. This was his chance to get the video his boss wanted destroyed. He should be able to log in to any online backup sites and delete them there too.

The area began to thin out as people loaded up in vehicles and went out to experience all the outdoor fun. Just before eleven, he was the only one sitting in the shade. Now was his chance.

He rose and stretched as if he had all the time in the world, then wandered over to the RV. He pulled out his lock-picking tools and bent over the door. In seconds he had it open.

He heard a growl and lunged back as a red dog leaped for him. He jumped out of the way, and the dog landed on the grass. In an instant he was inside with the door shut to keep the dog away.

Nice digs. Luxury all the way. He wouldn't mind having an RV tricked out like this one. Starting just behind the driver's seat, he opened every cabinet searching for computers. Nothing but board games and personal belongings. Leaving the main area, he checked the bedroom. Aha, there was a laptop in a drawer beside the bed. He turned it on but found it was password protected. He could take it with him and try to figure out the password.

That wouldn't solve the dilemma though unless he could delete the files online too. His boss was getting impatient. He stuck a GPS locator on the underside of a drawer so he didn't lose them again, then tucked the computer under his arm and headed to the door. Several people were nearby. He didn't want them to be able to ID him, so he slid into the driver's seat and exited that door, away from the people.

Crouching low, he darted through the parked campers to his

rental car and tossed the computer inside, then strolled back to his shady spot at the picnic table.

He would probably still have to take them out. It wasn't something he was looking forward to, but his boss was getting antsy. They were a week out from the planned event, and it was his job to make sure nothing happened to derail it.

TWENTY-FIVE

Her mother was dead.

The wind in Jane's face dried her tears. Somehow that hadn't been one of the possible ways she'd seen this day playing out. It was silly to cry, wasn't it? She hadn't seen her mother in fifteen years, and she hadn't been important enough for her mother to try to contact her. Not a card, not a phone call. Just heavy, painful silence.

So why did this hurt so much now? She'd been carrying some kind of hopeless dream around for years. It was time it died and she buried it.

It was a while before she realized Reid had taken her hand. She glanced over at him as he turned into the entrance to the campground. She nearly lost her composure completely when she saw the sympathy in his brown eyes. She sniffled and struggled to keep it together.

She lifted her hoarse voice above the wind and the sound of the engine. "Any word from the kids?"

"I don't think so. My phone didn't vibrate. They're probably having fun. I paid for a rafting trip before we left, and they should be under the spray of Cumberland Falls about now. We should go out tonight on the ten thirty moonbow trip."

"Moonbow? What's that?"

"The spray from the waterfall creates a rainbow illuminated by the full moon. This is the only place it occurs in the Western Hemisphere."

"Wow, I'd love to see that." Her voice sounded stronger to her own ears.

"Maybe we can." He parked the four-wheeler in the row of others like it, then consulted his watch. "It's only noon. We've got the rest of the day to enjoy ourselves. Anything fun jump out at you?"

Did she want to huddle in the motor home and mourn the loss of a dream, or did she want to push it all away and deal with it another day? "What are our choices?"

She'd always been good at running. Why change now? But no, she wasn't going to run. Not this time.

"Rafting. Zip lining, geocaching, hiking, tubing. The list goes on and on. I grabbed a brochure this morning when I paid for the kids' raft trip. I'll run the keys in and meet you back at the RV. The brochure is on the table. See if anything sounds intriguing." He tossed her the RV back door keys.

She nodded and climbed out. Trekking down the road to the RV, she turned over today's news. Would Dad be surprised, or had he known all along about Mom's death and didn't tell her? It was a hard thing not to trust your father. If only he would talk to her about it, but he clammed up every time.

She unlocked the door and tried to turn the handle, but it wouldn't open. She turned the key again, and this time it easily swung open. Had it been unlocked? Surely the kids would have locked it behind them. On high alert she climbed the steps into the RV and peered inside before entering. The kids had put their things away, and the place felt empty.

She took a step inside and sniffed the air. Nothing strange stood out—no unknown cologne or anything problematic. She was being jumpy for no good reason. "Parker?"

He didn't woof, and there was no movement. Where was her dog? A quick survey of the motor home showed he wasn't inside.

Her chest compressed, and she rushed for the door and exited into the sunshine. "Parker!"

A movement from the trees caught her attention, and Parker came running to her. She knelt and threw her arms around him. "How'd you get out?" She took him back inside. Talking to Olivia might help her get past this jittery feeling, so she placed a quick call to her friend. "Hey, girl, how's your mom?"

"Doing better. Surgery is over, and the doctor thinks she'll be fine. How are the kids?"

Jane smiled at Olivia's normal voice. No slurring. "Out on a Cumberland Falls rafting trip. Um, we just got back from the compound."

"You sound funny. Did you talk to her?"

"No." Jane's throat thickened, and she cleared it with a quick cough. "The leader there said she's dead."

"Dead? Oh, Jane, I'm so sorry. I wasn't expecting that."

"I wasn't either. He didn't give me any details. There's no death certificate anywhere. I've been looking for any mention of her. Maybe they buried her and didn't report it."

She turned at a sound and Reid entered. "I'd better go. I wanted to tell you."

"I'm praying for you."

"I know you are. Thanks." She ended the call and set her phone on the table. "Olivia's mom is doing fine."

"That's good." His frown stayed in place. "I've been mulling over what Gabriel said. They believe they have the true religion, so why would he say your mom is in hell? Something doesn't jive."

Her eyes widened. "You're right. And he sounded like he hated her. What do you suppose she did to him? Could he have killed her?"

"I wondered the same thing. I wish we'd talked to one of the women who might have known her."

"You recognized him."

Reid went to the fridge and got out two root beers. He handed one to her and took a swig of his. "He was my bunkmate at Liberty's Children. He complained about Will crying all the time. I wouldn't be surprised if he was punished when I sneaked out. He didn't stop me, and he could have. He saw me go."

"He seemed to be the leader."

"His dad was the head of the sect when I was there. He'd only be in his late sixties now, but I didn't see him. Maybe he died."

"I don't know much more than I did before we came."

Reid set down his drink and wrapped his arms around her. "We knew it wasn't likely to be a good confrontation, honey. Let it go. Move on."

She nestled her head against his chest and listened to the slow, steady beat of his heart. "I'll try."

He pressed a kiss against her hair, then released her. "I forgot to get a brochure for the moonbow tour. I'm going back to the office to get it. Be back shortly."

———

He wasn't sure he'd make it much longer without sleep.

Reid walked across the lawn toward the RV. The side door stood open, and Jane passed in front of it. Had she opened it for fresh air?

Maybe it was hot inside, and he had the keyless fob to start it. He changed directions and went to the driver's door so he could kick on the air and cool off the interior.

He hit the button and the lock clicked, but it wouldn't open so he punched it again. This time it opened. It hadn't been locked when he first tried it, but that was impossible. He distinctly remembered checking all the front locks before they left. They'd told the kids to lock the one side door. This wasn't his property, and he wanted to make sure he didn't neglect security in any way.

He climbed in and started the engine, then turned the air on high. When he swiveled his chair to the back, he saw Jane closing the side door.

He frowned. "My door wasn't locked, and I know I checked the locks before I left."

"The side door was unlocked as well. I didn't see anything of mine missing. And Parker was outside somehow."

"I'd better check my stuff too."

He searched every nook and cranny before going to the bedroom. Will would have to check his things. Megan too. Reid had stashed his belongings in the side table to the right of the bed, and as soon as he slid open the second drawer, he saw his laptop was gone.

Everything was backed up, but having a thief rummaging through things torqued him off. His former videographer had stolen from him, too, and it never felt good.

He slammed the drawer and went to rejoin Jane. "Someone stole my laptop."

"Oh no! It was a nice one too. Will insurance cover it?"

"Maybe. Theft makes you feel so violated though. Someone watched until we left, then went through all of our things." He moved past her to the side door and stepped down a step to examine the lock. "There are scratches around the handle. Someone used tools to get in."

"I wonder if the place has security cameras. I'm going to go check."

"I'll come with you."

Even having her out of his sight made his chest tighten. The intruder could still be around. In fact, he probably was still around. Could it have anything to do with the threat back in Pelican Harbor? He didn't know how it could be possible, but something about this felt all wrong and entirely too coincidental.

He followed Jane into the campground office where she registered the complaint about the RV being burglarized.

Jane showed her badge. "Do you maintain security cameras around the campsite?"

"We do," the young man said.

"I'd like to see them."

He blinked and glanced around. "I'll have to ask the supervisor. No one has ever asked this before." He walked off to speak to an older man in the back before returning. "Follow me."

He led them to a cluttered back office and swept away the papers in the way of the monitor. "It happened today? What's your lot number?"

Reid told him, and he pulled up the camera facing that direction. "We were gone about two hours so start it about nine thirty."

The employee nodded and fast-forwarded to the right time. "I need to get back to work."

Reid sat at the desk with Jane leaning over his shoulder. The camera was old and the video wasn't as crisp as he would have wanted but clear enough to see a man approaching the RV a little after ten.

He paused the picture when the guy looked toward the camera as if to see if anyone was watching. "Recognize him?"

She studied the monitor. "No. How about you?"

"He sort of looks familiar. I've seen him, but I can't place him. Let me see if I can print this out." He fiddled with the machine and figured out how to print it. The printer whirred to life and spit out a grainy picture.

He started the video again, and they watched as the man managed to gain entry to the RV. He was inside ten minutes, and the camera recorded movement on the far side of the RV into the shadows.

Reid pointed at the screen. "I think that's him leaving out the driver's door."

"Check out the people standing around the motor home. He was probably afraid of being seen."

They watched a few more minutes until the man strolled around the back of the lots and settled at a picnic table under the trees. When the video ended, he was still sitting there.

Jane turned for the exit. "Come on! He might still be there."

They rushed through the store past other campers who stared at their hasty departure. Reid shoved open the door and turned toward the picnic area.

"He's still there."

Against his better judgment, he let Jane go ahead of him since she had the badge and authority to question the thief, but he wanted to grab the guy by the scruff of his neck and get his computer back. But more importantly, he wanted to know if he'd followed them from Pelican Harbor somehow.

He looked way too familiar for it to be a coincidence.

They hurried toward him, and the guy bolted to his feet and

ran the opposite way, disappearing into the trees. Reid sprinted past Jane and tried to catch him, but he reached a blue car and drove away before he could reach him. He memorized the license plate, then tapped it into his phone.

Jane caught up with him, and he showed her the number. "At least we can track him."

But a phone call later indicated he'd stolen a license plate. Reid had to remember where he'd seen the guy.

"I need to see the kids," Jane said.

"I was about to say the same thing. Their raft trip should be docking in a few minutes."

TWENTY-SIX

Jane's fingernails bit into her palms from her tight fists. She needed to see her boy.

The kids were pink from the sun and smiling from ear to ear as they got off the raft. Jane wanted to hug Will tight, but she didn't want to embarrass him. She drank in the sight of his broad shoulders, so like his father's.

Will lifted his hand when he saw them waiting. "Hey, Mom. Dad. It was a great trip. We went right under the spray of the falls. See?" He shook his wet hair all over Jane.

She laughed and gave his arm a playful punch. "Looks like you had a good time. You hungry?"

"Starving. We have any hot dogs to throw on the grill?"

"I packed some unless you ate them cold last night."

"Yuck." Megan was holding Will's hand as they moved toward the RV.

Jane followed behind them and hid a frown at the sight of their linked hands. She wasn't ready to lose Will to another woman yet. They were just finding the rhythm of their relationship. She loved Megan, but was it wrong to want to have her newfound son to herself for a while?

Reid moved close and took her hand before he leaned down to speak in her ear. "Lower the hackles, Mama. They'll be fine."

She slanted a glance up at him. "What if she hurts him?"

"What if he hurts her? It's young love. They have to find their own way."

"This parenting stuff is hard."

"I know. All we can do is guide him as best we can and let him be his own person. I grew up with an overbearing father, so I never want to be that dad."

She understood that sentiment all too well. If not for her dad, would she have ended up in law enforcement? It was hard to know since that was all she'd ever known. By the time she was ten, she could break down and reassemble a gun in minutes. She was a crack shot, too, thanks to her dad's training. While she loved to draw, that interest had never been encouraged, and she only did it for pleasure because it relaxed her.

She didn't see herself ever leaving law enforcement—it was too much a part of her now. But if she'd grown up in different circumstances, she might be a completely different person.

She didn't want that for Will—she wanted him to follow his dreams and passion, to be his own man.

Reid gestured for her to go ahead of him into the RV. The kids were already raiding the fridge, and the hot dogs were on the counter.

Reid grabbed them. "I've got grill duty."

She followed him out to the grill with her sketch pad in hand. "Any recollection of where you know that guy who broke in?"

He shook his head. "I think it's fairly recent though."

"Your computer seems to be the only thing taken. And if you recognize him from somewhere—that's troubling. What if he's the same one who shot at us?"

"I don't know if he's familiar from Pelican Harbor or from somewhere else. And my computer was worth more than anything else."

True enough, but it still didn't sit right with Jane. Her fingers moving almost on their own, she sketched Reid at the grill as she sat in the sunshine. He grinned at her and she held it in her memory long enough to capture.

He glanced at it. "You're good."

"Just a hobby. It helps me relax."

The kids exited the RV, and Will wore an eager expression as he stopped. "Dad, I looked it up, and Wabash is only about five hours away. What if we go meet my grandparents? We could leave after we eat and get there early enough to see them yet today. We could spend tomorrow morning with them, then start for home."

Jane glanced at Reid. "We wouldn't be sitting ducks here."

Will frowned. "Sitting ducks? What's going on?"

"Someone broke into the RV while we were gone this morning. Security video showed the guy breaking in, and your dad thought he looked familiar. You'd better check your things and see if anything is missing."

The kids rushed to go through their things as if they had jewels stashed somewhere. A few minutes later they returned wearing identical grins.

"My iPad's still here," Will announced.

"Mine too," Megan said. "Nothing seems missing. Was the guy someone from home, Mr. Dixon?"

"I can't place him at the moment."

"You get a printout? Maybe I know him."

"We did." Jane pulled the folded picture from her handbag. She unfolded it and passed it to Megan.

She studied it and showed it to Will. "I've seen him hanging around the school. I think he works for the town. He wears a shirt with a town employee logo on it."

Reid nodded. "That's why he looks familiar. I saw him throwing trash in the barrel by the basketball court a few days ago."

So he *was* from Pelican Harbor. That information upped the danger factor.

Jane studied the picture again and shook her head. "I've never seen him, and I know most of the locals. When did you first notice him, kids?"

"Just before you locked me up in the bunker," Will said.

Jane winced, and her gaze collided with Reid's. She supposed they had that coming. They had acted like jailers, but it was for Will's good. What were they supposed to do with a threat like that? Any parent would react the same way.

Indecision filled Reid's face. They could go back to the safety of the bunker, or they could get on the road and stay ahead of whoever had been here. She knew he wanted to connect with his family, and they were so close. Now it was Reid's turn to wonder how a meeting would turn out. He might be as jumpy as she had been about it.

At least he knew his grandparents were still alive. He wouldn't be facing the same kind of shock she was today.

"Let's do it," she said. "Who knows when you'll have the opportunity again."

His gaze cleared, and Reid dropped one arm around her in an embrace. "Have I told you lately you're pretty wonderful?"

Her face warmed but not from the sun baking down. "Are you going to call first?"

"I should, but some part of me wants to see their initial reaction. I need to sleep a couple of hours first."

All too soon this time away would come to an end, and the weight of law enforcement would be squarely on her shoulders again. She intended to enjoy this time with Reid and Will for as long as she could. Her job had been everything to her, but a family made everything different.

Her gaze lingered on Reid's broad shoulders and handsome face. What did the future hold for them? If she faced facts head-on, it might break her heart.

———

Reid's knuckles whitened with his grip on the steering wheel. Wabash stood in the distance.

The trip to Indiana had been without drama. Jane had played Yahtzee with the kids, and he'd listened to their banter with a smile most of the way.

And here they were. Listening to his phone's directions, he slowed to make the turn onto Falls Avenue at a brick church. He followed directions to Hill Street. It was a cute town with tree-lined streets, people walking dogs, and historical architecture.

In front of a Craftsman home with a big front porch, he heard, "You have reached your destination."

He jammed on the brakes. The home resembled something out of a fifties TV show with its hanging flower baskets on the porch and the neat rows of posies along the sidewalk. Parking this behemoth might be a problem. He let the RV roll forward until the front tire bumped the curb, then shut off the engine.

It had grown quiet in the back, and he swiveled his chair to face Jane and the kids. "This is it." His voice quavered, and he cleared his throat. "Maybe you all better stay here and let me scope it out."

"I want to go too," Will said.

"We don't want you to do this alone." Jane stood.

Megan nodded. "Let's do this together."

He couldn't speak past the lump in his throat, so he just nodded and got out. Sunset hadn't come yet, but the shadows had lengthened. A mower cut off somewhere, and he caught the aroma of freshly mown grass and flowers. Through the screen door, he heard a woman's voice singing along with the radio. His grandmother? He was too rattled to identify the song but recognized a few strains as a familiar hymn.

He raised his hand to knock on the screen door frame, then dropped it back to his side. "What do I say?" he whispered to Jane, who pressed close to his left side. She kept her hand on Parker's head to keep him quiet.

"Just say hi and tell her who you are. Smile. She'll love you."

He felt flushed. Awkward. Raising his hand, he looked through the screen door into a living room with traditional Craftsman built-ins and wide oak trim. Pretty and so homey. He let his hand fall on the door, then knocked again for good measure.

The kids were to his back, so at least he felt he could protect them a bit if his grandmother hurled obscenities at him. The solidarity from the three of them stiffened his spine and lifted his chin.

A woman in her seventies with a salt-and-pepper bob smiled as she saw him in front of the screen door. She wore khaki slacks and a black T-shirt with New Life Baptist Church printed on the front in white.

"Can I help you?" Her gaze swept over Jane and the kids, and her smile broadened. "Well, hello. I'm a sucker for supporting the schools. What are you selling?"

"Um, you're Gretchen Parks?"

She tilted her head to the side, a slight wrinkle on her brow. "I am. And you are?"

"I'm Reid. Reid Dixon."

Her eyes didn't change for a long moment, then her mouth dropped and she cracked open the screen door. "Reid? My grandson, Reid?"

"I-I think so, ma'am."

Tears gathered in her blue eyes, and she rushed out the door to take him by the shoulders. "Let me look at you."

Her gaze drank him in with a thirst that made moisture flood his eyes.

"I haven't seen you since you were four years old. You have your mother's nose and mouth. You probably thought you resembled your dad, but let me show you some pictures and you'll change your mind."

She released him and wiped her wet eyes, then stared at Jane and the kids standing behind him. "This is your family?"

"The boy is mine. His name is Will. This is his mother, Jane, and Megan is a friend."

She stepped back and held open the door. "I don't know what's the matter with me. Come in. I didn't mean for the whole neighborhood to witness our reunion."

He stepped inside and smelled something with cinnamon and apple, probably the candle flickering on the mantel. Comfortable tweed furniture sat atop an area rug over oak floors, and the family pictures adorned soft gray-green walls. He felt at home instantly.

Jane and the kids crowded in behind him. His grandmother beckoned them forward, and they trailed her through the dining room to the kitchen, where a whole chicken waited on a tray to be carved. Beaters rested in a bowl of potatoes to be mashed, and steam curled from green beans with bacon in a saucepan on the stove.

"I was just finishing dinner, and there's plenty to share. Your grandpa is out back waiting for me. Let's introduce you." Her voice clogged with emotion.

She took his hand and led him out the back door to a large deck that held patio furniture. A white-haired man sat in a rocker with a fat French bulldog at his feet. Parker's tail began to wag, but Jane kept a hand on his collar.

"Philip," his grandmother said.

The man's gaze traveled from Reid to the rest of the group, then back to him. "We've got company."

"Philip. It's Reid, Denise's boy. He's come back to us. And his son, Will."

The man stood and grabbed a cane to limp toward them. He opened his mouth, then closed it again before choking out the words, "I never thought I'd see the day you walked through these doors, son."

He opened his arms, and Reid stepped into them. He inhaled the somehow familiar scent of his grandfather's cologne and knew he'd come home.

TWENTY-SEVEN

The remains of a delicious dinner lay on the outside table where they'd stuffed themselves in the shade of a pergola. Sunset limned the trees surrounding the backyard with red and gold, and Reid couldn't remember when he'd been more content. Traces of his mother were recognizable in his grandmother: the lilt of her voice, her expressions, and especially her blue eyes. It was almost like being with Mom again.

Will was eating up the attention. His great-grandmother plied him with more and more food until he cried uncle and pushed his plate away.

Reid took a sip of his iced tea, unsweetened since he was this far north, and regarded the lush backyard. "Did Mom live here too?"

"She did. I'll show you her room later," his grandmother said. "We bought this place right after we got married. You haven't said anything about your mom. When did you see her last, and when did you leave the cult?"

A rock formed in his belly. This was a topic he'd dreaded. "I think she's dead, Grandma. She was furious when my dad took another woman into the house, and they had a huge fight. She threw things and he hit her. She left and slammed the door. He followed her outside, and there was more yelling. I saw him drag her toward the woods, and I never saw her again. When I asked about her, he told me she'd left us. I don't believe she would have left me there. And I-I found a shovel the next day with blood on it."

The words rushed out, details he hadn't realized he remembered. The terror rose in a tide as visions of that awful night came back.

Tears pooled in his grandmother's eyes, and his grandfather's head dropped forward. Reid wished he could take back the words, make them less harsh and kinder somehow. But truth was truth. His mom had died up in the Michigan woods, and his dad had buried her there.

Jane reached over and took his hand, and he wrapped his fingers around hers. He'd been the one to offer comfort earlier in the day, and her gesture touched him. When she pulled her hand away and reached for her sketch pad, he wanted to protest, but her portraits were always wonderful, and he couldn't wait to see the results. He'd always have a memory of this special day.

"Did you hear about the raid that destroyed Mount Sinai?" he asked.

They both shook their heads. "It's gone?"

"About fifteen years ago. Federal agents and state police swarmed the place to rescue a woman Dad had kidnapped. The place burned to the ground. Dad and many others died that night. Those of us who were left joined up with a sister group, Liberty's Children. I only stayed about a year before sneaking off. I've been on my own ever since."

"With me," Will said.

He'd hoped to avoid talking about Jane's involvement in that night, but his boy wanted them to know they'd been together all that time. "Will and me. We got out, and I got a job."

His grandfather reached down and petted his Frenchie, Wally. "I wish you'd come to us. We would have helped you."

Reid rushed to answer before he asked about Will's remark. "My dad always said my grandparents were dead. It took years for me to question what I'd been told. I just found out your whereabouts a few days ago."

His grandmother reached over and touched his free hand. "I'm glad you came straight to us. We don't want to presume, but we have three spare rooms if you want to spend the night."

"We came in a motor home, so lodging is no problem. We thought we'd spend tomorrow morning with you before starting back to Pelican Harbor."

"I could feed you one more time. Your uncle Randy and his family live here, too, and they're due back from a trip tonight. You'd get to meet his wife and two daughters. Your uncle Rick lives in Arizona, and he has two boys about Will's age. They're twins."

While they could stay in the RV, they might be safer in a house if that guy had followed them. He had no way of knowing if that guy was back there with all the traffic running up I-65.

Jane squeezed his hand and smiled at his grandmother. "We'd be honored to stay with you. Thank you for having us."

There were three bedrooms and four of them. "Will and I can share a room, and the girls can each take one."

"Wonderful," Gretchen said.

"Um, I wonder if you'd mind telling me about how my parents met and why they went off to join a cult like Mount Sinai."

Gretchen stilled. "It's not a pretty story, Reid, and we're not blameless in it."

"That's okay. I'd just like to understand."

She sighed. "Moses came to town her senior year of high school.

He saw Denise at Kroger one day and followed her to the car to talk to her. He was five years older and already had a good job at Ford Meter Box in the sales department. Dark, handsome, and arrogant. I didn't much like him from the minute she brought him home. I told her he was too old for her and tried to slow things down, but she'd sneak out to see him.

"She got pregnant. I think he wanted her pregnant because he knew we'd drop our objections. And it seemed we had no choice. They got married, and you were born. When you were six months old, they went on a camping trip to Michigan. They came back—different. We later found out they'd met some people from Mount Sinai on that trip. They started to go back to Michigan about once a month. Moses started spouting crazy stuff about doomsday coming and religious babble that made no sense. We're Christians, and we know truth when we hear it—his ravings didn't have anything to do with the Bible. I couldn't see how Denise would swallow all that. She was taught better."

"But love can change things," Reid said.

Gretchen nodded. "You were five years old when they packed up and moved away. Denise promised to stay in touch, but we never saw her or you again. We went up to the compound several times, but we weren't allowed to go farther than the gate, and she never came out to talk to us. The last time we went there, no one was at the compound, and we didn't know where they'd gone."

Reid touched her hand. "You didn't know about the fire and deaths."

She shook her head. "We have wondered all these years." She wiped a tear from her cheek. "We prayed every day that we'd see you and your mother again. They had no other children?"

"No."

"That's good." Gretchen looked at her husband. "You should probably call Randy and tell him."

Jane rose and began to clear the dishes. "Let Megan and me help you clean up. Philip, maybe you could show Reid and Will where to stash our things. I'm sure you'll be interested in seeing the motor home we came in. It's spectacular."

Seeing the curiosity on his grandmother's face, Reid was sure she'd pump Jane for information through the washing up. Jane could handle it though. He motioned for Will to join him, and the three of them went outside where the stars were beginning to twinkle in the velvet sky. The air smelled fresh and clean.

His grandfather whistled at the RV. "Wow, I never saw one like this. Looks like a tank."

Reid barely heard him as he stared down the street to a car parked in the shadows. Had that guy followed them here? His heart pounded and he walked that direction. He was still two houses away when the vehicle's engine roared to life, and the car raced away.

It was too dark to make out the license plate, and he wanted to believe he was wrong. It would bring some peace of mind to be in a house tonight, though he would need to tell Jane they had to take turns standing watch.

This was the home life she'd been missing.

Jane dried the last dish and put it in the cupboard. Being with Reid's grandmother was everything Jane had craved all her life. The older woman mothered her in ways she'd never experienced. Lots of pats, a hug here and there, approval shining from her blue eyes at every moment. Jane felt like she'd stepped through a time warp.

This was what she and Reid had both missed. She didn't want to leave, and she knew it would be hard on Reid and Will.

"I'm going to go see what Will's doing." Megan took Parker with her and stepped out onto the back patio where the guys sat laughing and talking.

"Good. It's just the two of us," Gretchen said. "I'm dying to know what happened between you. It's clear you're crazy about each other."

Jane's face went hot. "We're just friends now. The past is . . . complicated."

"I've got time to listen." Gretchen gestured to the small table for two in the corner of the cozy kitchen.

Would Gretchen hate her when she learned she'd deserted Will and Reid? Jane pulled out a chair and considered how to tell the story. There was no way to spill the truth without appearing like a terrible person.

"It's not a pretty story."

Gretchen settled in the other chair. "The one I had to tell Reid wasn't either."

Jane clasped her hands together and told Gretchen of her great-grandson's birth and the fire. Of running for her life and always feeling lost without her child. Of finding him again and learning the truth. By the time she finished, they were both crying.

Gretchen reached across the table and took her hand. "Thank you for your honesty. You're a good person, Jane Hardy. You and Reid belong together."

Jane gave a watery smile. "That's to be determined yet. He didn't tell me the truth when he got to town, and I'm having trouble getting past the lies."

Gretchen kept hold of her hand. "Have you never done the same,

Jane? Withheld information until you could trust a person? Never given the benefit of the doubt and then found out later you should have? Mistakes are human. And Reid has stuck around to try to make it up to you. I've seen the way he looks at you—like a starving man staring at a filet mignon."

Jane wanted to laugh, but she'd seen that look on Reid's face too. What would it be like to be a real family? To have vacations like this together where she had a life outside her job? There was an uncle as well as a nephew and niece to meet.

"You're going to try, aren't you?" Gretchen sounded worried.

"I'll try. It might take some time though."

"I suspect he'll wait." Gretchen released her and stood. "Let's see what our men are up to."

Our men. What a homey, wonderful term. She already loved Reid's grandparents and longed to be part of an extended family like this. Her isolation for so many years seemed to be fading like the last bit of the night.

She stepped out under strands of twinkling lights hanging from the pergola and stopped beside Reid where he stood talking to Will and his grandfather. She slipped her hand into his, and he turned with surprise in his eyes.

He smiled. "You seem tired. It's been a long day."

"I think I'll turn in if you want to show me which room."

"Sure thing, but I think I'll stay up and talk awhile. The kids probably will too. Let me show you where I put your stuff." He led her through the house to the living room and up the open stairway to the first room off the hall. "I could have told you where to go, but I want to show you something. Don't turn on the light."

The warmth in her chest dissipated at his serious tone. "Trouble?"

"Maybe."

He led her to the window facing the street. "There was a car out there when I went to get our things. I think the guy from Pelican Harbor followed us here."

She put her hand to her throat. "Oh no. Are you sure?"

"Not positive, but it looked like him. I told Grandpa about it, and he and I are going to take turns watching the house. He's got a rifle and is a crack shot." He sounded proud.

"I'll take a turn too. You guys will be up awhile. Wake me when you go to bed." She bit her lip and glanced out on the street again. "I hate to tear you away from such a happy homecoming, but maybe we should head home. Get Will back to safety."

Reid's smile vanished. "Put him under lock and key again." He sighed. "He's having such a great time. What are we going to do about the danger he's in? We can't keep him locked up forever."

"Maybe another week will give us more answers."

"And maybe it won't. Then what?"

Good question, and she had no answers. "We'll figure it out as we go along." She touched his arm. "Your family is great, Reid. I'm glad you found them. You're already calling them Grandma and Grandpa. You stepped into a ready-made family that already loves you." She winced at the way her voice wobbled. She didn't want him to think she begrudged him the happy ending she hadn't gotten. "I'm really happy for you and Will."

His arms circled her and drew her into an embrace. "I know we didn't find your mom, but you are part of all of this. I can tell they like you already."

While it was all true, she still mourned the loss of the dream, that happy ending where her mother told her she thought about her every day. That had been a mirage though. If it were true, her mother would have come with them. Or she would have found them later.

It was time to grow up.

She pulled away and pushed him toward the door. "Go talk to your grandparents. Don't forget to wake me."

Closing the door felt wrong, but she knew it was the right thing to do. This wasn't going to change overnight.

TWENTY-EIGHT

The GPS tracker worked like it was supposed to. He'd been able to drive at an undetectable distance and follow the blip on his phone. They ended up in this quaint Indiana town he'd never heard of. Once he'd driven past the parked RV, he cruised through town and ended up eating a leisurely dinner at a Mexican restaurant called Mi Pueblo.

People said hello and smiled, and he spoke back as if he belonged here.

As it got dark he made a swath through the downtown and exited south to evaluate how he might get out of town if he was able to execute his plan. Around nine, he made his way back to Hill Street and parked half a block away from the well-maintained Craftsman house until Reid saw him. He'd driven off before he could be identified and had hung out in the city park down the street for a while, where he'd browsed the internet on his phone.

Patrons of a kids' softball game left the diamond, and he watched the stars come out above the oak trees. When he phone rang, he grimaced. "Yo, Boss."

"Where are you and what is the status?"

"I'm in Indiana." He told the man about escaping from the bunker and finding his quarry. "I got the laptop and nearly came on

211

back, but I couldn't crack the iCloud password to destroy backups of the files. I decided to hang here and see what they are up to."

"Have you destroyed all the physical copies on the computers?"

"The only guy who might have copies on a hard drive is his videographer. I didn't think he'd do anything with them if he had them since Dixon is the one making the documentary."

"There's no guarantee of that. Would he know the Cloud password?"

"I don't know. He might have his files backed up elsewhere."

A long silence followed. "Right now, the safest thing to do would be to eliminate Dixon. It's ideal that he's away from town. It might muddy the investigation. With him dead, the files will likely go unused. To be on the safe side, eliminate the videographer as well. With them both out of the way, no one should be able to access any online backups."

The man winced. "I'd hoped to avoid murder."

"Your bank account will thank you."

And accolades from his friends if he shut down the oil platform. "All right."

"Check in when it's over."

"Will do." He ended the call and ran his seat back to stretch out his legs.

A burglary gone wrong might work. Especially so far from Pelican Harbor. He could make sure to take items of value so the small-town police here would assume it was theft related. It would have to do.

At midnight, he yawned and started the car to return to Hill Street. He parked down the other direction and peered back at the house. The streetlights shone down more than he'd like. One in front of the porch lit up the front yard way too much. He got out and walked down the side street where he could see into the backyard. Nope, wouldn't work. The security light left few shadows and there was practically a spotlight at the back door. An awake neighbor would spot him in a heartbeat and call the cops.

He returned to the car and checked his supplies. Kerosene and a lighter should be enough. Two sides of the house caught too much light from the streetlamps, and though he had a suppressor on his Glock, someone might hear the exploding glass. Too risky. He'd have to set the fires as best he could and hope they all got caught in the inferno.

He slung his pack over one shoulder and got out to make a cautious approach.

Showtime.

———

Something felt off.

With Grandpa keeping watch, Reid had prowled the house though he should have gone to sleep for a while. He paused to examine every family photo, every obvious hand-me-down like knick-knacks and lace doilies. His grandmother had put him and Will in the room where his mom had grown up, and the three of them had pored over her high school yearbooks, old pictures, and the articles of clothing his grandparents still had in the closet before his grandmother and Will had finally gone to bed.

The time here had brought the dim memories of his mother surging back again, and the pain of her loss had sharpened as well. She'd been such an easy pawn for Moses. Gentle, loving, easily controlled.

He hated his father.

He sent his grandfather on to bed, then took up his post in

the darkened living room. Sneaking in through the back wouldn't be hard, so he occasionally padded to the kitchen and looked out. He didn't think the man would sneak in that way with the bright halo of the security light turning night into day, but he couldn't ignore the possibility.

Were there any other points of entry? The east and west sides didn't have doors, only windows. He would likely hear breaking glass if an intruder tried to get in that way.

Maybe he was jumpy for no good reason. He still wasn't sure that car was the same one they'd seen in Kentucky.

He yawned, but he wasn't sleepy.

He heard a noise and turned to see Jane coming down the stairs. She wore dark-blue cotton pajamas, and her feet were bare.

"I thought you were sleeping," he said.

"I tried. You should have gone to bed first. You've had two hours of sleep. Anything going on?"

"Nothing. I haven't seen the car come back."

When she reached him, he looped his arm around her and drew her into his side. She didn't pull away but slipped her arm around his waist.

"Anything from your detectives back home? They making headway?"

"I had an update from Augusta, but there's nothing new. She's asking questions and poking around, but we've hit a wall. No match on the fingerprints found on Keith's laptop. They also haven't been able to track the person he was emailing. Some kind of sophisticated cloaking was used. No telling what Homeland Security is finding. They don't keep me in the loop."

She tensed and her arm dropped away. He let her go with a sense of regret. "Something wrong?"

"What if I found my grandparents?"

"Your dad says they're all dead, right?"

"That's what he says, but he's not exactly the paragon of truth."

"You haven't looked before?"

"I was focused on finding my mom. But grandparents would be great if they are anything like yours."

"I'll help you."

"Thanks, I thought you might say th—" She stopped and tipped her head. "Did you hear that?" Her voice was a whisper.

"What? I didn't hear anything."

She didn't answer but moved toward the west side of the house toward the dining room. He pulled out his gun and followed her. She held out her hand so he passed it over. She must have left hers in the bedroom upstairs. Barely breathing, they stood in the hallway between the living room and dining room.

He strained to listen, and there was a soft tinkle of noise. Glass maybe? Or maybe his grandmother had a wind chime. The hair stood taut on the back of his neck, and he felt a whisper of air as if a window was open.

Someone was inside the house.

He reached for anything heavy. He found a table lamp by the armchair against the wall a few feet away and unplugged it. Hefting it by its neck, he went back to stand with Jane.

She was rigid as she stared at a corner just past the table and chairs. A sideboard was there, but Reid didn't see anyone in the dark. He didn't dare ask her either, since he was sure a presence was in the house they hadn't felt before.

He strained to listen, to see where the danger lay. She had the gun up and ready, and the danger was palpable.

A soft, sliding movement sounded to their left, nearer than

the corner with the sideboard. He swung that way with the lamp aloft.

Jane pivoted too. "Show yourself!"

A bullet plowed into the woodwork by Reid's head, and he flinched. Fire spat from the end of the gun in Jane's hand, then a dark shadow rushed past them toward the kitchen. Reid sprang after the figure and managed to snag the arm of his jacket. The guy left it behind as he exited the back door.

Jane rushed after him and the guy disappeared into the shadows of the neighbor's backyard.

"I smell smoke!" Reid ran for the back door and spotted the flames licking up the back wall in the kitchen.

Under the stench of smoke, he caught a whiff of kerosene. He flung open the door and ran for the sink, where he'd spotted a fire extinguisher attached to the side of the cabinet.

Jane rushed past him. "I'll get everyone out!"

White foam spat from the wand and began to smother the fire. Once it was out, he went in search of any more spots and found one at the side wall to the dining room. It was smaller and didn't take long to put out.

He went through the dining room, and Jane had assembled the rest of the family. His grandmother's hair was askew, and she trembled when he put his arm around her. "It's okay," he soothed. "I don't think there's much damage. It's all in the kitchen."

"I want to see." The older man marched past into the kitchen.

Reid led his grandmother after him and blinked in the bright overhead light. The flames had licked up the back wall directly under the bedroom where his son had been. Left unchecked, the fire would have destroyed the upstairs.

His grandmother hugged him. "It's a good thing you found the fire."

"It wasn't an accident, Grandma. A man was in here setting it."

Her eyes went huge, and she put her hand to her mouth. "Mercy sakes. Who would be so evil?"

"We're going to find out."

Jane's voice was grim. "We need to get back to Pelican Harbor and solve this case. I'm going to nail him. He could have killed your grandparents or one of the kids."

Reid couldn't argue with her. "I never saw him behind us."

"He might have put a GPS tracker on the RV. I'll check it out now while you pack up the kids. We're leaving as soon as possible."

While he hated to leave without meeting his uncle, they could come back when this was over.

TWENTY-NINE

The man was back in Foley by 2:00 a.m. on Monday, and the RV wouldn't be back for hours. He put his plane in the hangar and got into his truck in the parking lot.

The heat and humidity nearly suffocated him, and he tossed his cigarette out the window before he started the engine. He turned on the air-conditioning, then called his boss to report in.

"I was unable to eliminate the threat in Indiana last night, sir."

"What? Tell me what happened."

The man went over the details. "They are crafty and were keeping watch. I barely got out without being shot."

"Where are you now?"

"About to head to Hastings's place. I'll take care of that first."

"I want this all done by nightfall. Too much is at stake. Understood?"

"Yes, sir." He hung up and sighed.

He'd gotten little sleep for the past few days, and he'd hoped to catch a few z's. He drove to Hastings's place, which luckily had no near neighbors. The videographer's car was in the drive next to the pier where the houseboat bobbed in its dock. He'd hoped to prowl the house undetected to plan his next move first. On the off chance the guy would leave, he drove to the marina and parked, then got out to feed the seagulls with a stale loaf of bread he had in the backseat. He settled on a bench and stared out over the water as he threw crumbs to the gulls.

He was beginning to regret he'd gotten involved in this. He'd done it for all the right reasons in his mind, but his boss's fixation on revenge might see it all blow up in their faces.

He bought a lobster roll from a street vendor and ate it, relishing the sweet meat on his tongue, while he killed time. He tossed the last of it to the gulls and leaned back on the bench. The gentle sound of the waves and the distant creaking of boats bobbing in the water lulled him, and his eyes grew heavy. Maybe he'd close them for a few minutes.

He awoke with a start and glanced at his watch. Nearly an hour had passed since he'd driven by Hastings's house, so he went back to his truck and retraced his route. This time there was no vehicle in the drive. He drove on past and parked in a copse of trees where his vehicle was partially hidden, then strode back to the houseboat. He picked the lock and was inside in moments. From a former reconnaissance with binoculars, he knew one of the bedrooms was where most of the equipment was kept, but he made a quick scan of the living room.

No laptop. He went down the hall and smiled as he scooped up the laptop. For good measure, he grabbed the desktop computer and carried both to his truck before loading up every piece of equipment he could find, just to be sure he could destroy every byte of the footage.

He turned toward the door and came face-to-face with Hastings, who stood wide-eyed in the doorway.

Hastings lunged back the way he'd come, and the man dropped

the equipment to spring after him. Great timing. He'd be done here once the videographer was dead.

Hastings darted into his bedroom and slammed the door. A lock clicked into place, and the man cursed. He tried to shoulder open the door, but it held. In a fury he kicked it and nearly toppled to the floor when his foot stuck in the splintered wood.

He regained his balance and shoved his aching shoulder into the door again. His previous blows had weakened the wood, and it splintered open this time. He rushed into the room and snatched up a heavy lamp.

Hastings had a gun in his hand, but he was trembling so badly he'd never be able to hit anything. He clicked off the safety. "Stand back!"

Almost casually, the man threw the lamp in his hand, and it walloped the videographer in the head. He went down without a sound and struck the other side of his head on the corner of the bedside table. Blood began to pool under his head.

Should he finish him off? The man reached for the lamp again, but he jumped and stepped back when the phone on the table rang. Maybe he should get out of here. No way Hastings would survive the blood loss. He'd get rid of the file, collect his money, and forget about this job.

He found a cloth in the bathroom and wiped down the lamp and everything else he'd touched as the pool of blood grew around Hastings's head. When the man was done, he gathered up the equipment he'd dropped, then exited the back door and circled back to his truck. When he returned to his hotel, he'd make sure everything was in order.

He would be glad to see the back of this job. It had strung along longer than he'd expected, and he was starting to hate this place. And the nagging of his boss.

Had anyone followed them?

Jane rubbed scratchy eyes as they drove through Pelican Harbor before pulling into her dad's lane just after four that afternoon. "I don't know how you managed to drive straight back without sleep. You barely slept the last two nights."

She'd found a GPS tracker in the RV's bedroom and left it with Reid's grandparents, who promised to overnight it to the police station. She wanted to check it for clues, but she didn't want their attacker to be able to use it on the way home. It had been a tense thirteen-hour drive back with Jane and the kids checking for pursuit from their tormenter. There had been no further sighting of the guy's car.

"You didn't sleep either." Reid yawned. "I won't say no to some eye drops and a nap." He punched the door opener and pulled the RV into the barn, then closed the door behind them before he unlocked the doors. "Go through the tunnel straight to the bunker, Will."

Will rolled his eyes. "This is getting old, you guys."

"It can't be helped. Your mom will do what she can to figure this out, but we want to keep you safe."

"I'd be better off dead than penned up," Will muttered as he exited with his duffel bag on one shoulder and stomped toward the tunnel.

Megan followed without looking at either of them. Even Parker's look back seemed reproachful as he followed Will out of the barn. The kids didn't understand, but Jane didn't know what else to do.

She shoved open her door and got out. "You go on inside, and I'll bring in our stuff."

"I'll grab the two bags if you want to bring in what's left of the food."

She nodded and pulled the plastic sacks of leftover food out of the fridge. The two of them walked toward the passageway to the bunker, then made their way toward the light at the end where Will had left the door standing open.

"You going to tell your dad about your mom's death right away?"

"Yes. Maybe the shock will shake loose some truth about her."

But she wasn't holding her breath. She stopped him before they entered the bunker. "I have something for you." She pulled out the sketch she'd done of him with his grandparents.

His gaze lingered on the drawing. "This is special. I can keep it?"

"If you want."

"Thank you, Jane. I love it." He seemed like he wanted to say more, but her father approached them.

He pulled the door shut behind them and put the bar across it, then carried the bags away toward the bedrooms. She didn't know how to tell her dad what she'd found out.

He took the bag of food. "Well? How'd it go?"

Was that trepidation in his voice? Charles Hardy was the type of man who never seemed surprised by any events, but today, his eyes held uncertainty. Maybe he didn't know she was dead. He'd loved her once. Would the news wreck him like it had destroyed Jane?

She held his gaze. "The leader of Liberty's Children told me she was dead, Dad. And he seemed to hate her. He said she was in hell. Why would he harbor such anger?"

His gaze dropped, and he showed no emotion before he turned to go to the kitchen. She followed him and waited for him to respond. Pushing him would make him clam up even more.

He put away the chips and canned goods before turning to look her in the face. "Your mom was always a strong soul. Maybe they clashed."

She studied his face. "You know more than you're saying. Did you know the leader of Liberty's Children? Reid called him Gabriel."

Her dad shrugged. "Sure. Gabriel's dad and Moses had so many clashes that he finally moved off with his cohorts. Your mom didn't like Gabriel's dad, so I'm not surprised they didn't get along once she joined up with him. Did Gabriel tell you anything else?"

"Like what?"

He shrugged again. "Anything. Like when or how she died."

"No details. He threw us off the property, and he had the right because the group owns it. We ran into more trouble."

She told him about the shooter who followed them to Kentucky and Indiana. She detected a hint of relief in his eyes that they'd left the subject of her mother behind. Why was he so reluctant to talk about the past? It was killing her.

When he went to welcome Will home, she started for her bedroom, but when she passed his office, it stood open a crack. It was always locked. Their return must have surprised him.

He told Will he was going outside to finish planting his garden. He'd be gone awhile, probably at least an hour. Parker must have exited the attic floor with her dad because he came down the hall toward her. Good. She could use the comfort of his presence. Once the creak of the front door opening and closing came, she slipped inside the office door with Parker and locked it behind her.

Her heart jackhammered in her chest as she approached his desk. Privacy and respect for property had been pounded into her all her life, but she had to find out if he knew more than he was saying. Any information was unlikely to be on his computer. He didn't trust them much, and anything of importance was always printed out. Besides, her mother's death was likely to have been years ago, before he did much of anything on a computer.

The desk drawers weren't locked. She went through everything and found nothing of interest. The closet held only guns and ammunition. She started to shut the doors until she spied a cardboard file on the shelf. It was the kind with multiple dividers with a rubber band wound around it. She pulled it down and opened it.

In the first compartment she pulled out a sheaf of papers. She turned over the first page, and the face of her mother leaped out at her. She stared into her mother's eyes. She was older, weary. The next page was a report from a private detective. Her legs shook as she carried it back to the desk chair and sat before she fell down.

The report was dated 2010, and the PI had found her living in Maine. She was married.

Her mother was alive! Gabriel had lied. But why? The paper shook in her hand as the backside of the news hit her.

The paper fell from her hands, and she buried her face in her hands. Just as she thought, her dad had known all along where Mom was. And had chosen to keep that information from her.

Another lie from her father—as big as the first.

THIRTY

The pain would wreck her.

Jane sat on a bench in the sunshine with her arms around Parker and closed her eyes, willing the pain to ebb, but it only intensified. She'd come out here to try to wrap her head around what she'd discovered, but the shock and disbelief had come with her. The facade of a capable, in-control chief of police had crumbled at her feet, and she didn't want Will or Megan to see this poor farce.

Gradually, she became aware she'd brought the file with her. Dad would know she'd discovered the truth. Not that she planned to hide it from him.

"Jane?"

She opened her eyes when Reid called her name and rose to rush for the protection of the trees before he could see her. Too late. His footsteps pounded after her, and her short stride was no match for his long legs.

He caught her arm. "Jane, what's happened?"

Parker whined, and she put her free hand on his head. "I need to be alone, Reid." Her voice sounded high and strangled to her ears.

He didn't let her go but turned her to face him. "Tell me what's wrong. Did your dad say something?"

She made a derisive growl but couldn't meet his gaze. "Talking has never been his problem. He won't talk—that's the issue. Instead I have to find out everything important to me either from someone else or accidentally."

"He knew your mom was dead?"

She lifted her gaze to lock with his. "She's not dead, Reid. She left the compound in 2010 and married. Not only did she not care if I went off with my dad, she was perfectly happy to create a new life and leave me out of it."

"No. Not even your dad would keep that from you."

"Oh, he did all right. I found this in his office." She thrust the file into his hand. "He hired a private investigator to find her."

She stared at the leaves blowing in the wind while he studied the evidence. What made her think she was any kind of a cop? She'd missed the most important evidence all her life, and it had been right under her nose.

She sank to her knees and embraced Parker again. You knew where you stood with a dog. You didn't have to guess because a dog didn't know subterfuge or deception. Had her father ever really loved her? How could he when he'd lied to her all these years? And not little lies—but huge, life-changing ones.

Everything in her wanted to get in her SUV and drive away from here until she reached some place far away where she could forget how gullible she'd been. Some place where she didn't have to wonder who was lying to her.

Reid settled beside her and tried to pull her into his embrace, but she shook him off. His lie had been just as bad as her father's. Until today, she'd thought they might have a future. She'd begun to get past the way he'd kept Will's identity from her, but her father's second betrayal reminded her that trust was dangerous. That one moment in time could rip away everything she thought she knew.

"Honey, look at me."

She raised her gaze, letting her anger show through her eyes and not caring if he flinched from it. "I'm not your *honey*."

"You're mad at me again. I swear I didn't know about this."

"No, but you're part and parcel of the web of lies I've been trapped in for my entire life. Every time I think I can break free, the sticky strands wrap me tight again." Her voice trembled.

He didn't make another attempt to embrace her. "Did you talk to your dad?"

"Not yet. I need to get my feet under me again."

"Where does she live now? I just skimmed the documents."

"Maine, of all places. I don't know if she's still there. At the time of the report she lived up in Sunset Cove."

"You thinking of going to see her? I'd go with you."

Right now going off with him sounded like the worst thing possible to her. Who did she trust in the world right now? Olivia and Will were about the only ones. Finding out she was wrong about people had undercut her confidence. Her father's constant lies left her with no foundation for recognizing truth.

Love wasn't safe. For a little while she'd allowed herself to dream that maybe real love existed. That maybe Reid was the true love of her life. That maybe they could find their way past all the deceit to create a family that wouldn't be splintered apart.

She'd been wrong.

She rose with her fingers curling around Parker's collar. "I'd better talk to my dad. I don't know if I'll ever speak to him after today. It will be all I can do to look in his face and listen to his excuses."

"I'm sorry, Jane. Please, let me be your backup."

"The only thing I need from you is to keep the kids occupied so I can talk to him in private."

"He'd been in the garden, but I saw him heading into the munitions room a few minutes ago."

She nodded and left him in the shady grove.

His hurt was palpable, but she wasn't even sure it was real. People feigned emotion all the time. The past few weeks had proven that. Her former deputy Brian's simmering hatred had been completely hidden from her for years. She would have staked her life on his authenticity and commitment to her, but she'd been wrong once again.

It would take a lot for her to believe anyone again.

———

It was all his fault.

Reid tried to put himself in Jane's place to understand what she was feeling, but his own hurt kept swamping him with guilt. If he'd handled things differently right from the start, they wouldn't be here. She would have known she could trust him. Instead, he was tarred with the same brush as her dad.

He forced himself to rise from the grass and head for the bunker, the incriminating papers still in his hand. Her only request was to occupy the kids, and he could do that much for her.

Will held up a package of pepperoni when Reid entered the bunker's kitchen. "Hey, Dad, we're making pizza. Megan got a text from her mom, and she's going to pick her up on the way back from the hospital in a couple of hours."

"Need some help?"

"Nah, we've got it." Will shot a besotted glance at Megan.

Translation: He wanted to be alone with Megan. Reid nodded. "I'm going to get a movie ready to watch over dinner."

Unwanted wherever he turned. He could stand guard at least and make sure the kids didn't go into the munitions room to disturb Jane during the confrontation. This kind of discussion wasn't anything Will and Megan needed to hear. The boy loved both his grandfather and his mother. Witnessing conflict between them would be upsetting, and Will might try to take sides without knowing the full story.

Reid put the papers Jane had found on the coffee table, then got out his other computer and checked email. There were a couple of messages from his network about some documentaries he'd proposed. They wanted him to go ahead. Good news because they would keep him from thinking about how his dreams were dissolving like fog.

The aroma of garlic, tomato sauce, and melting cheese wafted toward him. He was hungrier than he'd realized. They all needed a good meal and some rest. It would bring perspective and strength to face all of these revelations. His world had been rocked too. Maybe not as much as Jane's, but he was still reeling from all he'd discovered from his grandparents.

He checked his phone and found several missed calls. One from his grandmother telling him she loved him and couldn't wait to see him again. Her gentle voice was balm on his aching heart. He clicked on the voice mail Elliot had left.

"Hey, man, I was looking at the footage again, and I found something. Call me."

Even though Reid would rather wallow in his pain for a while, Elliot's voice had skirted on the edge of panic or alarm. He clicked the Call Back button, but it went to voice mail after four rings.

"Tag, you're it, Elliot. I'm back in town. Call me when you get this."

It was apt to be uncomfortable to be around Jane and Charles tonight. Maybe he'd slip out after Will went to bed and see what Elliot had discovered.

The bathroom door opened, and Jane exited. Her cheeks were damp, and her eyes didn't hold their spark. She saw him fiddling with the television remote.

He held it up. "Just setting up a movie. The kids didn't want me around, so I thought I could stand guard here and make sure you weren't interrupted. I thought you were already with him."

She shook her head. "I'm still trying to calm down. The last thing I want to do in front of him is cry. He'll think I'm weak."

"You're the strongest person I know, Jane. Don't ever doubt your own strength."

"Yeah, right."

She didn't believe him, and he didn't know how to assure her he would never lie to her. Yes, he'd kept his identity a secret, but he'd never told her a lie. If the situation had taught him anything, it was that truth was more important than his comfort or his pride.

"Smells like the kids are making pizza."

"They are."

"I can see the wheels turning," she said. "You think I'm over-reacting?"

"Not at all. I'm angry for you, and I'd like to wring your dad's neck." He raised his voice more than he'd intended.

She blinked at his vehement statement. "Okay then." She inhaled and let it out. "Where did I put the papers?" she muttered.

"They're here." He picked them up from the table. "You left them with me. I'll pray for you."

"I don't think anything is going to make this easy." She took the papers from his hand and headed for the munitions room.

At least it was soundproof back there. The kids wouldn't be able to hear the yelling, but he wished he could hear what was being said.

THIRTY-ONE

Her dad was a liar and always had been.

Jane didn't knock but walked straight into the munitions room with the proof in her hands. The cavernous room smelled of metal and gunpowder, even though it was spotless. Her dad didn't look up from his task of loading bullets at the stainless-steel table.

She planted her feet and stared at him. "I need to talk to you."

"In a sec. I want to finish this."

"Now, Dad. Right now."

He turned to face her. "What's happened? Is Will all right?"

"Did you ever love me, Dad? You've never said it, not even once." Her voice broke, and she fisted her hands as she took several deep breaths to calm herself.

"What's this all about, Jane? You sound hysterical."

His contemptuous tone snapped her control, and she stepped forward and slapped the papers down on the table. Her mother's face stared up at him on the top sheet.

He paled. "You've been snooping in my office?"

"Oh, that's adult. Trying to turn it back on me like I'm a child who went snooping where I wasn't allowed. You're a coward, Dad. And a cheat." Her voice quivered again, and she cleared her throat. "You knew all along she was alive. That's why you seemed a little startled to hear she was 'dead.'" She made air quotes with her fingers. "But even seeing my pain about it, you couldn't tell me the truth, could you?"

"It's not what you think."

"What I think is that it's about not sharing me with my own mother. It's about you maintaining control to make sure things went the way you wanted."

"She doesn't have a soul, Jane. She didn't want us and let us go without a backward look. I don't understand why you wanted to find her. Rejection is never pleasant, and I wanted to spare you that."

"She rejected you, Dad. How do you know she doesn't want to see me?"

"She told me."

She reeled at that and took a step back. "I don't believe you."

"You don't think I let it go at this report, do you? I had her new name, her address, her phone number. I went to see her, and she wouldn't open the door. She told me never to come back and never to tell you where she was. I was honoring her wishes." He spread out his hands. "And I wanted to protect you."

"And when was this?"

"I flew to Maine when you were in college."

It felt like a convenient lie. Her dad hated to travel, and she didn't think he'd ever flown. She'd tried to get him to take a vacation, and he didn't like to leave the compound. Not ever.

"I don't like to travel, but these were extenuating circumstances. Ask Elizabeth if you don't believe me. She knows all about it. It was during spring break in 2010, the year you went to the Bahamas with friends."

She remembered. He'd been eager for her to go to the Bahamas, which had surprised her. Now she knew why. "Yet you never told me."

His lip curled. "Your mother didn't want me to. She's got a new family, and she doesn't want anything to mess up her happy new life."

"Why should I believe you now when all you've done is lie to me? I can't trust a word you say, Dad! I'm not sure I want you to be around Will any longer. What kind of a role model are you for my son?"

His eyes narrowed, and he clenched his fists. "He's my grandson. I'll take you to court for my rights."

It was an idle threat, but she didn't tell him that. She didn't have the heart to hurt her son that way, but she could make sure Will knew his grandfather was a liar and not to be trusted.

But was that even fair to her son? This parenting business was hard to navigate.

She forced her fists to open and relax. "Have you heard anything from her since you saw her?"

He looked down at the floor, then held her gaze. "I called her in 2013. I offered to buy her a ticket to come to your graduation. It would have been a great surprise for you."

Her lips felt numb. "She refused."

"She wouldn't hear of it. She and her husband were having some marital problems, and she didn't want to stir the waters more. Her girls were six and eight at that time, and she said she couldn't leave them even if she wanted to."

Sisters. She had two younger sisters. They'd be thirteen and fifteen now. "They don't know about me?"

"No. Your mother didn't want you in their lives. Or hers. I know that seems harsh, but it's the truth, and it's why I didn't want you to know. You had her on a pedestal, and I'd rather let you keep her there instead of knowing what kind of person she really is."

"Why should I believe you?"

He shrugged. "It's the truth."

"Truth isn't in your vocabulary."

"I know it appears that way, but it was only for your happiness and peace of mind, Jane. I wanted you to grow up untainted by her abandonment."

She let that statement alone like a copperhead. "Who's her husband? And did she divorce you?"

He raised a brow. "No. She never told him about me, just married him and pretended we never existed. That probably has a lot to do with her panic to avoid having me show up in her life. She could go to jail for bigamy."

"Her husband?"

"He's an attorney." Her father gave a faint smile. "Wouldn't that hit the newspapers?"

She felt a sickening lump in her stomach that everything he was saying was true. "Why would Gabriel tell me she's dead?"

"Probably because she abandoned the group. She might have stolen money. Hard to know." He hesitated. "One of the reasons we joined Mount Sinai was to get away from the cops. She had embezzled money at the job she had in Detroit. Hiding there seemed like a good option, but she quickly came to believe the lies Moses preached. I wanted to leave long before the fire."

He reached out toward her, but she backed away and rushed for the door.

———

Jane's face was white when she returned to the living room. Reid wasn't sure what he was supposed to say. *How'd it go? Are you all right?* The unspoken questions died on his tongue when she didn't look at him or speak.

"Pizza's ready!" Will called from the kitchen.

Jane bolted from the room and headed for her bedroom, and Reid let her go. Somehow he'd try to maintain a normal evening so the kids didn't know anything was wrong.

His phone rang as he started toward the kitchen. Elliot. "You caught me."

There was a strangled sound on the other end.

"Elliot?"

The only response was panting and another strangled sound.

"Elliot!"

He heard a sound like someone falling or maybe the phone tumbling out of his hand. Rushing for Jane's door, he pounded on it with his fist. "Jane!"

She threw open the door to reveal tousled light-brown hair and a tearstained face. "What's wrong?" Parker lifted his head from the bed behind her, then jumped down to come to her side.

"Elliot called, but he couldn't talk. It sounded like he might be injured."

"At his place?"

"I'm not sure. He couldn't speak."

She whipped around and grabbed her phone. "I'll send Jackson to his place to check on him. He'll get there faster than we can. I'll meet you at my vehicle."

While she placed the call for help and headed outside, he went to tell Charles what was happening and found him exiting the munitions room. He didn't seem to be perturbed by the talk with Jane and simply nodded when Reid told him to watch the kids while they went to check on Elliot.

In moments he hopped into the passenger seat of Jane's SUV. "Was Jackson close?"

"He'd gotten a call about some vandalism at the marina and has to finish what he's doing. We'll get there first, I think. I tried Augusta, too, but she didn't pick up. I left a message."

Dust roiled behind them as she drove toward the road. He got out and opened the gates along the way until they were speeding toward Elliot's. The lights whirled, and the siren screamed as the SUV barreled for the houseboat Elliot had rented on the Bon Secour River. Reid strained forward in his seat, mentally urging Jane to go faster as other vehicles pulled off the highway to allow them to pass.

He directed her where to turn, and he pointed out Elliot's houseboat. "There's his car."

"Good. I was worried he might have been somewhere else when he called." She pulled behind Elliot's car and turned off the engine. "You have a key to get in?"

"No." He threw open the door and rushed to the entry.

His gut took a dip when he saw the door swaying unlatched.

Jane's gaze took it in, and she pulled her gun from its holster. "Stand back, Reid. I'll let you know when it's clear."

He obeyed her steely command, but he couldn't wait for her to allow him in. Elliot might be hurt inside, and desperation had him ignoring Jane's frown. His gaze went past her to the disarray in the living room. The place had been tossed. Had Elliot interrupted a burglary?

Jane advanced through the living room to the kitchen, which was in the same sorry state as the living room. He itched to dart down the hall to the bedroom, but he stayed behind her as she checked for an intruder before moving to the bedroom.

The doorjamb on the bedroom door was splintered and broken, and the door had a large hole kicked in the bottom of it. He noticed the smell when he neared the doorway: a thick and cloying stench of blood.

Jane pushed the door open all the way. Elliot lay sprawled on the floor with a pool of red spreading from his head, and his blond curls were matted. His phone lay by his outstretched hand.

She knelt beside him with her gun still ready and touched his neck with the fingers on her left hand. "There's a pulse! Call for an ambulance." She grabbed a T-shirt on the floor and pressed it to his head wound.

Reid dialed 911 and told the dispatcher where to send the ambulance, then knelt beside Jane. "Is he going to make it?"

"Keep pressure on the wound. I need to check the rest of the house."

His mouth went dry when she didn't answer his question. He took over trying to stop the bleeding while she rose and prowled the closet, then exited into the hall. He heard her checking the bathroom and other bedroom Elliot used as an office.

His gaze roamed the room. There was so much blood. Could anyone survive so much blood loss? Someone had tossed this room too. All the contents of the dresser and closet lay strewn on the floor.

What was the intruder looking for and was this related to whoever had followed them to Kentucky and Indiana? Or was it a random burglary Elliot had interrupted?

It seemed forever before he heard the wail of the ambulance. Footsteps rushed inside, and two paramedics shouldered into the room.

"We've got this," one of them said, and Reid relinquished his spot beside Elliot.

He watched them work on him for a moment, then went to find Jane in the kitchen. "Anything?"

"I think the guy picked the lock." She pointed to the front door standing open. "I'm not sure what was taken. Do you see anything missing?"

"Let me check his office."

As he went back down the hall, he glanced into the bedroom. The paramedics were putting Elliot on a stretcher. At least he was still alive. He stepped into the office and saw in an instant that all the video equipment was gone. The bank of computers, the cameras, and the editing equipment.

Somehow he didn't think the intruder had taken it all to sell it.

THIRTY-TWO

This might become a murder scene, so everything had to be done right.

Nora squinted in the sunlight in the backyard and pushed her glasses up on her nose to study the ground under a water oak tree. Jane had little hope of finding anything valuable in the grass, but she loped across the uneven ground to join the forensic tech.

Nora straightened. "Some crushed grass here, Chief. I think the perp hid a vehicle in the trees. I found several butts, and I think he was watching our vic a while." She held up a baggie containing the remains of a cigarette. "Not enough of a print to take a cast, but this looks fresh. I'll run DNA on the butt and see if we get a hit. Does the vic smoke?"

"I don't know." Jane motioned to Reid, who loped across the yard to join her. "Does Elliot smoke?"

"No, he's a health nut and hates cigarettes."

Nora tucked it in her evidence bag. "It might give us something."

Jane willed Reid to walk away, but he stayed too close for her peace of mind. "What about inside?"

"Hairs, fiber, blood. We'll check it all. The place was pretty neat, so maybe some of the DNA will be the perp's."

"Elliot vacuums every day. He is a germophobe," Reid said.

Nora's smile appeared. "Excellent. I'll get to work."

Jane turned to follow her, but Reid put his hand on her arm. "Is Elliot going to make it?"

Her discomfort vanished at his worried tone. "I don't know, Reid. He lost a lot of blood."

"The attacker took our video equipment. What if all of this is about the video we shot aboard the oil rig? Elliot's message said he'd found something."

She considered his theory. "You've looked at all of it, haven't you?"

"Not every frame. Elliot is the one who edits it to look good."

"Do you have all the files somewhere?"

He shook his head. "My laptop that was stolen had what Elliot sent me, but he had the complete files."

"On his equipment that was stolen. What about backups?"

"They took the backup hard drive."

"Online backup?"

"I'm sure he had that, but I'm not sure where or what password he used."

"Were your files backed up online?"

"Sure, on my iCloud."

"We can start there and take a look at what he sent you."

"I've seen it, and nothing jumped out at me, but maybe you'll notice something I didn't."

Time spent with him made it hard to hold her distance. "Let's go to the war room and put it up on a large screen."

Other people would be there, too, which might make it easier for her. He nodded, and they walked back to her SUV and got in. She felt his gaze on her as she started her vehicle and drove toward the station.

"How'd it go with your dad?"

"Fine."

"Your tone says otherwise. Did he give you a reason for not telling you she'd left the cult?"

She gripped the steering wheel with both hands. Was the man obtuse? "I don't want to talk about it."

"You need to though. It's eating you up, and keeping it inside will make it worse."

"He wasn't a bit sorry, okay?" Her voice rose and ended on a sob she barely choked back. "He had no remorse. None. All I got were excuses as if I should thank him for saving me from hurt." That was the worst of it—that he hadn't regretted what he'd done. "He was defensive and self-righteous. According to him my mom told him not to tell me because she has a new life and didn't want me to spoil it."

"Do you believe him?"

Reid's calm voice grounded her, and she swallowed. "No. I don't think he'd know the truth if it bit him. For a man who has dedicated his life to the law and justice, he's clueless about truth and honesty. He's like a copperhead hiding in the leaves—he fits in with honest people, but he doesn't know what it is. Not really."

Reid reached over and put his hand over her right one where it lay on her leg. "I'm sorry, Jane. Where is she living?"

"Maine. At least she was in 2010. Dad visited her."

"We can go there—you, me, and Will. He'd be excited to meet his grandmother."

"She probably won't want to see me, and I don't want him hurt."

The betrayal was a huge rock in her chest, pressing in and closing off her air. It was better not to think, not to feel. She pushed his hand away. He stared out the window, and she knew her action hurt him. What did he expect though? He'd hidden Will from her. Two major lies had slammed into her life and splintered it into pieces.

He blew out a heavy sigh and looked back at her. "Did your dad keep in contact with her?"

"No. She told him to leave her alone. At least according to Dad. And get this—he said she was wanted for embezzlement so that was why they first joined Mount Sinai. I'm not sure what to believe."

"Wow, that's a surprise."

"And supposedly she never divorced Dad—just married some attorney. If we show up, it will come out that she's a bigamist. Again, according to Dad."

"You can find out for sure. You have the resources."

True enough, but did she want to? It would be easier to hide all this in a cave and never look at it again, but she doubted she could do that. Truth had always been important to her, and these secrets would fester like an infected splinter.

"You won't be able to leave it alone, Jane. Isn't it better to know the truth for sure?"

He knew her better than she'd realized. "Is it? My search for truth has brought nothing but pain."

"That's not true. You have Will now. I know how much you love him. He was worth all the pain you felt."

"Will is worth everything."

"Once you're on the other side of this pain, it will be worth whatever you go through too. Valleys and mountaintops. That's what life is all about. It's how we grow."

"I'd like to stay the same, thank you." She pulled into the parking lot and parked. "Let's go look at the video."

She needed to find Keith's killer and get the part of her life she could control back.

This had better tell them something.

The mammoth screen nearly covered the wall. Reid logged into his Cloud backup from a computer at the police station and found the three video files Elliot had sent him. They were dated just this morning, May 11. Before getting started, he'd called to check on his videographer and had learned he'd been taken to Mobile and was in surgery. His condition was critical. Reid had also spoken with Elliot's mother in Seattle, and she was on her way to the airport. She wasn't due in until late tonight. He'd offered to let her stay at his house, but she planned to take a cab straight to the hospital.

Augusta passed around coffees from Pelican Brews, and he accepted one. "Thanks. I've got the files downloaded," he told Jane and her team assembled in the war room. "Here's the first one."

The screen flashed to life, and there he was talking to Dex. The thirty-minute video held no surprises since Reid had watched it several times. He slowed it down in spots, but nothing jumped out at any of them. He queued up the next one and let it run.

"There!" Jane reached over and froze the frame. "Is that someone standing in the shadows?"

Reid squinted and nodded. "Maybe. If we had the stolen equipment, I'd be able to enhance it."

"I can do it." Nora moved over to the computer and emailed the video to herself. "It will take a little while. Let's look at the rest of this in case there are more frames for me to enhance."

They watched the rest of the second video, then moved on to the final one. Again, no surprises.

Nora rose and moved toward the door. "I'll do what I can with the clip and let you know when I have it ready."

She nearly collided with a young redhead in the doorway. Reid didn't remember her name, but she often manned the front desk, and Jane had mentioned she was a temp.

She rushed into the room. "Chief, Olivia's been in an accident! She could barely talk and is still connected with 911. She's in the ditch a mile from your dad's house."

Jane jumped up. "How bad, Rachel?"

"I don't know. The ambulance isn't there yet."

Jane ran for the door, and Reid was right behind her. He pulled out his phone. "You drive, and I'll call your dad. He can get there before anyone else."

He had Charles on the phone by the time they reached the SUV. Reid told him the situation.

Reid started to tell him not to take Will, but the boy would refuse to stay behind, and no one was big enough to make him now. Charles never left the house unarmed either, so his son should be safe enough in his grandfather's care.

"We're on our way, and the ambulance is ahead of us."

"Leaving now."

"Your dad is on his way."

"You should have told him not to let Will out of the house."

"I started to and realized it would be a waste of breath. Will wouldn't stay behind any more than I would if you'd been in an accident." He turned and looked out into the downtown lights twinkling in the dark.

There was no sense in hiding his feelings. She might not want his love, but he was powerless to take it back no matter how much she pushed him away.

"Megan is in the car too?"

"Your dad said Olivia picked her up fifteen minutes ago. The accident must have happened right after they left."

"She seemed okay the past few days, but the stress might have worsened her condition. At some point she'll have to quit driving."

Reid could only pray it hadn't been Olivia's fault. If anything happened to Megan because Olivia shouldn't have been driving, she'd never live with herself.

The lights on Jane's vehicle strobed, and the siren drowned out all other sounds. The speedometer topped out at eighty miles per hour. The accident site was five miles out of town, and he soon saw the ambulance lights ahead. Jane accelerated even more at the flashing red lights, then slammed on her brakes and pulled in behind the ambulance.

She had her belt off and was out of the SUV in an instant. Reid rushed after her to find two paramedics tending to Olivia, who lay in the grass in the wash of light from her open car door.

He caught sight of two figures over at the tree line. Will and Charles. What were they doing clear over there?

Jane knelt at her head and put her hand on her cheek. "I'm here, Olivia. You're going to be okay."

The paramedic pressing gauze to a wound on her arm nodded as the second rescuer brought out the stretcher.

"Megan," Olivia muttered. "He took Megan."

Reid froze, and his gaze locked with Jane's. He moved closer. "What about Megan?"

Olivia licked her lips and opened her eyes. "Tyler. He forced me off the road and took her."

Jane's eyes went wide, and she looked at the paramedic. "Is she lucid?"

"She has a cut from broken glass and a minor head wound that briefly knocked her out. There's no one else in the car. You're sure her daughter was with her?"

"Yes," Reid said. "Charles said she picked her up from his house fifteen minutes before we heard about the accident." He pointed to the dense forest. "Will and Charles are in the trees. I'd guess they're searching for Megan since they didn't see her, assuming she wandered off injured."

"We'll be transporting Olivia now," one of the paramedics said.

Reid started for the woods and Jane followed. The dark woods welcomed him with the scent of pine from the fallen needles underfoot. An owl hooted off to his left. "Will, Charles!"

Charles's gruff voice answered. "I'm here. The boy went that way looking for Megan."

They moved toward his shadowy figure. Parker came to nose at Jane's hand, and she petted him. "Tyler has Megan. He forced Olivia off the road and kidnapped her. Get Will to safety. I'm going to find Tyler and Megan."

"He won't go back until he knows she's safe," Charles said. "You might as well take him with you."

"Will!" Reid called.

He started off in the direction Charles had indicated. Where was his boy?

THIRTY-THREE

He didn't like grabbing a kid. He'd been watching from the woods when the Price boy forced the woman's car off the road and took the girl. He could have stopped it, but it wasn't his problem. His job was to eliminate the threat to the attack, and the girl's fate held no reward for him.

But this . . . He watched the old man and the kid wander into the woods calling Megan's name. The fortress was undefended now, and he could slip inside and root around for backups, but taking the boy seemed logical. His dad would do anything to protect him—even give up every byte of video taken aboard the oil platform. And his life.

And his job here would be done. Just one more day.

He hunkered behind a large tree and swatted at the mosquitoes buzzing his head. The boy wasn't with his grandfather now, and the man calculated how far he'd have to carry the kid to his truck. Not fun but doable. Maybe he could coax him closer.

He rose and retreated toward his truck with as much noise as he could. Will stepped into a patch of clearing in the moonlight behind him. Should he call to the boy? No, not until he was sure they were out of earshot of the old man.

"Megan, where are you?" Will sounded frantic.

He stepped on twigs and leaves to attract the kid's attention, and the boy started that direction. The sound was probably faint enough that he wasn't sure what it was but only hoped it might be the girl.

When he was fifty feet from his hidden truck, he rummaged in his backpack and removed the sedative shot he always carried. He knelt on the ground by a log that might appear to be a prone body in the dim light.

"Will, over here! I found her!"

The boy broke into a run and rushed over the uneven ground to where he knelt. "Is she all right?"

He stood and moved back. "I can't tell. See what you think."

When Will dropped to his knees, he plunged the needle into his arm. The boy yelped and grabbed his arm, then struggled to his feet and spun on his heel as if to run. The sedative began to loosen his muscles, and he stumbled for a few feet before collapsing to the ground and blinking.

He touched the kid's shoulder. "It's okay, Will. Go to sleep. It will all be over when you wake."

He took the teen's arm, and Will tried to shake off his grip but was too weak. Finally his eyes closed, and he slumped into a pile of dry pine needles.

He smiled and, grabbing Will under the arms, dragged him to the waiting truck. It took more work than he'd anticipated to heft the kid into the passenger seat and buckle him in, but he managed it. He arranged Will so he appeared to be sleeping, then went around and climbed behind the wheel.

He'd get him to a secure place, then make his demands to the dad. With any luck, he'd be out of this wretched town by morning.

She had to find her boy.

When Will didn't answer their calling, Jane started deeper into the woods, fragrant with wildflowers and mossy scents, with Parker, Reid, and her dad. "Find Will, boy. Go find Will."

Before she lost signal, she shot off a text to Augusta with details of what happened and told her to put out a BOLO on Tyler's car.

Tail high, Parker barked and pranced in a Z pattern. He didn't have the scent yet, but Will had been here. He'd get it.

"What's he doing?" Reid asked.

"He's an air sniffer. He's trying to pick up the scent. It's faster than sniffing the ground. There are skin rafts in the air he'll be able to detect."

Parker growled, and when his tail flattened, Jane's pulse jumped. There was another scent here, one he perceived as dangerous. "Find Will."

The dog woofed, and his tail went back up. He was off in a flash. Jane ran after him. "He's got the scent!"

Reid's tension and worry was palpable, and Jane tried to stay calm. They'd find him. He'd just wandered deeper into the woods. Parker's alarm was over an animal and nothing to worry about. But no matter how much she self-talked confidence, her fear mounted.

They could barely keep up with the dog, who bounded over fallen logs and plowed through low-hanging branches and bushes. She was scratched, sweating, and breathless when they broke through to a clearing.

Her dad knelt. "Footprints here, fresh ones. He went that way, toward the road." He pointed to their right.

The dog had already darted that way, and they followed. In another smaller clearing Dad knelt again and touched a flattened spot. "Something or someone lay here." He studied the ground more and made a sound of dismay. "Looks like something was dragged this way."

"Something or someone?" Jane's gaze met her father's.

His mouth went grim. "Someone. I see heel marks to the road there."

She and Reid trailed after Parker and her father to a spot beside the road. She saw the tire tracks before her dad said anything. "Appears like a truck parked here. The drag marks go to this side."

"The guy put Will in the truck and drove off." Her dad gestured to the dog. "He's lost the scent."

Jane nodded, and her mouth went dry. She reached for Reid's hand.

His fingers closed around hers. "Keep the faith, Jane. I've been praying. Will's going to be okay." But in spite of his assurances, his voice wobbled.

Jane gave a jerky nod and squeezed his hand. "Tyler wouldn't have been able to drag him anywhere. He's not nearly as big or as strong as Will."

Her dad swept a hand over the ground. "The footprints are at least size twelve. Tyler's is about an eight. Has anyone called his father?"

Steve. Jane hadn't even thought to notify him. Maybe he'd know what Tyler had done with Megan, and if they talked to the two of them, they might know who took Will. This scene was a dead end. She'd call Nora to search for evidence, but it would be hard to find in the dark.

"Not yet." She checked her phone. "I've got a signal. Let me tell Augusta to be looking at trucks that might have Will." She called her detective and told her what had happened. It was all she could do to keep her voice steady as she instructed her to put out the BOLO and to send Nora to the scene.

Who had taken Will? It had to be the same person who'd threatened him. The thought of her son being harmed nearly buckled her knees. He could be dead even now. But no, she couldn't face that, couldn't entertain the thought.

She found Steve's number and placed a call, but it went straight to voice mail. Her terse message simply said Tyler and Megan were missing and to please call. He might be avoiding her because of the earlier pointed questions about his behavior with young women.

He called back in thirty seconds. "Jane? What do you mean Tyler is missing?"

"Have you seen him?"

"Not since this morning. He should have been back by now, but he's been spending a lot of time with Will. I assumed that's where he was."

"We haven't seen him since we got back in town." She told him what she knew. "Do you know where he might have taken Megan? And why?"

"He's not been himself since his head injury. He forgets they aren't together any longer. It upsets him. I know he wouldn't hurt her."

Jane knew no such thing. "He hurt Olivia, Steve. She's on her way to the hospital with injuries."

"I'm sure he didn't mean to. He's just a kid, Jane. You have to find him."

"Where might he have gone? Does he have a favorite place? Do you have a cabin somewhere or a vacation home? A favorite camping spot?"

When Steve went silent, she would have thought she'd lost the signal except for the sound of a sports game in the background. "Steve?"

"I'm thinking."

Was he figuring out where they might be, or was he deciding if he should tell her? "It's best if we find him quickly, Steve. It will go easier on him."

"He gave her his ring out at Dinosaurs in the Woods."

Jane knew the place out by Elberta. She'd been there a time or two herself. "Thanks, Steve. I'll let you know when we find them."

"I'll go look too. He'll listen to me. I can talk him down off just about anything."

Jane's gut was to keep everyone else out and let her handle it, but Tyler was just a kid, and a wounded one at that. Maybe having Steve along would help. "I'll pick you up on the way there."

She ended the call and updated Reid and her dad. "Our best chance to find Will is to get to Tyler and Megan. They might know something."

The hope was flimsy at best, but it was all she had. She looked down and realized she'd taken Reid's hand again. Their clasped hands symbolized their promise to work together to find their son, and she would cling to the strength of their unity in this moment.

THIRTY-FOUR

R ain blew in from an offshore storm and pummeled the SUV. Reid held it together somehow as Jane's SUV hurtled toward Dinosaurs in the Woods. Steve, Charles, and Parker were in the backseat, and the mood in the vehicle was as black as the night sky.

Will had to be all right. Must be. He and his son had faced many adversities together, and they'd weather this one. They'd be together again soon. A prayer for his son's safety was on constant repeat in his head. *Please, God, please.*

The tires slid on the wet, narrow road as Jane squinted into the misty beam of the headlamps. "This wretched rain," she muttered.

"What's this dinosaur place?" Reid asked.

She turned right on Fish Trap Road. "There are four dinosaur statues there that Mark Cline made years ago." She turned left onto a road at a Berber Marina sign. The rain began to lighten. "Look there. That's Bamahenge."

He squinted in the distance. "I don't see anything. What's Bamahenge?"

"A Stonehenge recreation, also done by Mark Cline. The dinosaurs are just ahead."

Steve leaned forward from the backseat. "Tyler likes the T-rex one the best."

"It's pouring down rain. I can't see the kids out wandering in the storm," Jane said.

Lightning flashed across the sky, and the shudder of thunder came. Her headlamps swept the road ahead as she slowed.

Steve pointed to their right. "That's his car!"

The blue Toyota Corolla was half hidden in a spot off the road. As soon as Jane parked behind it, Reid leaped from the car, ignoring her call for him to hang back. Will was his boy. Yes, she was his mother, but she hadn't spent every hour of her life seeing to Will's needs like Reid had. He had to find his son no matter who was unhappy at his presence.

He checked the car and found it empty. "Tyler, Megan!" The rain, now more mist than anything, dampened his shout as well as his shirt.

Jane and Parker reached him. She led the dog around to the passenger seat and had him sniff around. "Search, Parker. Find Tyler."

The dog whined and turned to trot around the road. He started down the beaten-down path. A T-rex rose in front of him, and Parker stopped to sniff around it.

"I think Tyler has been here. Parker has the scent." Jane put her hand on Reid's arm. "Reid, I need you to let me and Parker do our jobs."

"I need to find Will." His voice broke, and so did his composure. "They have to know where he is."

She took his hand. "I'm going to find him."

The warm press of her hand was his lifeline, but he forced himself to let her go and turn back to the pine needle path. Charles and Steve approached, but Reid left them behind and followed with Jane after Parker, who was moving toward the other dinosaurs. They found the triceratops near the T-rex. No one there either.

"The stegosaurus is next, and that seems to be where they were heading." She took him along a well-worn path.

He nodded and followed her and Parker. The statue glistened from the rain, but nothing moved. No Tyler, no Megan.

Parker nosed around, then turned back toward the car with his tail high. He barked and raced the way they'd come.

Reid's legs were wet from the vegetation, and bugs buzzed in his ears now that the rain had ended. They followed the dog a ways down the road. "I don't see anything."

"It's hidden in the woods," Jane said.

Charles hadn't said much, and Reid suspected he blamed himself for taking Will out. He wanted to comfort the older man, but he didn't have it in him. Once he found his boy, he'd talk to Charles.

"There it is."

Reid peered through the dark at the head rising into the tree-tops. "That thing is big."

"It's my favorite." She picked up her pace. "I think Parker's found Tyler. There's someone under it."

Hope kicked his chest, and he broke into a long lope past her. He found Tyler curled up under the dinosaur's belly, Parker licking his face.

"It's Tyler!" He reached under and pulled the boy out.

Tyler's eyes opened, and he blinked up at Reid. "Megan?"

"Where is she? What have you done with her?" He wanted to shake the kid, but Tyler was as much of a victim as the other two.

"She ran off. I wouldn't hurt her." Tyler's face puckered as if he was going to cry, but his gaze went past Reid to Steve. "Dad!"

Steve helped him up. "Are you hurt, Tyler? What happened?"

"I wanted to talk to Megan without anyone around. This used to be her favorite place. We'd come here all the time. But she yelled at me. She wouldn't listen at all. She finally shoved me and ran off. I tried to find her, but it started raining so I got under the brontosaurus. I couldn't remember where I parked the car."

Reid grabbed Tyler's arm and spun him around. "Do you know where Will is?"

Jane broke his grip on the boy and got between them. "Tyler, someone took Will. Do you have any idea who it was? Did you see anyone when you forced Olivia's car off the road?"

His forehead wrinkled. "I didn't do anything to Olivia's car." He looked at his dad. "Did I?"

"Don't say anything, son. We'll get you an attorney."

Reid wanted to wring the guy's neck. "My son is still out there. Megan is still missing too. He has to tell us what he knows."

Steve's hands curled into fists. "No, he doesn't. He has rights."

Reid forced himself to take a deep breath and turn. "Megan! Where are you?" He walked across the street toward where she'd likely run, and Jane followed him with Parker.

"Dad, put them in my vehicle until we get back."

"I want to get to town," Steve protested.

"Walk," she told him.

Reid followed her through the mud. "What else is here?"

"We can check Bamahenge."

He had a sinking feeling this search wouldn't lead to his boy. Someone else had him.

———

The kid's dead weight was a boat anchor.

The remote house he'd rented along Oyster Bay had served him well, and he lugged the kid inside and tied him to a chair.

COLLEEN COBLE

After checking to make sure the windows were locked and the boy couldn't escape, he left Will sleeping off the tranquilizer.

He retrieved a beer from the fridge and walked out onto the porch gazing out on the bay. The storm had stolen the moonlight, and the water was a dark pool just beyond his sight. Something splashed to his left—probably a dolphin or flounder—and the lights of a shrimp trawler glimmered.

He called his boss. "It's me. I managed to grab the kid. I'm going to ask for all copies of the files as ransom."

The long pause should have warned him, but he shouldn't have been smiling.

"You idiot! You can't do that. Dixon will know our interest is in the video footage. And you could never be sure he gave you all the files."

His boss was the idiot. The man took a long swig of his beer. "He's a dad. He'll do anything to get the boy back. And then I kill him."

"And I presume the boy has seen your face?"

"No, he hasn't. I drugged him in the dark."

Take that, boss man.

"You'll have to destroy the evidence. All of it."

He got the gist. "No, I don't. The kid doesn't know anything."

"This has gone too far now. We only have a few hours before the explosion. I can't have anything go wrong now. I want to see Steve suffer like I've suffered. I want to hear him scream as the flames take him. I've come too far to see my plan crumble now. Once he steps foot on the platform tomorrow, I'll have my revenge."

"I don't want to hurt the kid."

"If I have to call in someone else, you'll be on the evidence list too."

He shuddered at the cold, pointed words. He either took care of it or someone else would take care of him. While he could leave town, he didn't have a plan for hiding long-term. The Boss was the sort who had the patience to make sure he was tracked down and eliminated.

Did he have any options? He examined the situation. He released a heavy sigh. "I don't like it, but there's not much I can do. Make it look like an accident?"

"I don't know how an accident could take out three people. And what about that videographer? I heard he survived."

He'd messed up there. "For now. He's critical and not expected to make it."

And what if he didn't? That would be four people killed. Was he ready for that? He threw back another pull of beer and clenched his teeth. What choice did he have?

"I'll figure out a way to do it. Maybe a fire."

"I like that. Use the boy to lure them somewhere, then torch the place. It will destroy a lot of evidence too. Maybe you're not an idiot after all."

The man ended the call and glanced at the TV as a storm surge warning broke into the programming. Storm surge. He had a better idea for how to deal with the problem, but it would take more beer to gather his courage. Luckily, he had two cases in his fridge.

The boy muttered something and raised his head. He blinked and focused his eyes. "I know you, don't I? I've seen you around the school. You work for the city."

He smiled. "That's what I wanted you to think. It's nighty-night time again."

He plunged another needle into Will's arm, and the kid went out like a light again. Perfect.

THIRTY-FIVE

The sky cried for Will too.

The clouds parted and the moon peeked out, illuminating the path Reid, Jane, and Parker traversed with trees on both sides. The recent rain released the scent of pine and mud.

"Bamahenge is a replica of Stonehenge made out of fiberglass," Charles said. "It's twenty-one feet tall and one hundred and four feet across just like the original and is aligned to the summer solstice. Schoolkids come out here all the time."

Reid didn't want a history lesson right now—he wanted to feel his son's arms around his neck and to know he was alive and well. His hands curled into fists, and he wished he could smash them into whoever had taken Will.

He darted ahead of Charles and caught up with Jane, who trailed Parker as the dog, tail high, raced toward the looming fiberglass stones. "Any word from your team on that truck?"

"Not yet. I know they're looking, but it's impossible to say where the guy took Will. I'm pinning my hopes on Megan knowing something."

Something moved near the base of three standing stones stacked with one on top of the other two. "There!"

Jane's flashlight probed the shadows, and a white face turned their way as Parker reached her. "Megan!"

The girl's face crumbled, and a sob came from deep in her chest. "Parker!" She threw her arms around the dog and hugged him, then scrambled to her feet and stumbled toward them with her fingers curled in Parker's collar.

Jane enveloped her in an embrace. "It's okay, honey. You're okay."

While Reid knew Megan needed comfort, he had to bite his tongue and hold himself in check to give Jane the time she needed to calm the girl. The question *Where is Will?* echoed over and over in his head. Jane had to be impatient as well, but he gave her credit for the way she was hugging and patting Megan.

Megan's sobs tapered off. "Is Mom okay? She was bleeding when Tyler dragged me out of the car."

"She's going to be okay. She has a concussion and some minor cuts, but nothing life-threatening," Jane said. "I don't think the hospital is even keeping her."

"Thank the Lord." Megan wiped at the moisture on her face.

Reid couldn't take it any longer. "Someone took Will, Megan. He arrived at the scene, and when he didn't find you, he and Charles went into the woods in case you wandered off. We believe someone in a truck snatched him. Did you see anything or anyone on the road as Tyler took you away?"

Megan's eyes grew huge, and the tears welled again. "Oh no!"

"Think, Megan," Jane urged. "If you saw the truck, maybe we'd have some kind of description. We only found tire tracks."

Megan's shoulders shook, and she pulled away, hugging herself. "I didn't see anything. I was screaming at Tyler and trying to jump out of the car. I kept unlocking the door, and he kept locking it until he was going so fast I couldn't get out. I was hysterical about Mom."

Reid's throat closed. She hadn't seen anything. His boy was still out there, in danger, with no way to locate him. His constant prayers were hitting the ceiling, and he didn't know what to do. Where was God right now when he needed him like he'd never needed him before?

His boy, his boy. The agony expanded in his chest until his knees weakened. He leaned against one of the stones to steady himself.

In the next instant Jane was there, wrapping her arms around him, murmuring broken sobs herself. He buried his face in her neck. The scent and feel of her was a balm on the pain enveloping him.

His phone vibrated and rang, and he pulled back to reach for it. The number wasn't familiar, but with Will missing, it could be important. "Dixon."

"Dad?"

"Will!" He turned toward Jane, whose eyes had gone huge. "Are you all right?"

"I-I'm okay. This guy, h-he says he's going to kill me if you don't bring your computer and all your backups of the video you took aboard the oil platform."

"Done. Where should I come?"

"You and Mom have to come alone. You can't bring Parker either."

"Your mom too?"

"That's what he says." Will sounded younger, vulnerable. "If he sees anyone else, any other cars, any people skulking around, he'll k-kill me and disappear."

"We'll take no chances, Will. We'll be there. Tell me where to come. My laptop was stolen, remember? Tell him I'll bring your mom's computer so he can see me delete the files on the Cloud."

"You need to drive out west on Oyster Road. There's a turnoff onto a dirt road." Will parroted what a muted voice was saying about landmarks. "He says to come now. You have an hour or I'm dead."

"Okay, we're on our way."

"Dad, did you find Megan? Is she all r—" His voice cut off.

Reid stared at his phone. No connection. The kidnapper must have cut him off.

Jane was hanging on to his arm. "He's all right?"

"At the moment." He told her the demands.

"I don't like it. No backup, no guarantee. Parker could help us, and I don't like leaving him behind. And his plan doesn't make sense, Reid. The guy could have no possible way of making sure we don't have backup. The files are already being analyzed on several computers at the office. That cat is out of the bag. We could be walking into a trap."

"We have to do what he says, or he'll kill Will."

"I'm not saying we aren't going—just that I think there's more to this than we know. We need to have a plan in place. Maybe Dad could circle around through the trees with my officers."

"This guy seems to have been watching everything at the compound. He might have cameras around the house. If we blow this, our son won't survive."

It hurt to say the words, but he couldn't take any chances with Will's life because she wanted to play it like the cop handbook. This was their *son*.

He wheeled and headed for the SUV. "We've only got an hour."

⸻

They had to save their son.

Once a squad car had arrived to take everyone else back to town,

Jane and Reid drove toward Oyster Road. She didn't like it, and she especially disliked leaving Parker behind. It felt wrong to keep her plans from her team, but Reid was right—they couldn't risk their son's life.

The wet roads glistened in the wash of headlamps as she drove out Oyster Road. The forecast warned of a tropical storm with some surge, especially into Oyster Bay, which was where they were headed. This time of night, her SUV was the only vehicle traveling out here.

They were on their own.

She touched the butt of her gun. It wouldn't be much help if they were ambushed by more than one person.

Reid turned away from his perusal of the dark abyss outside his window. "I have my gun too. Do you have a plan on how to approach this?"

"There's been no time to even think." She glanced at the green display on the dash. "We've only got fifteen minutes now."

She'd chewed the inside of her bottom lip raw, but she was no closer to figuring out how to keep them all safe than the first moment she'd heard the kidnapper's demands.

She recognized the sign of the turn ahead. "Here's the road."

Pulling to a stop along the side of the road, she pulled up the map now that she knew the exact location. She switched to satellite view so she could study the terrain around the property. "I've never been back there. Trees all around and maybe swamp too. The surge might hit hard back here. I've got boots in the back. We'll go in prepared for the worst."

"What are you thinking? We walk in off the road?"

Thirteen minutes. "We'd have to drive back at least partway, or we won't get there by the deadline." She traced the narrow lane back to the house. "It makes a turn here. We could park and walk from there, but I'm not sure what that will gain us, other than maybe a more secretive arrival."

"It's worth a shot. I know I pushed you to do what the kidnapper said, but we don't have to walk in like sitting ducks either. That won't save Will."

"No, it won't." She pulled back onto the road and turned left onto the muddy drive, which was getting more treacherous as the downpour started again. The vegetation scraped the side of her vehicle like nails on a chalkboard. She handed her phone to Reid to navigate as she peered through the blurry windshield.

"The curve is right here," Reid said.

A break in the vegetation showed flattened grass, and she nosed in, then executed a turnaround that took several tries. "I want us in a position to make a quick getaway if we have to."

She parked and reached into the back for her laptop, then hopped out in the pounding rain and opened the hatch to grab rubber boots. The spare pair were men's twelves, and she tossed them to Reid when he joined her. The large droplets plastered her hair to her head and ran down in rivulets over her face. It was a warm night, and the moisture rose like fog around them. Frogs croaked from the woods.

She stamped her feet into the boots, then handed him a yellow slicker before she pulled one over her head. "I'll circle around from the north. You go in from the south. Let's try to get near enough to peek in the windows before we go barging in there."

He pulled on the slicker. "I'll take out my gun when I get close. I want to protect it from the moisture as much as possible."

She turned to start for the house, but he caught her by the arm. "Jane, you might not want to hear it, especially now, but I love you. I've always loved you. I-If I don't come back from this . . ."

She turned and burrowed against him. The smell of the rubber filled her nose, and she fought the tears threatening to weaken her resolve. The words *I love you too* wouldn't come out no matter how hard she tried.

She swallowed the lump in her throat and tried again. "I-I—"

He took her by the shoulders and held her away to look into her eyes. "It's okay. You don't have to say anything. I know you'll take good care of Will if this goes badly."

His dear face, so earnest and loving, blurred through the tears and the rain. He bent his head and kissed her, a quick, hard press of his lips.

She gasped as he released her, tucked the computer under the slicker, and strode into the trees. The hand she raised toward his disappearing back trembled, and she gritted her teeth. *Pull yourself together.* She needed every ounce of courage and cunning she could muster.

She couldn't lose Reid or Will. This was on her shoulders, and she couldn't fail them. Taking a deep breath, she went the other way and fought through the thick brambles and heavy vegetation. The slippery red mud and decreased visibility made the trek miserable.

A structure finally emerged in a clearing. A dim light glimmered through a first-floor window of the old farmhouse, and she struggled to see if Will moved past the gleam of glass.

Nothing.

He had to be there, and she had to save him. She crouched down and went forward.

THIRTY-SIX

The flood surged to Reid's knees.

He was soaking wet through and through, and even his feet squished inside his boots. Would Jane even be able to get through this fast-running water?

She and Will had to come out of this alive.

A wet tree branch slithered across his arm and face, and he thrust it away to step into a clearing. The house, a two-story with a steep roof, loomed ahead, and he crouched to approach the closest back window.

A loud snap sounded, and pain grabbed his ankle, so excruciating he shouted as he fell. He closed his eyes and gritted his teeth as it hit in wave after wave.

He opened his eyes. When he smelled metal, he touched his ankle and felt around the device holding him in its grip. A trap of some kind. Maybe a bear trap? He wrenched at the jaws that held him fast, and the pain was so severe he thought he might pass out. He took deep, steadying breaths until the next wave of pain passed. Sweat beaded his forehead and mixed with the moisture driving into his face.

He had to do this.

The light still shone dimly through the windows of the house, and he'd heard no outcry. Maybe the sound of the rain on the metal roof had muffled it.

He put his foot out in front of him and examined it in the dim light. Two springs, a pan where his foot rested between the jaws. Though he'd never seen a bear trap, if he compressed the springs, he'd be able to pull his foot free. Taking a deep breath, he pressed down on the springs with all his might. The jaws eased open, and he maneuvered his ankle free.

The sudden release brought another throb of pain, and he rubbed his ankle. He didn't feel any blood, but his ankle was swelling fast. Was it broken? He rolled to his knees, wincing, then managed to stand. His left foot wouldn't take much weight, so he hopped back to the tree line to find a stick to use.

He hobbled into the woods. He leaned against a tree and wiped the rain from his eyes, then looked around for a sturdy branch for several moments. Nothing. He stared overhead and saw an attached branch that might work. He wrenched it off and stripped it of leaves before testing it for a few steps. It would have to do. He hobbled back toward the house.

Where was his boy? And Jane? There was nothing moving but the downpour sluicing from the sky in torrential buckets. Thunder rumbled in the distance, and lightning flashed across the dark clouds.

A whisper of movement was followed by something striking him in the head before darkness claimed him.

When he opened his eyes some time later, he lay on his back on something hard. Stifling a groan, he turned his head to the right and saw the distant lights of a trawler in the bay. When he tried to get up, chains rattled on his uninjured leg. The other end of the chain linked to one of the dock's support piers.

Water sluiced over the tops of the boards, soaking his back even through the yellow slicker he still wore. The storm surge that had been forecast seemed to be on its way. He moved closer to the pier to see if he could free the chain that tied him, but another strong set of links ran from post to post, and his bonds were snapped into one of those.

He tried to pull the chain apart with his hands, but it didn't budge. He stood on the chain and tried again. Nothing. Was there anything nearby he could use? The gas can he saw was empty and useless with its half-rusted-out metal. No boat bobbed at the dock. He stopped and looked back toward the house, obscured by the curtain of rain except for a dim outline.

Where was Jane? He could only pray she was still out there focused on rescuing their son. He'd happily drown if it meant she and Will survived this. But what if they needed his help? What if they were in a desperate situation in that house?

He attacked the chain with renewed determination. They needed him.

The deluge blocked out Jane's vision except for a few feet in front of her, and the raging wind snatched most noise away before she could identify it. She thought she'd heard someone cry out once, but it had to be an animal somewhere. No human made a noise like that.

The floodwaters rolled across a dip in the yard, and it was deep enough she feared she might be swept away. How did she get to the house from here? She retreated back the way she'd come. She thought a small hill ran to the left of the house. She might be able to make her way through there.

The wind struck with full force as she climbed the hill, and it seemed to take forever battling the weather before she stood above the backyard. A sudden slide in the ground beneath her sent her arms flying above her head as she slid down the hillside to land in the yard. She lay there stunned for several long moments before she struggled to her feet.

She inched along the side of the house to a window, then stood on tiptoe, cursing her short stature the whole time, to peer in. Her breath caught at the sight of Will, arms tied behind him, in a wooden chair by a table. Her first warning of alarm came when she saw no captor nearby. The kidnapper could be prowling around the exterior of the house.

She wanted to drink in the sight of her son, alive and well. No bruises, no bleeding. As if he felt her gaze on him, he strained at his bonds, and chafing marked his wrists. He'd tried before and failed.

Though she wanted to climb through the window, she forced herself to drop back down with her back against the wall. Someone could be creeping up on her, and she'd never know it with the din of the storm swirling around her.

Where was the kidnapper? She touched the butt of her gun and studied the darkness around her. The back of her neck prickled as if someone was watching her, but her gaze couldn't penetrate the darkness of the stormy night.

Keeping her back against the wall, she sidled toward the back-yard. If she could get inside without being seen . . . The wind picked up, sending twigs, leaves, and branches scudding to land at her feet.

She picked her way through the debris until she rounded the corner where the wind grew even more ferocious.

Her phone vibrated and conveyed a storm surge warning. And this house was right on the water.

With no way of knowing how high the tide would rise, she needed to get Will to higher ground even if it was the upstairs of this place. It might be too late to run for the SUV and get out of here.

The wind hammered at her back and billowed her yellow slicker. She struggled to keep on her feet as she searched the darkness for movement. Where was Reid? Could he be inside? She went to the back door and tried the knob. Locked. If Reid had gone in this way, he would have left it unlocked.

The wind shrieked with fury. It might mask what she had to do. The yellow slicker wasn't much protection, so she pulled it over her head, then wrapped her hand in it and struck her fist through the windowpane. The glass cut through a spot in the slicker but spared her hand. She reached through and unlocked the door, then stepped inside.

The vague outline of a washer and dryer coupled with the scent of fabric softener told her she was in the utility room. The floor sloped a little as if it had once been a back porch, and she lurched as she moved toward the door into the rest of the house.

The lurch sent her stumbling forward as a whoosh went by her ear. Her phone fell onto the floor, and a brick smashed on top of it, splintering it. She whirled with her gun in her hand to see who had thrown it.

She was too slow, and a figure came at her from the shadows and knocked the gun from her hand.

Still unsteady from the slanted floor, she fell onto her backside as he loomed over her. He aimed a kick at her, but her training kicked in, and she caught his leg and sent him sprawling. She rolled over and grabbed her gun, then regained her feet as he got up and faced her again.

She didn't recognize the twentysomething guy with his ropy muscles and hard brown eyes, but she brought her gun up at the determination on his face. "Hold it right there."

He grimaced, then held his hands up in slow motion. "Take it easy, Chief. Unless you want lover boy to drown." He held another brick in one hand.

A weight pressed on her chest. "Where's Reid?"

"Shoot me, and you'll find his dead body after this storm is over." He lowered his hands. "In fact, I don't think you are in any shape to threaten me. Which is kind of a shame because I would like to have seen your face when the oil platform blows up. It has to be hard to be such a monumental failure."

It was true. There was a plot to take out the oil platform. She had to get the workers off the rig.

She lowered her gun, but as he smiled with a satisfied gleam in his eyes, she kicked out with her right foot and planted it on his chest. He reeled back and crashed into a freestanding cabinet, then toppled to the floor. The cabinet door opened, spilling its contents on his head.

He grabbed something from along the wall, and she saw the gleam of a rifle barrel as he brought it up to her chest level and fired. She had just enough reaction time to dive to her left. It wasn't until he fired again that she felt the heat in her shoulder. She'd been hit.

The fire spread to her neck and down her arm. The gun dropped from her numb fingers no matter how hard she tried to hang on to it and return fire. She grabbed at her injured shoulder with her left hand and dove through the door into the next room. She kicked the door shut with her foot, then clicked the dead bolt into place.

The man rattled it from the other side, but she didn't wait for him to blast through the lock. Will needed to get out. Her head felt woozy as blood pulsed down her arm. She staggered through the kitchen to the living room, where her son was on his feet straining at the bonds tying his hands to a chair.

"Mom!"

She propped her leg on the chair and let go of her wound long enough to grab the knife from the sheath on her left ankle. She sawed through the rope, then thrust the knife at him. "My SUV is parked just down the lane. Hurry!"

A rifle blast came from behind her. "Go!"

His eyes wide, Will looked at her for a moment, then bolted to the front door, unlocked it, and vanished into the deluge.

She could only pray the storm surge wouldn't sweep him away. Clutching her injured shoulder, she staggered after her boy into the night.

THIRTY-SEVEN

Don't pass out. Stay awake.

The rain sluiced over her as Jane stood swaying at the pathway to the SUV. Her shoulder pain was of epic proportions and made it hard to think. Lightning struck a tree nearby, and the thunder rumbled through her body before the sharp tang of ozone cleared her head.

Should she make sure Will made it out or try to find Reid? It was hard to think past the wooziness and pain, and she fought the lethargy slowing her muscles and dulling her brain. She was losing blood quickly no matter how hard she pressed against the wound in her shoulder.

Reid would expect her to take care of their son no matter what, but she couldn't just walk away from Reid. The kidnapper had said he was going to drown. Where was he?

Another flash of lightning flickered through the swirling black clouds, and she flinched. Such an impossible decision, but she had to take five minutes to find Reid. She had to.

She turned toward the bay, but a hard shoulder crashed into her and she fell headlong onto her injured shoulder in the rising water. She screamed as pain seized her in its jaws. She must have passed out a few seconds because she wasn't conscious of the man hauling her to his shoulder until she realized her head was dangling down his back, and her legs were draped over his chest. She couldn't think, couldn't plan past the horrific pain, but she had to push past it or she and Reid would be dead.

The man's legs sloshed through water nearly to his knees. The storm surge. Where were Will and Reid?

She shook her head to clear it, then struggled to extricate herself from the man's grip. His hands tightened on her knees, and he hefted her forward and onto her back in the water. The salty waves covered her nose and mouth as he held her under the water.

She kicked out her strong right knee, and it connected with his body. He reeled back with an *oof*, and she came up gasping for air. He'd fallen into the water and gotten tangled in branches and debris. While he struggled to free himself, she lurched to her feet and reached with her left hand for the cuffs on her waist. Gone. She must have lost them somewhere in her struggles.

If only she had a rope or some other way to restrain him. Her shoulder was on fire, and she was getting weaker and weaker.

He threw off the last of the clinging vines and branches and got to his feet. Bellowing, he put his head down to charge her again, and she knew this time would be the end. She had no strength left to fight.

An engine roared behind her, and she jumped back as her SUV splashed through twelve inches of water toward him. She glimpsed Will's determined face in the wash of dashboard lights for an instant before the grille smashed into the man. He flew over the hood and slid across the roof before landing face-first in the water.

Somehow she managed to find the strength to stumble toward him and flip him over before he could drown. He was no use to her dead. He was the only one who knew how to stop the attack on the oil platform. He was woozy but conscious as she sat him up and rested him against her leg while she tried to find the strength to do what she had to do.

Will jumped out of the vehicle. "Mom!"

"Grab the handcuffs in the back of my SUV."

She was holding on to consciousness by a thread. Will retrieved the handcuffs and brought them to her.

"Can you cuff him, Will? I-I don't think I can."

She barely kept to her feet as he pulled the man's hands behind him and slapped on the handcuffs. "We need to get him in the back of the SUV. And make sure he has no weapons on him."

"I can do it." Will frisked the man, then dragged him to his feet and hustled him into the backseat. He slammed the door. "Where's Dad?"

"I haven't found him yet, but the guy said something about a plan to drown him. I think that's what he was going to do with me too. He was taking me toward the water."

Will pointed. "There's a dock."

She tried to stagger toward him, but her knees gave out, and she was barely aware of her son's strong arms lifting her and carrying her to the passenger seat.

He brushed a kiss over her cheek. "I'm going after Dad. Pray, Mom."

Pray? Would God even listen to her? She wanted to spring into action, to be the warrior she'd always been. But she'd lost too much blood. Prayer was all she had. She thought she whispered a prayer before darkness claimed her.

By the time the rising water covered Reid's leg, it was bloody from efforts to free himself. His other ankle was swollen, and it was hard to stand, though he didn't think it was broken. The salt stung the open wound, but he couldn't get out of his bonds no matter how much he tried.

The ocean had reached his knees, and the strong current kept throwing him down into the waves. He'd struggled to his feet multiple times only to be tossed down again. His hands were numb from clinging to the dock post, and he was barely aware of the prayer he kept whispering.

Save Will and Jane, Lord. I'm ready. Just save them.

Thunder and lightning raged in the heavens, and the noise drowned out everything else. He staggered to his feet as yet another crash of waves threw him down, and as he rose dripping and exhausted, he spotted a light moving toward him.

He squinted in the darkness. "Here, over here!"

Jane's SUV. He waved his hands. "Go back! The water's too deep."

The SUV stopped, and a figure got out. At first Reid thought it was the kidnapper until he realized this guy was taller and broader. Will?

Terror gripped him. "Go back, Will! It's not safe." The wind whirled his words away before he could be sure his son had heard the warning.

Will wouldn't have a chain to hold him onto the dock, and the next big wave would sweep him out to sea. The boy went around to the back of the SUV and opened it. He took something out and came toward the dock. In the next flicker of lightning, Reid saw he'd tied one end of a coil of rope to the grille before wrapping the other end around his waist.

The first stab of hope lifted Reid. "We need something to cut a chain," he called above the sound of the storm. "I think there are bolt cutters in the back of the SUV."

Will waved and went to the back of the SUV again. Something gleamed in his hand when he returned. Bolt cutters. The boy tied them into the rope, too, then started for the dock.

But where was Jane? Dead? The dread Reid had been fighting for an hour seized him again.

He couldn't lose her again, not when he'd just found her.

With his feet wide Will inched toward Reid. Every time the current tossed a fresh wave toward him, he grabbed hold of a support post and held on until it passed. The water was rising fast, and they both might drown at any moment.

"Save yourself, son! Go back!"

Will shook his head and inched closer. "I'm not leaving you, Dad."

With agonizing slowness the teenager finally reached the post Reid clung to. A massive wave swamped them both and tossed them into deeper water. The rope had too much slack in it for Will to use it to haul himself back to the dock. With one hand on the chain holding him, Reid reached out blindly for his boy, and his hand brushed something. He lurched forward and managed to grip Will's arm.

"Hang on to me." He wrapped the chain around his wrist and pulled as soon as Will had both arms around him.

His muscles ached with the strain, but he managed to get close enough for them to feel the dock with their feet. "Climb, Will! Grab the post."

The boy obeyed, and they stood trembling next to the pier. The water was to their waists.

Will unwrapped the bolt cutters from the rope and cut the chain. "Let's get out of here, Dad. Hang on to me."

"Let's both hang on to the rope. Wrap it around your wrist until it's taut."

He showed his boy how to use the rope to steady him as they half-swam, half-stumbled back to the land. The water was still rising, but it was not as deep yet where the SUV was parked.

"Where's your mother?"

"In the SUV. She's hurt bad, Dad. Lost a lot of blood. We've got to get her to a hospital."

"The kidnapper?"

"In custody in the back of the SUV."

They reached the SUV, and Reid released the rope and helped Will unwind it from his wrists. Barely able to walk, Reid limped to the passenger side of the SUV. Jane was slumped unconscious in the seat.

He turned toward his boy. "You think you can drive in this? Both of my legs are injured, and it's going to be tricky."

Will nodded. "I can do it, Dad. You've had me out in fields and rough terrain lots of times."

"But never in this kind of water."

"I got it here. I can get us out. I have to." Will got behind the wheel.

God had gotten them this far. Reid climbed into the back where the kidnapper sat with his hands cuffed behind him. He was barely conscious and kept moaning, but Reid barely spared a glance his way.

Reid leaned forward to look at Jane through the cage keeping the backseat secure. "Jane?" He wanted to touch her, to make sure she was still alive, but he couldn't poke his fingers through.

"She's still breathing, Dad." Will cranked the engine, and it coughed several times before it caught.

He put the SUV into Drive and began to drive back the way he'd come. The water was nearly up to the engine compartment a few times as he navigated the vehicle through dips.

Reid held his breath and prayed whenever the engine sputtered. It somehow kept going, and they reached the main road on higher ground. Even there, several inches of water stood on the pavement.

Reid didn't have his phone any longer. "Your mom have her phone? Or you?"

Will shook his head. "I already looked. Yours is gone too?"

"Yeah." Reid felt the prisoner's pockets. "He's got his." He pulled it from the man's pocket. "Turn on the lights and siren, Will." He dialed 911 and asked for an ambulance and a squad car. "We're going to keep driving," he told the dispatcher. "Tell the ambulance to look for our lights and siren. We'll pull over when we see it."

He prayed Jane survived until then. Her breathing had grown more and more shallow, and her pallor terrified him. She had to live.

THIRTY-EIGHT

Had Jane lost too much blood to survive?

In a bed in the ER, Reid lay with Will and Charles in chairs beside him. Parker lay sleeping on the cool tile floor. Reid listened to the squeak of nurses' shoes and the beep of machines as he prayed. Megan and Olivia were on their way here now.

His last glimpse of Jane had been in a bed with her face nearly as pale as the pillowcase. She'd lost a lot of blood. It was a flat-out miracle she hadn't died en route, and even more amazing that she'd managed to fight the guy off as long as she had.

He raised the head of his bed with the lever and looked at his boy, so grown up and strong at fifteen. "Will, you saved us. Me and your mom both. I'm so proud of you."

Will had been staring unblinkingly at a game show on TV, and he turned an anguished face to Reid. "It's my fault though, Dad. I shouldn't have wandered off into the woods. I wanted to find Megan, but I disregarded all the warnings about someone trying to hurt us."

"It's not your fault, son. You've got your mom's heroic impulses. The same drive to help others that drove you to look for Megan made you push through in the face of incredible danger to save us."

Charles clapped the boy on the shoulder. "You're a chip off the old block, Will."

Will still looked troubled. "Maybe. Is she going to make it?" His voice wobbled.

It was the same question Reid had avoided asking the doctor who wasn't in control of this anyway. God was. "I hope so."

A white-coated doctor stepped into the room and his gaze landed on Charles. "Mr. Hardy, your daughter is out of surgery." He hesitated as he glanced at the other two occupants in the room.

"I'm her son. And this is my dad."

Charles nodded. "They can hear whatever it is you have to say."

The doctor eased into a green plastic chair across from them. "I got the bullet. It nicked an artery, which is why she lost so much blood, but luckily it hit no major organs. I've given her three units, and her color is better. She should survive, but she's in ICU now for closer monitoring. You can go back one at a time to see her but just for five minutes. She's waking up and asking for Will and Reid." He glanced at the boy. "That would be you and your dad?"

Will shot to his feet. "Yes! Can I go back right now?"

"Sure. Stop at the nurses' station for directions."

When Will rushed from the room, the doctor turned his attention back to Reid. "I hear that bear trap didn't break any bones. You were lucky. Elevation, ice, and rest."

"That's what I was told. And they cleaned the abrasions on my other ankle. Nothing broken there either."

Not that he intended to do much resting. Jane would need care. The doctor had cleaned and dressed his skin flayed by the chain, and an elastic bandage encased his bruised ankle. All he wanted to do was get out of this bed and see Jane.

"You can go see her, Charles."

The man shook his white head. "My girl needs you right now. Your strength and your love. I'll wait. You can take a wheelchair down."

It was more like ten minutes by the time Will returned, his dark eyes somber. "She's still pale and washed out, Dad. She tried to smile though, and she took my hand."

"She's probably still groggy from the anesthetic."

"Maybe. You want to go next?"

"Yes, I need to see her."

"There's a wheelchair by the desk. I'll grab it for you and wheel you down."

Will stepped out of the room and returned in moments with the chair he moved close to the bed. "Let me help you."

Reid leaned on his son's strong arm and got in the chair without as much effort as he'd thought it might take. He probably could have walked. Will wheeled him out and down the hall to the ICU. The stink of antiseptic stung Reid's nose and eyes, and he leaned forward as Will pushed him into Jane's room.

"I'll be right outside, Dad." Will left him beside the bed and stepped out into the hall but didn't go far.

She was attached to a bunch of machines, and the lines and numbers didn't mean anything to Reid so he stared into her beautiful face. Dirt and debris matted her hair, and scratches and bruises aplenty decorated her face and arms. He picked up her closest hand, and she felt cool to the touch.

She startled awake and turned her head toward him. "Reid? You're all right?"

"Thanks to Will. He saved us both, Jane. You were out of it, but our boy figured out how to get out to me on the dock and cut my chains. I'd be dead now if not for him."

A smile curved her lips, and her gaze went to Will standing on the other side of the glass door. "That's some kid you raised."

He squeezed her hand gently. "He got your superhero genes."

Her smile widened a bit. "He might have a bit of his mama in him." She clutched his hand, and her smile faded. "I should have been the one to get to you. I couldn't figure out what to do—whether to make sure Will had made it to the SUV or to go look for you."

"Will, always Will."

"I couldn't leave without trying to find you. I-I don't quite know what that means." Her gaze skittered away. "I couldn't bear the thought of walking away and letting you drown." Her voice wobbled, and tears trickled down her cheeks.

Her admission squeezed his heart, and he lifted her hand to his lips. "I was chained to the dock with the water rising. I wish you'd seen Will. He was amazing."

"What about the kidnapper?"

"Augusta is questioning him as we speak."

Her eyes widened. "The oil platform! It has to be evacuated. The kidnapper said the explosion is in a few hours. What time is it? How long have I been out?"

Reid glanced at his watch. "Four a.m. on the twelfth."

"Tuesday?"

"Yes."

She struggled to sit up. "I need a phone. This is bigger than my department can handle, but the state police can intervene. Or the Coast Guard and Homeland Security. We have to move quickly."

"I don't have a phone either. I'll step out now and find one for you, and I'll go get you a new phone when I get out of here."

"The department will reimburse you."

The silence of so much unspoken stretched between them, but

he wasn't willing to risk saying anything more of what was in his heart. It could wait.

How long did they have before people died?

The urgency in Jane's voice had Reid leaning forward in the wheelchair as Will rolled him back to the ER. Charles would have a phone.

Charles was leaning back in the small room's recliner with his eyes closed, and he sat up when they entered. "How is she?"

"Doing fine. Can I borrow your phone? Jane says an attack on the oil platform is imminent. The whole thing needs to be evacuated."

Charles's eyes widened, and he pulled out his phone. "It takes time to get that many people off. Let me call the state police and warn them. This is bigger than Jane's department can handle."

"That's what she said. She planned to call the state."

Charles hesitated. "I'm not sure she should jump back into work with that injury."

"I'm not so sure either, but we both know Jane. She'll want to handle it."

"I'll take it to her. I want to see her anyway." Charles exited the room almost at a run.

Reid felt the urgency too. Who could he call to move things along more quickly? Even one life lost would be too many. Maybe Jane would have an idea. "Let's go talk to your mom, Will."

"Sure thing, Dad." He grabbed the chair's handles and maneuvered Reid into the hall.

As they neared the nurses' station, he heard a familiar voice and saw Olivia and Megan standing at the counter.

"Megan!" Will left Reid sitting in the chair and rushed toward the two.

Megan ran into Will's arms. She was crying and incoherent. Olivia followed at a more sedate pace and reached Reid. There was a bruise on her forehead, but she was smiling.

Her gaze traveled to his bandaged feet. "How's Jane? You look a little worse for the wear."

"Mine was minor stuff. Jane was shot in the shoulder, and she lost a lot of blood. She came through surgery okay, and she's conscious. Weak though. Can you ask Augusta to come see Jane? She is fretting about this whole thing, and I think she'll rest better if she hands some direction to Augusta."

"Of course." Olivia made the call and walked away a few feet.

A sense of unease haunted Reid as he waited. Maybe he should call his buddy in the Coast Guard about this. They could order extra patrols to keep intruders off. Reid tried to imagine the different law enforcement branches springing into action when Jane called, but even that mental exercise didn't calm his foreboding.

He might feel better after he talked to Jane. Reassuring her might reassure him too. He left Will talking with Megan and wheeled himself back to ICU.

Olivia caught up with him and limped alongside him. Her muscles were stiffer than the last time he'd seen her, but her speech was better than the other day.

"Augusta is on her way," Olivia said. "She'll be here in five minutes. I got the enhanced picture of the person in the shadows from the video, but I haven't looked at it."

She held the door to ICU open for him, and they found Jane sitting on the edge of her bed. The blood transfusion was done, and only saline hooked her in place.

He recognized the determination on her face. "Jane, what are you doing?"

"I just called to have them unhook me. I'm fine. I can't lie here when people are in danger."

"It's under control. Augusta is on her way here, and you can tell her what to do," Olivia said. "You're in ICU, and you just had surgery. You can't just check yourself out of the hospital. I've got something to show you too. Just lie down and wait on Augusta."

Jane frowned. "Show me what?"

Olivia pulled out her phone. "Augusta sent me a copy of the enhanced picture. I haven't looked at it yet." She called up the picture and handed it to Jane.

Jane looked at it and gasped. "It's Victor Armstrong. What would he be doing on the platform? I don't get it." She showed Reid the picture.

Reid stared at the man's face. "He's a real estate agent, right? And on the city council."

Jane exhaled. "I've got to find out what he knows."

THIRTY-NINE

This was crazy, and Jane knew it. Reid had been kicked out of her room, and she used the quiet time to think things through.

She'd just been shot and her shoulder still felt on fire. But it wasn't bleeding. She'd had the blood loss replenished, and the doctor said no major organs had been hit. She would go crazy if she waited in the hospital as all this went down.

It seemed preposterous that Victor could be involved, yet he seemed to be implicated in this plot, and she had to get to the truth.

How did she find out what was happening? Who could help? She stared out the window into the dark parking lot, then looked at the nurses' station and pressed the call button.

A young male nurse hurried in. "What can I do for you, Chief? You have pain?"

While her shoulder felt like it was on fire, Jane shook her head. She needed to be alert. "I want to be discharged."

The guy seemed like he'd spent a lot of time in the gym. "You've lost a lot of blood. We'll see what the doctor says later today."

She swung her legs over the edge of the bed. "The blood was replaced. Either you take out the IV, or I'll do it myself. Lives are on the line—many lives. I have to go. Now."

The nurse frowned and held up his hands. "I can't do it, Chief. Sorry."

"Okay." She'd seen it done before, so how hard could it be to pull out a needle?

Jane peeled the tape cage thing away, and the nurse reached out to grab at her arm. "You can't do that!"

"Yes, I can." She pulled out the IV. "Got a Band-Aid?"

Muttering to himself, the guy whirled around and left the room. Jane feared he was going after security so she stood and paused until her vision cleared. She'd have to hurry, but she couldn't go out in this gown.

Sure enough, the nurse returned with a guard. "Chief Hardy, you must get back in bed."

"You can't hold me, guys. It's illegal. I'm leaving. Either get me a wheelchair, or I'll walk out on my own, and you'll be in trouble with your insurance company."

The nurse scowled. "I'll get a chair. And some scrubs. You can't walk around like that. And a prescription for pain meds and your antibiotic. You'll need both."

Jane sat on the side chair to wait and pulled out Olivia's phone. "Augusta? Come pick me up. We've got work to do."

She was prepared for Augusta's objections, but her detective didn't argue. "Already on my way. I saw the enhanced picture, and Nora passed along some interesting information. I'll tell you when I see you. I'm in the parking lot now."

"Meet me at the entrance. I'm on my way down."

The nurse brought in the wheelchair and scrubs. Jane had him leave long enough for her to pull up the pants under the gown. She eased her arm out of the sling and slid it into the short sleeve top. Perspiration popped out on her forehead from the pain, but she managed to get dressed. The exertion left her weak and shaky, and she nearly fell into the chair.

The nurse glowered as he wheeled her down to the exit, and she didn't bother to try to ease his anger. Too many people might die if she didn't get to the bottom of this.

"There's my detective."

The sun gilded the tops of the French Quarter buildings as Augusta stopped the car in front of Jane and got out to help her in. "You shouldn't be doing this."

"I know." She told her detective about the suspicions surrounding Victor. "I want to talk to him myself."

Augusta buckled Jane's seat belt since her right arm was in a sling. "I'm a good detective, Chief."

"I know you are—that's why I hired you. Too many lives are at stake, so it's all hands on deck. What did Nora tell you?"

"Were you aware Victor had a daughter who drowned?"

Jane thought back, then nodded. "I might have heard something about it, maybe five years ago? She didn't live here. She'd gone swimming out off Fort Morgan and was caught by a riptide."

"His daughter, Belle, was friends with Nora's cousin, and when she was investigating who might have come in contact with Steve at college, her cousin said she always thought Belle's death wasn't an accident. She suspected Belle swam out and drowned on purpose because she was so despondent."

"Does she know why?"

"She'd been having an affair with an older man, and he dumped her. Steve Price."

Jane turned the radio down. "And Victor wants revenge?"

"It's possible."

"Any idea why the explosion is scheduled for later today?"

Augusta nodded. "There's an important inspection happening, and Steve has to be there."

"Victor wants to kill Steve and doesn't care what he does to other people or the environment. Does it happen to be the anniversary of her death?"

"Yep."

"We need to shut this down."

Augusta nodded and shut Jane's door before going around the front of the car and getting in. Jane used Olivia's phone to call Homeland Security, but she got voice mail and left a message. How did she find out what was happening? Who could help? She stared out the window into the dark parking lot.

Senator Jessica Fox.

Jane had helped save her daughter and grandson a few weeks ago, and she was sure the senator would do anything she could to help in a situation like this.

She reached for the phone Olivia had left for her. Her efficient friend would have the senator's number. Jane found it in the digital phonebook and placed the call even though it was five o'clock in the morning.

The call dropped into voice mail, and Jane left a brief message about needing urgent help. Did she dare call again, hoping the senator would pick up this time? While the matter was urgent, there was no guarantee the senator kept her phone nearby. What should she do?

By now, her family might know she'd checked herself out. She had no idea where to find Victor for sure, but his home would be the best place to start since it was closest.

Jane looked around Augusta's car. "You have an extra gun?"

"Sure, but you can't shoot it. Your arm is immobilized."

And she was a lousy shot with her left hand. "Good point, but I don't like going in without protection."

"You have me. I can outshoot you, boss lady. You saw my stats."

True again. "Okay, you got me. You're the designated shooter if any firearms need to be drawn." She put her hand on Augusta's arm. "Good work, Augusta."

"Thanks. We could call in Jackson too."

"Yes, you're right. I don't know what we're going to find at Victor's." She grabbed the handset on the dash and called dispatch to tell them to send backup. Jackson should be only fifteen minutes or so behind them.

***

What a stupid, pigheaded thing to do. When the nurse had told him that Jane had left the hospital, he couldn't believe it.

If Jane were here right now, Reid would have chewed her out. But her tenaciousness was one of the traits that made her so endearing. When no one answered Augusta's number, he sat on the edge of his bed and swung his legs over.

Will's dark eyes filled with alarm. "What are you doing, Dad?"

"Get the wheelchair, son. We're busting out of here too."

The doctor had released him for discharge, but the paperwork was too slow in coming for Reid's peace of mind. Charles had already left with Parker, and nothing was holding him here. Well, other than the fact he'd find it difficult to drive. Will couldn't legally drive, and though he'd done a fine job last night in the heat of danger, he couldn't let him break the law today.

Megan and Olivia had gone to the cafeteria for breakfast and were bringing back food for Reid and Will. They should be back any minute. Reid expected them to argue with him too.

He couldn't ask Olivia to drive. She was getting weaker by the day, and he couldn't put that stress on her.

Could he drive? While Will went after a chair, Reid flexed his right foot, the one scraped by the chain. He could flex it okay. He eased to his feet and tried to put some weight on it. A little pain and it felt like a lump of lead, but not bad. He wiggled it some more. The more he moved it around, the better it was getting. He could drive.

His instructions were to elevate and rest his feet and ankles as much as possible, but there were no broken bones. The leg caught in the bear trap was more painful when he tested it, but it wasn't excruciating. Will still had Jane's keys, so Reid could take her SUV.

The problem was finding where she'd gone.

Jackson.

Olivia and Megan returned with a bag of beignets and a tray of coffees. "Megan, could I borrow your phone? I'd like to talk to Jackson."

She didn't ask questions but handed it over. Olivia told him the number, and he punched it in. Will came back with the wheelchair and stood waiting for Reid to climb in, and he held up his index finger in a *one second* motion.

"Officer Brown."

"This is Reid Dixon. I need to catch up with Chief Hardy. I've got her gun and personal belongings."

Not a lie because the bag with her firearm and dirty, wet clothing was right beside him. What had she worn out of here? Maybe she'd had spare clothing in the SUV. At least she'd had enough sense to make sure Augusta was driving.

They would make a sorry army with both of them injured. And she'd be furious with him if he showed up.

"I'll let her know," Brown said.

"She might need her gun right away."

"She's with Detective Richards, sir. She'll be fine. And from what I understand, she can't use her right arm, so I don't think she needs her sidearm."

Reid slumped and sighed. "Look, Officer Brown, I'm worried about her. I think she's going to need backup."

"She already asked for backup, and I'm on it. It's not your job, sir. It's mine."

The officer wasn't going to divulge any information, and Reid curled his other hand into a fist. "Take good care of her, Officer Brown."

"Take some advice from someone who has watched this worry play out in his own family, Mr. Dixon. My dad is a police officer, and I've watched my mom worry every day until he comes through the door at night. Trust Chief Hardy to do her job and do it well. She is one of the most qualified officers I've ever met. And leave her welfare in God's hands."

The words struck Reid square in the chest. He hadn't been doing a good job of trusting God lately. Love fermented worry in ways he hadn't realized until he'd gotten to Pelican Harbor. For all his talk to Jane about trusting God, he'd picked up his worry every time he'd put it down.

"Thank you, Officer Brown, I'll keep that in mind. You're a good man."

Reid ended the call and handed the phone back to Megan, then looked at his son waiting so patiently. "If we're going to love a police officer, Will, I guess we'll have to learn not to worry."

Will's eyes widened, and he shook his head. "You're worried about *Mom*? Dad, she's a freakin' giant when it comes to justice. There isn't a criminal strong enough to kill her. Look at her. She ripped out her own IV and walked out of here. I'd be worrying about the guy she's after."

Reid grinned. "Well said, Will. Well said."

FORTY

Jane swiped on Olivia's phone when she saw Senator Fox's name. She motioned for Augusta to head out in the predawn darkness of the quiet town. "Senator, I apologize for calling so early, but I've got an urgent situation that affects many lives."

"Chief, I owe you, and that's the only reason I'm calling at this hour. What's so urgent?" At five thirty in the morning, Senator Fox's voice was rough and sleepy.

"A possible terrorist attack on the Zeus oil platform."

Jane plunged into the details she'd learned. "Do you happen to know Victor Armstrong? He sells commercial real estate here in town and is on the city council."

"I've met him."

"He lost a daughter a few years ago. Very tragic."

Jane heard rustling in the background, the sound of a coffee grinder. Pelican Brews wasn't open yet, but she could use a shot of caffeine herself. The lingering effects of the anesthesia made her feel numb and sluggish.

"I think I heard a little about Belle's death at the time. She drowned off Fort Morgan? The riptides can be dangerous out there."

"I have it from a reliable source that Belle deliberately swam far from shore, too far to be able to make it back even without a riptide. She'd been despondent after an incident at college."

"What kind of incident?"

"It appears she was having an affair with Steve Price, and he dumped her."

"How would he be able to punish Steve by blowing up the platform? Your theory is a little wonky, Chief Hardy."

"There's an important inspection happening today, and Steve will be there. I need your help, Senator. That platform needs to be evacuated immediately, and Homeland Security is more apt to move fast with your backing."

"I'll call them right away. Do you know where Armstrong is?"

"I'd hoped he was at his home, but I haven't gotten there yet. I need to interrogate his associate."

"All right. I'll get Zeus evacuated and the threat shut down while you gather evidence on your end."

"I'll talk to him first. I have no real evidence for an arrest."

"Keep me posted."

When the call ended, Jane laid the phone in her lap. "Before we talk to Victor, I want to speak with the guy who kidnapped Will."

Augusta nodded and turned into a parking lot to head to the jail. "I couldn't get anywhere with him, but you can try."

The SUV hit a pothole exiting the parking lot, and Jane gritted her teeth against the pain that jolted through her shoulder. The pain meds were wearing off, but it was too early to get the prescription filled for more.

She'd get through the next few hours and then tend to her injuries.

Jane looked through the interrogation room door at the man who'd nearly killed them all. Jonathan Cook looked smaller and not so dangerous dressed in prison garb.

"Stay close," she told Augusta. "I'm no match for him if he comes over the table at me."

She swallowed four ibuprofen with a sip from the bottle of water in her hand. She had one for Jonathan, too, though she doubted something so mundane would soften him up.

Augusta nodded and opened the door. She let Jane enter first, and Jane wished she'd had time to change out of the hospital scrubs. A uniform would have held more authority, and he would remember how much he'd hurt her.

His hard brown eyes swept over her. "You look a little worse for wear, Chief."

"I'm fine." The fire in Jane's shoulder intensified as she remembered that first moment the bullet had slammed into her shoulder.

His smirk made her want to pummel him, but she settled in the chair and slid a bottle of water in front of him. "When did Victor Armstrong first contact you about this project?"

His smile faded. "You have him in custody?"

"It took a while to figure out, but you're his patsy, aren't you? He's throwing you under the bus."

"I always knew he would." Cook's dark eyes flashed, and he clenched his fists in his lap. "I didn't have anything to do with the McDonald murder. It was all Victor. I just disposed of the body."

"Keith drowned before you tied him to the girder?"

"Dex threw him overboard. No one can survive a fall from that high up."

Dex. She'd thought he might be more than a courier, but he was in this up to his eyeballs.

His evasive answer told Jane everything she needed to know. "Was Dex your contact, or did Armstrong give you orders directly?"

"I don't deal with lackeys. You've found all this out a little too late, Chief." The mockery was back in his eyes. "The rig will begin to malfunction any time now."

Jane showed no emotion. "Homeland Security has it under control and disabled the rogue program."

Cook blinked. "Armstrong said it couldn't be detected."

Her guess based on the little she'd learned from Keith's emails had been correct. They had to stop the program from executing. She nodded to Augusta, who pulled out her phone and shot off a text to Senator Fox to alert her how the sabotage was planned to play out. Jane could only hope Homeland Security had the best computer specialist in the country on it. Would shutting everything down stop it?

The pain in her shoulder intensified as more of the pain med wore off, and she winced as she rose and nodded to Augusta. "Detective Richards will take any other information. Cooperate with us, and we'll reduce the charges."

Murder, attempted murder, kidnapping, the list went on and on. She called Jackson and told him to get an arrest warrant for Dex. "He killed Keith and took the pictures of Bonnie. He's a big part of this."

"I'll get right on it, Chief."

Leaving Augusta to finish up, she went to her office, where she sank into a chair. Her eyes were gritty, and every muscle in her body protested at the abuse they'd suffered in the past few hours. The thought of a comfy bed enticed her, but she couldn't rest. Not until Zeus was locked down, and her beautiful Gulf was safe.

She longed to talk to Reid, to rest in his strength, but he'd try to talk her out of what she had to do. He might be sleeping and not even know she'd checked herself out of the hospital. She hoped so.

She leaned back in her desk chair and thought through the next steps. The senator had promised to call with any news on her end, and Jane needed to make sure she'd gotten Augusta's text about the plan's details. She reached for the phone and called.

"Chief, I was about to call you." The senator's voice was brisk and alert. "Homeland Security raided Price's office and had him order the rig shut down and evacuated. The workers are being air-lifted off the rig as we speak. We sent out helicopters and boats. They should all be off in the next few minutes. Computer experts are onboard now as well, and I hear they've located the file and stopped its execution."

Jane closed her eyes briefly. "Thank you, God."

"Amen. And thank you, Jane. Well done, Chief Hardy, well done."

Jane's eyes burned, and she blinked back relieved tears. "Thanks to you, Senator. We'd have been too late without your intervention."

"I did very little, Jane. I merely informed the right people of your discoveries. Now get some rest, Chief."

"I still need to arrest Victor."

"Federal agents can do it unless you want to."

"He messed with my town. I want to get him."

"Have at it then."

"I'll do that, Senator. Thank you."

Jane gritted her teeth at the pain when she rose. The smart thing to do would have been to let federal agents arrest Victor, but this was personal.

FORTY-ONE

He'd better get used to worry.

Reid sat on a lounger to elevate his feet on the back deck. He listened to the bullfrogs as the sun came up over the trees. His ankles throbbed, but it wasn't too bad since he'd taken some ibuprofen with breakfast.

Will came through the door with a cup of coffee and handed it to Reid. "Have you heard anything from Mom?"

"No, but she can't really call me since I don't have a phone. As soon as the store opens, I'll get us new ones."

He wrapped his hands around the hot mug and sipped his coffee. It would be a perfect morning if Jane were here with them. He couldn't help worrying even though she was an excellent officer and had backup now. Things happened. Officers died in the line of duty. The only way to live with that day after day was to remember God knew the hour and day of each of their deaths. He could die in a car accident or from a brain tumor before Jane took a bullet.

Life was unpredictable, but death wasn't the end, just the beginning. That fact was often hard to remember.

"Megan's going to come and get me for church if that's okay."

"That's great. I'm going to keep my feet elevated today."

"Good plan. I'll wait out front for her. She should be here any minute." Will took his coffee with him and vanished around the side of the house.

A shower sounded great. Reid still had sea salt in his hair and on his skin. He'd get cleaned up when he was done with his coffee. He took a sip and heard tires on the crushed oyster-shell drive-way. He assumed it was Megan until Scott came around the side of the house.

"Saw your boy out front." The attorney wore gray slacks and a white button-down shirt. His hair still glistened from his morning shower. "I had something I needed to talk to you about, and I didn't want to wait until our next appointment. This isn't something I wanted to discuss over the phone."

When he approached, he looked at Reid's bandaged ankles and discolored skin, visible in the sport shorts he wore. "What happened to you?"

Reid told him what had happened. "We're all going to be okay though."

Scott settled on a chair beside Reid. "This is probably bad tim-ing then."

"No, it's fine. What's up? Did you hear from Lauren's attorney?"

"Unfortunately, I did. This will come as a shock, Reid, but you remember I told you about Nevada's funny law about death in absentia?"

"Yes." Reid didn't like the sound of the *unfortunately*.

"Lauren can make the case that she's actually still married to you. She came back in time to set aside the decree about her death, which also nullifies our assumption that the marriage is no longer in effect too."

Reid felt like he'd been punched in the gut. He straightened and shook his head. "That's not possible."

"I've done some research, and it's possible a judge could rule that way. The law hasn't been tested, and in other states if someone comes back, the marriage is as invalid as any claim to property. But her return basically nullified the death in absentia. You never filed for divorce while you waited to have her declared dead, correct?"

"Correct."

This was a nightmare. Just as he and Jane were getting closer, and he'd told her he loved her, they'd have to deal with this. And his faith had balked at the thought of filing for divorce. Which was why he didn't. Now what did he do? Lauren had committed adultery, which was an allowable reason in the Bible for divorce, but it still left a bad taste in his mouth.

"We can file for divorce now though, right?"

"Right. But it adds another wrinkle because she can sue for half your estate. Half the house in New Orleans, half this house, half your assets. Now, I don't think a judge would rule in her favor, but it's going to cost more to extricate you from all this in court costs. You might be better off to offer her a settlement and get it over with."

Everything in him balked at the idea of giving Lauren even one penny more than he had to. She'd hurt Will so badly that he didn't want to fund her to damage someone else.

"I'd rather see if a judge will rule in my favor and set aside the marriage."

"I thought you'd say that. I'll file the necessary paperwork, and we'll see what happens. I can understand you not wanting to deal with her and maybe have to give her more than you want."

How did he tell Jane this news? It would be hard to swallow. He'd seen the love in her face last night, even though she'd had trouble saying the words. He'd allowed himself to dream they would be a family soon and live here together.

Now all those plans were in jeopardy. They'd need to discuss it. If she wanted him to pay off Lauren, he'd do it.

―――――

Would she lose her job over arresting Victor?

Jane parked in the circle drive of the lavish estate overlooking Oyster Bay. She'd heard it was seven thousand square feet and had an indoor pool, but she'd never been inside. She only knew his wife in passing, and she'd met his son and deceased daughter a time or two.

His baby-blue Mercedes convertible was loaded with suitcases. Was he planning on fleeing as soon as the explosion went off?

She let Augusta lead the way to the door. With the personal issues between her and Victor, it would be best to let her detective take the lead. Her shoulder was on fire, too, in spite of the ibuprofen she'd taken.

Augusta rang the doorbell, and its deep chime echoed from the bowels of the house. When the door opened, she expected to see his wife, but it was Victor himself dressed in his usual gray suit.

His pale-blue eyes swept over Augusta's shoulder and dismissed Jane. "I'm too busy to talk, Jane."

He started to close the door, but Augusta thrust her foot in. "I'm afraid we have some questions that won't wait, sir."

He flung the door open and slammed it behind him before he stalked to his convertible. "Talk to the back."

Jane stepped past Augusta and seized his arm in her left hand. She nodded to Augusta, who snatched the handcuffs from her belt and slapped one on the arm Jane held.

Victor tried to twist away, but both women held him fast. "What's this? Let go of me or I'll have your job. Both your jobs."

304

"It's all over, Victor," Jane said. "Jonathan is singing as we speak. Steve isn't on his way to the platform, and the computer virus has been contained."

His mouth sagged, then he snapped it closed. "You don't know what he did to my daughter. You don't understand how much he deserves to suffer. I want him to burn, to hurt the way he hurt my family."

Jane let Augusta handle his thrashing and stepped back. "What about the innocent people you would've harmed, Victor? Did that make your revenge worth it? And it would have destroyed ocean life as well."

Augusta wrestled him to the back of her car and thrust him inside, then shut the door. He banged his head against the window, howling to be let out.

"Chief?" Augusta held open the passenger door.

"Go ahead and book him, Augusta. I'm going to have my guys pick me up so I can go to bed. My shoulder has endured all it can."

Augusta's kind brown eyes lit in a smile. "I approve."

Jane sank onto a bench and exhaled. It was done. She could go to her own house, sleep in her own bed. Maybe kiss Reid on the sofa like a teenager. Her pulse fluttered at the thought. The roses from the garden filled her nose with sweet fragrance, and she listened to the birds sing.

This was her town, her responsibility. And she'd acquitted herself well.

There was a honk, and she looked up to see Will and Reid getting out of the truck. Reid was pale with haggard eyes and his worried expression lightened after he sized her up.

He limped her way and stopped in front of her. "What's happened with the case?"

Will stood beside him. "Mom, you got him, didn't you? I can see it on your face. I told Dad you would. Who was it?"

She told her guys how she'd figured it out and about the senator's help. "Augusta is booking Victor now, but everyone is okay and the oil rig is safe. There's still going to be a big hoopla when it hits the news, and the congressman may get his wish with more attention put on the vulnerability of the oil platforms. I hope it beefs up security."

"How's your pain?" Reid asked.

"About a twelve out of ten. I need to get a pain prescription filled."

"You should go back to the hospital."

"And let someone else nurse me instead of my men? I don't think so."

A dawning hope lit Reid's eyes, and his smile emerged, slow and tender. "Will might be nursing both of us. I can hobble a little, but we might like ordering him around."

"That sounds like a lot of fun." Jane shot a teasing smile at their son.

Will's eyes glistened with moisture. "God's really good to have pulled us all through this, Mom. I hope you know that."

"Oh, I do, honey. I sure do." She held out her good arm and Will crouched by her. She tried to gesture to Reid with her bad arm and winced.

He leaned over and slipped his arm around her. "If I get down, Will might have to haul me up." He put his big hand on her back and bent over her in a tender gesture. "Thank you, God, for your mercy to us," he said in a choked voice.

"Amen." Tears of exhaustion and relief came then. Tears of what could have happened and how her life might have ended if anything had happened to Will or Reid. Tears of thanksgiving to God.

These guys meant everything to her, and she had a little more time to figure everything out.

There was some kind of tension in Reid's manner and embrace around her. It was nothing, just fatigue and his injury. What else could it be?

"Let's go home. I need coffee, food, and beignets. Only maybe not in that order."

Reid helped her up. "Coffee and chocolate beignets coming up. Our place or yours?"

"Ours," Will said. "Just the way it should be."

He knew her mind, just like his old man. The future looked bright in spite of her nerves right now.

To be concluded in *Three Missing
Days*, coming April 2021

A NOTE FROM THE AUTHOR

Dear Reader:

I hope you're enjoying this new series! It's a little different from the majority of my books since we are following Jane and Reid through the entire series. They have a lot of baggage to sort out, so it couldn't happen in one book! I'd love to hear what you think of the series so far.

When researching the Pelican Harbor series, I was struck by how many oil and natural gas platforms loom in the horizon out in the water. I knew I wanted to write a story around one of them, and *Two Reasons to Run* is the result. I've never been at the ocean after an oil spill, but the pictures are horrific, and it saddened me to think of Gulf Shores being spoiled, and I had to make sure it didn't happen in my fictional world.

The more time I have spent in Gulf Shores, the more I love it. I hope you have come to love it too. Let me know what you think! You can email me at colleen@colleencoble.com.

Love,

Colleen Coble

ACKNOWLEDGMENTS

My great thanks to the England family from the Gulf Shores area. Isaac gave me the idea for the first book, and Amy selflessly hauled me all over the area to experience the flavor of southern Alabama. You all are awesome!

Eighteen years and counting as part of the amazing HarperCollins Christian Publishing team as of the fall of 2020! I never take my great fortune to land there for granted. I have the best team in the industry (and I'm not a bit prejudiced), and I'm so grateful for all you've taught me and all you've done for me. My dear editor and publisher, Amanda Bostic, makes sure I'm taken care of in every way. My marketing and publicity team is fabulous (thank you, Paul Fisher, Kerri Potts, and Margaret Kercher). I'm truly blessed by all your hard work. My entire team works so hard, and I wish there was a way to reward you all for what you do for me.

Julee Schwarzburg is my freelance editor, and she has such fabulous expertise with suspense and story. She smooths out all my rough spots and makes me look better than I am. I learn something from you and Amanda with every book, so thank you!

My agent, Karen Solem, and I have been together for twenty-two years now. She has helped shape my career in many ways, and that includes kicking an idea to the curb when necessary. She and a bevy of wonderful authors helped brainstorm this new series. Thank you, Denise Hunter, Robin Caroll, Carrie Stuart Parks, Lynette Eason, Voni Harris, and Pam Hillman!

My critique partner and dear friend of over twenty-one years, Denise Hunter, is the best sounding board ever. Together we've created so many works of fiction. She reads every line of my work, and I read every one of hers. It's truly been a blessed partnership.

I'm so grateful for my husband, Dave, who carts me around from city to city, washes towels, and chases down dinner without complaint. My family is everything to me, and my three grandchildren make life wonderful. We try to split our time between Indiana and Arizona to be with them, but I'm constantly missing someone.

Most important, I give my thanks to God, who has opened such amazing doors for me and makes the journey a golden one.

DISCUSSION QUESTIONS

1. Do you find forgiveness hard or easy? What is the hardest thing for you to forgive?
2. Will is finding his way as a teenager. What was the hardest part of being a teenager for you?
3. Jane is a "fixer" and wants to fix Olivia's illness. What do you do when faced with a seemingly insurmountable problem?
4. Do you struggle with trusting God in hard situations?
5. Is there any circumstance that would make you doubt God's love?
6. Reid has a steadfast personality. Do you know anyone like that?
7. Does revenge satisfy the need for justice?
8. Reid found his grandparents. Have you ever gone searching for a lost family member?

THE PELICAN HARBOR SERIES

COMING
APRIL 2021

Available in print, e-book, and audio

THOMAS NELSON
Since 1798

PLEASE ENJOY THIS EXCERPT FROM
STRANDS OF TRUTH

Suspense, romance, and generational secrets meld when a DNA test helps Harper Taylor locate the family she's always longed for . . . but has it also put her in the crosshairs of a killer?

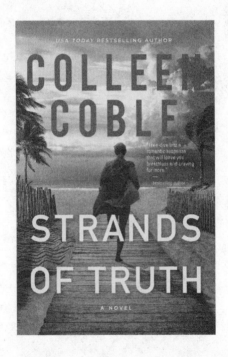

AVAILABLE IN PRINT, E-BOOK, AND AUDIO

THOMAS NELSON
Since 1798

PROLOGUE

Lisa ran to her Datsun Bluebird and jerked open the yellow door. Her pulse strummed in her neck, and she glanced behind her to make sure she wasn't being followed. She'd tried not to show fear during the confrontation, but it was all she could do not to cry. She couldn't face life without him.

She'd been on edge ever since yesterday.

Twilight backlit the treetops and highlighted the hanging moss. Instead of finding it beautiful, she saw frightening shadows and shuddered. She slid under the wheel and started the engine, then pulled out of her driveway onto the road.

She turned toward the Gulf. The water always calmed her when she was upset—and she had crossed upset moments ago and swerved into the scared zone.

Her belly barely fit under the wheel, but this baby would be born soon, and then she'd have her figure back. She accelerated away from her home, a dilapidated one-story house with peeling white paint, and switched on her headlights.

The radio blared full of the news about the Berlin Wall coming down, but Lisa didn't care about that, not now. She switched channels until she found Tom Petty's "Free Fallin'" playing, but even her favorite tune failed to sooth her shattered nerves. Could she seriously be murdered over this? She'd glimpsed madness in those eyes.

She pressed the brakes as she came to a four-way stop, but the brake pedal went clear to the floor. She gasped and pumped the pedal again. No response. The car shot through the intersection, barely missing the tail end of another vehicle that had entered it before her.

Hands gripping the steering wheel, she struggled to keep the car on the road as she frantically thought of a way to bring it to a stop that didn't involve hitting another car or a tree. The baby in her belly kicked as if he or she knew their lives hung suspended in time.

"We're going to make it, little one. We have to. I can't leave you alone." No one would love her baby if she died. Her mother couldn't care for her child. She cared more about her drugs than anything else.

Lisa tried to tamp down her rising emotions, but she'd never been so frightened. The car fishtailed on the sandy road as she forced it back from the shoulder. Huge trees lined the pavement in a dense formation. Where could she drive off into relative safety? A field sprawled over on the right, just past the four-way stop ahead. If she made it through, it seemed the only place where they might survive.

Had the brakes been cut? What else could it be? She'd just had the car serviced.

Lisa approached the stop sign much too fast. The slight downhill slope had only accelerated the speed that hovered at nearly seventy. Her mouth went bone dry.

Her future with her child and the love of her life depended on the next few moments.

She could do it—she had to.

The tires squealed as the car barely held on to the road through the slight turn at high speed. Before Lisa could breathe a sigh of relief, a lumbering truck approached from the right side, and she laid on her horn with all her strength. She unleashed a scream as the car hurtled toward the big dump truck.

The violent impact robbed her lungs of air, and she blacked out. When she came to, she was in an ambulance. She fought back the darkness long enough to tell the paramedic, "Save my baby. Please . . ."

She whispered a final prayer for God to take care of her child before a darker night claimed her.

1

The examination table was cold and hard under her back as Harper Taylor looked around the room. She focused on the picture of a familiar Florida beach, which helped block out the doctor's movements and the smell of antiseptic. She'd been on the beach at Honeymoon Island yesterday, and she could still smell the briny scent of the bay and hear the call of the gulls. The ocean always sang a siren song she found impossible to resist.

Calm. Peace. The smell of a newborn baby's head.

"All done." Dr. Cox's face came to her side, and she was smiling. "Lie here for about fifteen minutes, and then you can get dressed and go home." She tugged the paper sheet down over Harper's legs.

"How soon will I know if the embryo transfer was successful?" Though she'd researched the process to death, she wanted some assurance.

"Two weeks. I know right now it seems like an eternity, but those days will pass before you know it. I've already submitted the lab requisition for a beta-HCG test. If we get a positive, we'll track the counts every few days to make sure they are increasing properly."

Dr. Cox patted her hand. "Hang in there." She exited the room, leaving Harper alone to stare at the ceiling.

Her longing for a child brought tears to her eyes. She'd felt empty for so long. Alone. And she'd be a good mom—she knew she would. All the kids in the church nursery loved her, and she babysat for friends every chance she got. She had a wealth of patience, and she'd do everything in her power to make sure her child knew she or he was wanted.

She slipped her hand to her stomach. The gender didn't matter to her at all. She could love either a boy or a girl. It didn't matter that this baby wasn't her own blood. The little one would grow inside her, and the two of them would be inseparable.

Once the fifteen minutes were up, she was finally able to go to the bathroom and get dressed. She already felt different. Was that a good sign, or was it all in her head? She slipped her feet into flip-flops, then headed toward the reception area.

The tension she'd held inside melted when she saw her business partner, Oliver Jackson, in the waiting room, engrossed in conversation with an attractive woman in her fifties. She hadn't been sure he'd be here. He'd dropped her off, then gone to practice his bagpipes with the band for the Scottish Highland Games in April. He said he'd be back, but he often got caught up in what he was doing and lost track of time. It wouldn't have been the first time he'd stood her up.

Oliver was a big man, well over six feet tall, with broad shoulders and a firm stomach from the hours spent in his elaborate home gym. She'd always wondered if he colored his still-dark hair or if he was one of those lucky people who didn't gray early.

Even here in a fertility clinic, this man in his sixties turned women's heads. She'd watched them fawn over him for years, and he'd had his share of relationships over the fifteen years since his divorce. But Oliver never stuck with one woman for long. Was there even such a thing as a forever love? She hadn't seen any evidence of it, and it felt much safer to build her life without expecting that kind of faithfulness from any man. Having a child could fill that hole in her heart without the need to be on her guard around a man.

He saw her and ended his conversation, then joined her at the door. His dark-brown eyes held concern. "You changed your mind?"

She shook her head. "Not a chance."

"It seems an extreme way to go about having a family. You're only thirty. There's plenty of time to have children in the traditional way."

"Only thirty? There's not even a boyfriend in the wings. Besides, you don't know what it's like to long for a family all your life and never even have so much as a cousin to turn to." She knew better than to try to explain her reasons. No one could understand the guard she'd placed around her heart unless they'd lived her life.

His brow creased in a frown. "I tried to find your family."

"I know you did."

All he'd discovered was her mother, Lisa Taylor, had died moments after Harper's birth. Oliver had never been able to discover her father's name. Harper still had unpleasant memories of her grandmother, who had cared for Harper until she was eight before dying of a drug overdose at fifty. Hard as those years were, her grandmother's neglect had been better than the foster homes where Harper had landed.

This embryo adoption was going to change her life.

"I'll get the car."

She nodded and stepped outside into a beautiful February day that lacked the usual Florida humidity. Oliver drove under the porte cochere, and she climbed into his white Mercedes convertible. He'd put the top down, and the sound of the wind deterred further conversation as he drove her home.

He parked along the road by the inlet where she'd anchored her houseboat. "Want me to stay awhile?"

She shook her head. "I'm going to lie on the top deck in the sunshine and read a book. I'll think happy thoughts and try not to worry."

His white teeth flashed in an approving smile. "Sounds like a great idea."

She held his gaze. "You've always been there for me, Oliver. From the first moment Ridge dragged me out of the garage with his new sleeping bag in my hands. How did you see past the angry kid I was at fifteen?"

He shrugged and stared at the ground. "I'd just given my kids everything they could possibly want for Christmas, and they'd looked at the gifts with a cursory thank-you that didn't feel genuine. Willow was pouting about not getting a car. Then there you were. I looked in your eyes and saw the determination I'd felt myself when I was growing up poor in Alabama. I knew in that moment I had to help you or regret it for the rest of my life."

Tears burned her eyes. "You've done so much—making sure I had counseling, tutoring, a job, college. All of it would have been out of reach if not for you."

He touched her cheek. "You did me proud, Harper. Now go rest. Call me if you need me."

She blinked back the tears and waggled her fingers at him in a cheery good-bye, then got out and walked down the pier to where the *Sea Silk* bobbed in the waves. A pelican tipped its head to gawk at her, then flapped off on big wings. When she got closer to her houseboat, she slowed to a stop. The door to the cabin had been wrenched off. Someone had broken in.

She opened her purse to grab her phone to call the police, and then her gut clenched. She'd left her phone in the boat cabin. She'd have to go aboard to report the break-in. Could the intruder still be there?

She looked around and listened to the wind through the mangroves. There was no other sound, but she felt an ominous presence, and fear rippled down her back. She reversed course and went to her SUV parked in a small pull-off nearby. She'd drive into Dunedin and report it.

Ridge Jackson drove through downtown Dunedin at twilight to meet his father. His dad was usually straightforward and direct, but when Dad had called for a meeting, he'd been vague and distracted. Ridge couldn't still a niggle of uneasiness—it was as if Dad knew Ridge would be a hard sell on whatever new idea he'd come up with.

He had no doubt it was a new business scheme. Oliver Jackson had his finger in more pies of business enterprises than Ridge could count, but his dad's main company was Jackson Pharmaceuticals. The juggernaut business had grown immensely in the last ten years. He had the Midas touch. Everyone expected Ridge to be like his dad—charismatic and business oriented—but what Ridge wanted to do was pursue his work of studying mollusks in peace.

He smiled at the thought of telling his dad the great news about his new job. The offer had come through yesterday, and he still couldn't take it all in. Dad's distraction couldn't have come at a worse time. Ridge had to sell his place in Gainesville and find somewhere to live on Sanibel Island.

He parked and exited, ready to be out of the vehicle after the long drive from Gainesville. He went into The Dunedin Smokehouse, his favorite restaurant. The tangy aroma of beef brisket teased his nose and made his mouth water. They had the best brisket and pecan pie in the state.

He wound his way around the wooden tables until he found Dad chatting up a server in the back corner. He had never figured out how his dad could uncover someone's life story in thirty seconds flat. Ridge liked people, but he felt intrusive when he asked someone how their day was going.

Dad's grin split his genial face. "There you are, Ridge. I've already ordered our usual brisket nachos to share. How was your trip?"

"Good. Ran into some traffic in Tampa, but it wasn't too bad."

"Uh-huh." His dad stared off into the distance. "I've got a new project for you, son."

Ridge squared his shoulders and steeled himself for the coming battle. "Before you even get started, Dad, I've got a new job. I'm leaving the Florida Museum, and I'll be working at Bailey-Matthews Shell Museum on Sanibel Island. I'll get to work with one of the best malacologists in the country. I'm pretty stoked about it."

Most people heard the term *malacologist* and their eyes glazed over. He'd been fascinated with mollusks ever since he found his first shell at age two. It was a dream come true to work for the shell museum. He'd be in charge of shell exhibits from around the world.

His dad's mouth grew pinched. "I, ah, I'm sure it's a good job, son, but I've got something bigger in mind for you. It's a chance to use your knowledge of mollusks for something to benefit mankind. This isn't just growing collections, but something really valuable."

Dad always managed to get in his jabs. Preserving mollusks had its own kind of nobility. Ridge narrowed his eyes at his dad and shut up for a moment as the server brought their drinks. When she left, he leaned forward. "Okay, what is it?"

"I've bought a lab for you. You'll be able to study mollusks and snails to see if they hold any promise for medicinal uses. I'd like you to concentrate on curing dementia first. I don't want you or Willow to end up like my dad."

Ridge's grandfather had died of Alzheimer's last year, and it hit Dad hard.

Ridge held back his flicker of interest. His dad knew exactly which buttons to push, and Ridge didn't want to encourage him. Ridge had long believed the sea held treasures that would help mankind. Researchers thought mollusks might contain major neurological and antibiotic uses. "That sounds—interesting."

"I've already put out the call for lab assistants and researchers. You'll just oversee it and direct the research. I've even created a collection room for you to fully explore the different mollusks." His dad took a sip of his tea. "It will be a few weeks before we're up and running, but in the meantime, you can comb through research and see where you want to start."

"You're just now telling me about it?"

His dad shrugged. "I wanted you to see the lab in all its glory first. We can go take a look when we leave here. There's only one caveat."

Ah, finally the truth. Story of his life. Dad always held back the full truth about anything. He should be called the master manipulator.

Ridge took a swig of his drink. "What is it?"

"I want you to start with pen shells. They're already so versatile, and I believe there's more of their magic yet to be discovered."

White-hot anger shot up Ridge's spine. "This is about Harper instead of me, isn't it? It's been that way since you first saw her camping out in our backyard as a teenager. You're such a sucker for a sob story. I overheard you on the phone the other day, you know. You were telling her you'd be there for her and the baby. She used to get into trouble wherever she went, and I doubt that's changed. And you're still the same patsy." He spat out the last words with a sneer.

Dad's brows drew together in a dark frown. "I've never understood your hostility toward her. And she's long outgrown any kind of reckless behavior."

They'd had this discussion on many occasions, and he wasn't going to change his dad's mind about her. From the moment she'd shown up in Dad's life, Ridge had resented her and the way his father catered to her. Ridge had gone off to his freshman year of college when Dad took Harper under his wing. She'd been a runaway from the foster care system, and he'd done more for her than for his own kids. He'd gotten his secretary to agree to foster the girl. She hadn't had to work during her high school years like he and Willow had. Dad had hired tutors to help her catch up while they'd been expected to figure out their studies by themselves.

The woman had been a thorn in his side for fifteen years. No part of him wanted to have anything to do with her. "What's Harper have to say about it?"

"I haven't told her yet."

Ridge stared at his dad. Typical. Only reveal half of what you know and keep the other half for negotiation. He was sick of his father's half-truths.

But what if in working with Harper, he was able to find definitive proof that she was only hanging around Dad because of his money? Ridge knew it was true. His dad hated being used, and it wasn't often someone managed to get the best of him. Harper was that one exception.

He wanted to get to the bottom of whatever clever plan she'd hatched.

He reached for a nacho laden with smoked brisket and jalapeños. "Tell me more about the lab."

His resolve helped him walk through the lab after dinner. He would enjoy working with the impressive equipment and facilities, and it almost superseded his goal of bringing down Harper. Almost.

2

It should be easy to swim out there, grab her, and haul her back here to his vehicle. While there were several boats out there, he thought she was the only one diving. He swiped his wet hair off his forehead and reached for his mask. Diving was his passion, and he relished any chance he got to exercise his expertise.

He checked his dive computer. Plenty of air. In and out in twenty minutes. He adjusted his mask over his eyes, then slipped his mouthpiece into place before wading out into the water and plunging into the waves.

Visibility was about thirty feet with all the sand in the water, but he knew where he was headed and struck out for the mollusk beds north of Dunedin, about a hundred feet offshore and below twelve feet of water. Seaweed tried to snag his ankles as he swam through, and he spotted a bull shark off to his right. His hand went to the knife at his waist, but he hoped not to have to use it.

A diver off to his left snared his attention, and he paused. Where'd he come from? The older guy with dark hair was big. Not good. He would have to either wait until the guy was done here or take him out.

He didn't have time to waste waiting around. The Taylor woman was likely to finish her work on the mollusk beds soon.

Decision made, he pulled out his knife and swam quickly to the diver examining the cage over the mollusk beds. He didn't seem to notice anyone else was in the water, and by the time his head came up and his eyes widened behind his mask, the knife sliced his air hose.

Bubbles rose in the water as the older man fought hard to break free, but he didn't let him go until the diver's eyes rolled back in his head and his mouth slackened. He hauled him to the unidentified boat and shoved him onto the dive platform, then hauled up the anchor. The tide would carry it out to sea. He didn't want the guy's murder on his hands.

Perfect. Now to grab the woman, deliver her, and collect his money. His son's life was riding on his success. It was the only way to pay for Alex's surgery, so he had to do whatever was necessary, no matter how repugnant.

The warm Gulf water embraced her like a hug. Harper paused as a playful manatee came close enough to touch. The sea mammal she'd named Cyrus swam past her before perching on the sandy sea floor to scratch his bottom. Manatees were related to elephants, and Harper could spend time with one for hours.

She grinned and swam over to him. Today had been a fine day snorkeling above her pen shells, a bed of bivalve mollusks. The shells were about six inches tall and tapered to a sharp point. The fibers protruding from the pointed end helped anchor them into the beds. Their growth was progressing nicely. The netting designed to protect the beds from predators seemed to be in good shape, and she'd watched her best friend, Sara Kavanagh, dive down to secure one edge of a cage.

The first harvest would be in two weeks, and she was eager to see what kind of black pearls she'd find. A special file in her computer holding recipes for pen shell meat was growing as well, and with the new harvest, she'd have byssus. The filament produced by the shells to keep them in place in the sand would be ready for use.

Sara surfaced beside her and pushed up her mask. "Out of air and I'm beat. Let's head back to the boat."

"In just a minute. I can't just leave this handsome fellow floating by himself." She waggled her fingers at the manatee. "Have you seen Oliver?"

Sara shook her head. "He's the worst diving partner in the world. He never stays within eyesight."

"He thinks it's not necessary since the beds are so shallow."

"People have drowned in less water than this," Sara grumbled. As an EMT for the Coast Guard, she'd seen more than her fair share of drownings.

Sara shaded her eyes with her hand. "Looks like his boat is gone. The least he could have done was tell us he was leaving. Don't stay out too long without a rest." She struck out in strong strokes for their boat.

Sara was right. It wasn't like Oliver to be so thoughtless.

Harper frowned and swam nearer the manatee. She laughed out loud as the large creature floated on the waves as if he were body surfing. The minutes slipped away as she frolicked with the manatee. She glanced at her watch. Sara had left over forty-five minutes ago. Harper blew the manatee a kiss and headed for the boat.

A shadowy figure exploded from the murky water to her right

and swam toward her. She flinched as she caught sight of the silvery flash from a knife in the man's hand. What was happening? He waggled the knife in front of her mask as if he thought the sight would paralyze her, but it galvanized her into action.

Adrenaline kicked in, and her hand went for her own knife at her waist, but she couldn't unsheathe it before the guy reached her.

His hand clamped down in a painful grip on her arm, and he jerked her under the waves. She tried to pry his fingers loose but couldn't get him to release her.

A flurry of bubbles obscured his face, but she got an impression of dark hair and flinty eyes. He grabbed her hand to drag her toward the shore.

With renewed desperation she fought against him, and his grip slackened enough for her to swim from him. Panic gave strength to her long legs, and she kicked as hard as she could for the safety of her boat. If she could beat him there, she had flares and other things she could use as a weapon. Her lungs burned with the need to breathe, but she flutter-kicked her fins furiously and finally grabbed ahold of the ladder.

Her head broke the surface, and she dragged gulps of air into her lungs. She hauled herself up the ladder as fast as she could.

A hand seized her ankle as she scrambled for the last rung, and she kicked the guy in the face, then flung herself to the deck of the boat. Her little black schipperke, Bear, barked and leaped past her to snap at the man as he came after her.

"Get him, Bear!" She dove for the storage box where she kept the flare gun and grabbed it, then turned to see Bear sink his teeth into the man's hand as the guy hung on to the top rung.

The man yowled and let go of the ladder, then fell back into the water. Bear put his paws atop the railing and continued to bark. Her hair still damp, Sara came out of the wheelhouse with wide eyes.

"Start the engine!" Harper flung her five-eleven length toward Sara, who didn't ask any questions as she turned and switched on the engine.

In moments Sara had the boat speeding out to sea. The trembling started in Harper's arms and spread to her legs. She sank onto the deck as she stared out over the waves toward where they'd fled. There was no sign of another boat or of her attacker.

Sara flung her honey-colored hair out of her eyes and glanced back at her. "You okay? What happened?"

Harper swallowed hard and nodded. "There was a-a man. I don't know if he was trying to kill me or kidnap me."

The speed and silence of the attack had been unnerving and surreal. She told Sara what had happened, and her expression grew more somber. "Someone broke into my houseboat yesterday while I was gone. I reported it to the police, but they didn't find anything."

"It might be related." Sara reached for her phone. "Thank goodness Bear was there. We'd better call this in."

"I suppose so, but I don't have a good description. His wet hair could have been brown or light blond, and I didn't see his eye color. It happened so fast." Harper's voice wobbled. "And we have to call Oliver. His boat is gone, but I want to make sure he's okay."

"We'll head back in a minute. You're as white as sea foam." Sara rummaged for a bottle of water and handed it to her. "Take a drink and a few deep breaths. Did he cut you anywhere?"

Harper shook her head and tried to stop the trembling in her limbs. She took a swig of water. "I'm okay. It's just the adrenaline. I've never been attacked before. It seemed so random and senseless."

Sara and her fiancé, Josh Holman, were with the Coast Guard. They'd both transferred here after Josh had returned from a year's temporary assignment on the West Coast. Harper listened with half an ear as her friend called Josh and filled him in.

"Josh will be here in half an hour. Try calling Oliver."

"I didn't bring my phone with me."

"Of course you didn't." Sara handed hers over. The two of them had met their first year at Duke University when Harper needed to borrow Sara's cell phone outside Duke Gardens, and they had been fast friends for twelve years now.

Harper placed the call, but it went to voice mail. "He's not answering. Let's get back and make sure he hasn't been hurt."

She sipped her water, then scooped up her dog and cuddled him close. The warmth of his fur began to calm the nerves jittering up her spine.

"Could this be a warning to move my pen shell beds? I got a call two days ago about this being an ancient Native American burial site. Maybe Eric doesn't want to wait for me to figure out what to do."

"Seems extreme, but I suppose it's possible. I'll mention it to Josh." Sara waved. "Here he comes now."

ABOUT THE AUTHOR

Photo by Amber Zimmerman

Colleen Coble is a *USA TODAY* bestselling author and RITA finalist best known for her coastal romantic suspense novels, including *The Inn at Ocean's Edge, Twilight at Blueberry Barrens,* and the Lavender Tides, Sunset Cove, Hope Beach, and Rock Harbor series.

Connect with Colleen online at colleencoble.com
Facebook: @colleencoblebooks
Twitter: @colleencoble
Pinterest: @ColleenCoble